SMOKING GUN

by

J. S. Matlin

To my former partner & good friend, Paul

Don't let the story put you off North Carolina

Copyright© 2021 J. S. Matlin
J & S Publishing

J. S. Matlin has asserted his right under the Copyright Designs and Patent Act, 1988, to be identified as the author of this work.

All rights reserved include the right to reproduce this book, or portions thereof in any form. No part of this text may be reproduced, transmitted, downloaded, decompiled, reverse engineered or stored, in any form or introduced into any information and retrieval system, in any form or by any means, whether electronic or mechanical, without the express written permission of the author.

A number of historical figures appear as characters in this story. However, this book is a work of fiction. References to real people, events, establishments, organizations or locales are intended only to provide a sense of authenticity and are used fictitiously.

All other characters and all incidents and dialogue are drawn from the author's imagination and are not to be construed as real.

dearjsm@uwclub.net

ISBN: 9798 7019 25852

To Jessica and Susanna

Without you both, my life would have little meaning.

Also by J. S. Matlin

Truth to Power

*****

Awaiting Publication

Trade-Off

Injunction

Prologue.
<u>October, 1947.</u>

It was nearly eight at night when Edgar Butler drove his navy blue 1928 Essex Super Six onto the carport. After a long day, he was relieved to be home, even if home was just a wooden structure with two rooms and no running water. Edgar practically crawled out of the car. It had been another of those weeks, made even more exhausting by his clandestine conversations with the workers at the B & M factory. His back ached as he slid a stack of files from the back seat of the Essex and locked the doors. What a difference the Super Six made to his working life. A tobacco union rep can achieve so much more if he can drive the roads of North Carolina. That was his pitch to the bosses. The Union loaned $140 so Edgar could buy the car and deducted $2 a week from his pay. Edgar had scrimped and saved the additional $20. In less than two years, the Super Six would belong to him outright.

He looked up to see Millie by the front door, her legs crossed at the ankle and arms akimbo. After almost seven years of marriage, he still felt a jolt when he saw her. Those huge almond eyes would stir any man. That body!

"Your dinner is ready if you like it ruined," she told him, walking inside. Almost as an afterthought, she turned and added, "The girls are still awake. Go say goodnight to them. I'll get your plate."

Edgar walked through the main room that served as meeting place and kitchen and entered the bedroom where they all slept. The girls were in bed. They leapt up when they saw him.

He hugged Jen, who was clutching her doll and Nancy, two years younger. At three, she was at that age where she talked to her fingers as if they were friends.

Edgar cuddled and kissed his daughters. He felt so tired, he could barely remain upright. "Hush you two, it's late. Time to sleep, but I promise we'll play tomorrow."

Edgar returned to the main room, where he tidied the folders and began to sort through the papers. He came to one document, studied it and slapped it onto the table.

"Gotcha, you bastard!" he declared.

"Come on an' eat," Millie said, placing a plate of food and a glass of milk before him.

Edgar looked at her with gratitude. "Woman I'm so hungry I could eat the legs off this table."

She gave him a hug and pulled out a chair for herself. "So man of the house, how were things today?"

Edgar was about to answer when there was a screech of brakes and squeal of tires, followed by slamming doors. The front door was thrown open and two men wearing white-hoods stood before him. A third man was outside, hammering a large wooden cross into the dirt. Edgar heard his daughters running into the room with cries of fear as he stared at the intruders. They said nothing.

One of the men pulled out a Colt revolver. Edgar tried to speak, but he froze with fear. The man aimed the gun at the children. Edgar grabbed the girls and tried to push them behind him. He heard Millie yell, "no." Two shots rang out and the girls were prostrate, dying instantly. Millie screamed hysterically but her shock and grief was silenced by a bullet fired into her head. She died on the spot.

Edgar dropped to his knees, sobbing and pleading. All feelings of a lifetime were quelled with one last shot. Edgar was dead. Four bullets used. Four humans murdered. One room splattered and filled with Butler family blood and corpses.

The killers poured kerosene throughout the shack, lit a match and set the place on fire. Outside, they doused the Essex and torched it. Neighbors appeared, but more gunshots in the air forced them back inside. It had taken only seconds to wipe out the Butler family but more than two hours for the blaze and the cross to burn out. The town's fire department didn't visit the place.

Later that evening, three men sat in a roadhouse and drank quietly, their glasses refilled every now and then by a waitress who worked long hours for little pay and poor tips. A fourth man joined them, exchanged a few words and then produced a wad of cash. The three leaned in to divide the spoils. As the money was being shared out, the fourth man produced a Mauser and fired three quick shots. Standing over the men, he shot them again for good measure and retrieved the cash. The horrified waitress tried to disappear behind the counter, but she didn't stand a chance. Five seconds later she, too, was dead. The short order cook didn't last much longer. No witnesses.

Shortly after midnight, a County Police patrol car drove past the roadhouse. Surprised to see lights blazing, the cops entered and discovered a scene of carnage. Five people dead. Detectives arrived within thirty minutes and spent several hours studying the crime scene, but found few clues. Outside in a pickup truck, there were three white hoods. The fingerprints in the truck matched three of the dead men. Two days later, the truck's tires were matched to the tracks found outside the Butler shack. However, the truck had been stolen. The police were baffled by the killings.

The town's newspapers for the colored community ran the story of the Butler murders for almost a week. There was no apparent motive. The conclusion was another white supremacy outrage had occurred. There were no fresh clues. The newspapers for the whites gave the roadhouse killings a front page story with art but after the next day's report on an inside page, the story ended. Deaths of colored folk and white trash didn't sell newspapers.

BOOK ONE.
1947/1948 – Winter.
Chapter 1.

My name is David Driscoll. If you know the American newspaper world, you may well have heard of me. Back in the early 1930s, I bought the failed *St Luke Bugle* and brought it back from bankruptcy to rude health. I spearheaded the removal from power of the notorious St Luke boss, Mike Doyle, and most senior members of his political party machine. More than three hundred people who worked for him either ended up in jail or paid heavy fines.

By the end of the war, I was bored with the repetitive nature of running a Midwest newspaper. I missed new challenges. I yearned to write about federal politics. So when Nick Anslow, the owner/editor of *The Washington Mirror,* offered me a columnist role in D.C., I grabbed it.

My wife, Abby, took a little persuading but as she had grown up in Richmond, Virginia, she supported the move. Abby is no stay-at-home Mom. She is a college professor and in demand. The University of Richmond was happy to offer her a teaching position. Our two teenage children had quite a few friends in Richmond, not to mention cousins. They were easy.

I did a 'quick and dirty' deal, selling *The Bugle* to my senior management team. To sweeten the deal, I discounted the price and agreed to payment being spread over ten years. They deserved it. They had made me a wealthy man.

One of my early tasks at *The Mirror* was to lobby President Truman's people for an interview. He often stayed at 'The Little White House' in Key West between Christmas and New Year and I mentioned I would be in the vicinity. Arrangements were made.

The Key West house was military without any frills. The living room was just a comfy place with a small desk in one corner, some furniture and a large, round poker table in another corner with stacks of poker chips on it.

As we shook hands, the President noticed me looking at the poker table and asked, "Like a game, Mr. Driscoll?"

"I'd love to, Mr. President, but I think you would separate me from a lot of cash."

Truman laughed. "Want a cold drink? Let's get to business."

Over two hours, the President covered a whole range of issues: the economy, the dangers of inflation as America changed from a war to peace footing; race and civil rights; the Marshall Plan, foreign relations and the Cold War; how the atomic bomb was keeping the Russians in check. I was left in no doubt that the Commander-in-Chief was in control of his government, notwithstanding the hostile Congress he faced.

My final question: "Will you run again in November next year, sir?"

"You knew FDR, didn't you? He called this 'the best job in the world.' On the record, if I stay healthy and if Bess is willing, I'll seriously consider it. Off the record, of course."

Back at our Miami Beach hotel, Abby grinned as she asked me, "How is the President?"

"He is well. He asked after you."

"He did not!" she laughed.

"Sure he did. 'How is your family?' He wanted to know."

"How about that. Oh, Peter Garibaldi called. John Rayburn is trying to find you. Evidently, it's urgent."

Peter was one of the new owners of *The Bugle*. He had been my right hand man for years.

John Rayburn was a banker at the First Bank of Richmond. I had not seen him since I bought *The Bugle.* Well, Rayburn could wait. No banker was going to spoil my holiday. I wrote the Truman article that night and had it shipped to Washington.

Chapter 2.

When I returned to Richmond, I called John Rayburn. We arranged to meet at his bank later that week. When I first met John, he had an unimpressive office on the second floor of the building. Upon arriving, I was ushered to the top floor, where I waited in an outer office for a minute or two. John's secretary appeared and escorted me into a spacious corner office with large windows. The floors were covered in a plush claret carpet, the walls paneled in rosewood. On the walls were a myriad of certificates, diplomas and bank testimonials, all attesting to his qualifications, as well as photographs of John with politicians and celebrities. In pride of place, there was a shot of John shaking hands with Henry Morgenthau, Jr., FDR's Treasury Secretary.

Holding center stage was an oversized desk, topped in red leather and embossed in gold. The desk was bare, save for framed family photographs, a set of papers and three telephones in red, white and blue plastic.

John walked over to me. I greeted him with, "What patriotic phones you have!"

"Red is the intercom, white is my office line, blue is my private line. I'm an important man these days." The last was said with a grin.

"So I've heard," I responded, also with a smile.

John gestured for me to sit in one of two chairs near the window. "I read the Truman piece," he said, taking the other chair. "You've moved up in the world."

I nearly told him the same, but simply nodded. He had put on quite a few pounds since our last meeting. He looked the very picture of an opulent banker.

"I hear your family lives in Richmond," John said. "We should get together one night for dinner."

I had no idea where this conversation was going, although I doubted I was called to this lofty tower to plan a social visit. "That would be nice," I acknowledged, "but not easy. I spend a lot of time in D.C., Abby's a professor at Richmond and we keep weekends free for the children." I added, "I'll try, but don't be offended if we can't manage anything," which sounded better than the truth. I've never liked bankers. My old mentor, Sam Perkins, insisted that bankers are bloodsuckers. "They only lend money to people who don't need it," he insisted. "Remember this, David: journalism is a profession, banking is an industry."

John studied the sky outside the window and shifted in his chair. "You must be wondering why I wanted to see you. There's a newspaper in North Carolina, *The Durham Monitor*. Have you heard of it?" I shook my head. "No reason why you should. The newspaper is in serious financial difficulties. The bank has loaned substantial funds to its owner without any security except the borrower's Note. It's a kind of mortgage to secure the loan."

"I know what a Note is. I left the turnip farm a while back."

"Just so. Now the customer that signed the Note is a corporation owned by Jeremiah Burns."

"*The* Jeremiah Burns?" Now, Rayburn had my attention. There were four gigantic cigarette manufacturers in the United States and Burns owned one of them, Burns & Murphy Tobacco. By any definition, B & M was big business.

Rayburn leaned forward. "A year ago or so, Burns decided to buy *The Durham Monitor*. He set up his ownership in a complex corporate structure because he didn't want the newspaper's business tied in any way to B & M."

"But he guaranteed the loan, right?"

Rayburn took a deep breath and pursed his lips. "Burns' new corporation borrowed $700,000 from this bank to buy the paper. He put up $700,000 of his own funds, too, for working capital. Then the corporation borrowed a further $700,000 from the bank, supposedly for additional working capital. The only security for our loans was the borrowing corporation's Note."

I started to speak, but John held up both hands.

"I confess the loan terms were poorly thought through and poorly written as well. Burns pocketed that second $700,000 loan, then he drained the newspaper of funds. So, we found ourselves a creditor for $1,400,000, plus interest. The loan is effectively unsecured. Burns has no personal liability whatsoever."

At first, I wasn't sure how to respond. When did a reputable bank make such poor decisions? "If you don't mind my saying, this is astonishing. The bank has certainly changed since I last did business with you."

John looked increasingly miserable and a film of perspiration appeared on his lip. "It gets worse. Not only has Burns no personal financial exposure, nor any other obligation to the bank, but he has deliberately run the newspaper into the ground. Its staff was just under two hundred when he bought it and at the last count, it was less than thirty. Circulation has dropped by more than three quarters. *The Durham Monitor* is dying."

If not already dead, I thought. "Why would Burns do this?" I asked. "I assume the paper was a sound prospect when the loan was made, so what would make Burns want to destroy it?"

"I honestly don't know," said John. "This wasn't my deal. I took over here as CEO just a few months ago. The circumstances of the loan weren't brought to my attention until recently."

I stared at Rayburn. There was something in his expression that made me think he wasn't telling me the whole story. Years ago, I had known him as a straight shooter, a good egg, but time and the banking business might have changed him.

Rayburn spoke again, this time his voice stronger, more decisive. "The bank doesn't want to write off the fat end of one-point-five million bucks, so here's what we'd like to happen. You take over management of the paper and nurse it back to health. I know this is a big ask but we'll be more than generous. Of all the people we know, you are the one who surprised and impressed us the most when you brought *The Bugle* back to life. If you can't save *The Monitor,* no one can."

I felt flattered by his praise and trust, but wasn't that exactly what he wanted? Build up my ego and make me feel indispensable. How could I say 'no'?

"Have you got the latest management accounts?" I asked.

He walked back to his desk, opened a drawer and removed a set of papers. "They make ugly reading," he warned, handing them to me. "Without the bank's support, this newspaper is insolvent."

I gave the accounts a quick look but long enough to realize the task would be Herculean. Knowing this, why would I take on *The Monitor?* I had extricated myself from *The Bugle* to be free from the chains of running a local newspaper. Here I stared at the frying pan and the fire. Why give up my Washington role, which was promising to flourish in this presidential election year? One more unsettling question: how could I disrupt my family yet again, so soon after the last move?

"I'm flattered, John," I said, "but I don't think this is for me."

"Don't be too hasty. Give it some thought."

He was appealing to my vanity to be sure, but we both knew that if I accepted this challenge and turned the paper around, it would be a grand slam for me. I would likely be the talk of the newspaper world. "Let me discuss it with Abby. If she is opposed, that's an end to it."

John stood and extended his hand. "Fair enough. I can give you a little time, but we need to move on this quickly."

On the journey home, I was anxious about how to approach Abby. We had lived in Richmond for little more than a year and had decided to stay. Abby was looking for a house to buy. Would she go through the roof at the thought of moving again so quickly? And what would the children say?

I found Abby in the kitchen. I opened with, "Is the rolling pin handy?" and waited for her to respond.

Her eyes widened. "Okay, buster, what have you done this time? Tell me everything."

This is why I love Abby. No accusations, no distrust, just a request that I lay it out, full disclosure.

"Do you know the name Jeremiah Burns?"

"The tobacco baron?" she asked.

"That's him." I took a deep breath. "It seems he screwed First Bank out of one and a half million bucks." I tried to sound casual when I added: "He also ran a local newspaper, *The Durham Monitor,* into the ground."

Now I had her attention. "Where this is going, David?"

"I haven't agreed to anything. The first thing I told Rayburn was that I'd talk to you. If you said *no*, my answer would be 'no'."

"No to what?"

I looked at her for a moment, detecting a little twist to her mouth. "Now you're playing with me."

"Oh, is this a game?"

Abby opened a cupboard and took out a bottle of Californian Cabernet. "So they want you to rescue the paper." I watched her insert the corkscrew and pull the cork out. "I can see what's in it for the bank, but what's in it for you, for us?"

"I haven't discussed terms yet."

Abby carried two glasses to the table and sat down, humming. I think the lyrics of the song were 'After you get what you want you don't want it.' I waited for her.

"So let me work it out," she said. "Eighteen months ago you sold *The Bugle* because you felt stale and didn't want to play editor anymore at a town paper. You wanted to write on the big political scene, which you're now doing. And you tell me you're thinking of going back to being what you didn't want to be. You, my dear, are an enigma."

"All those years ago when I took on *The Bugle,* I made some terrible mistakes, especially with our marriage, but if I'm honest, I never felt so alive when I was working twenty-hour days to bring that newspaper back to health. I had a real sense of what my life was meant to be. I know I made our personal lives hell. I promise this time it will be different. I do get things balanced better now, don't I?"

Abby turned her glass a few times, seemingly inspecting the color of the wine. "Aren't you forgetting that terrible beating you took from Doyle's people?" This was true. I was hospitalized for months and my hearing will never properly recover. "But what I can't fathom is why you'd take a backwards step when you already have the newspaper world at your feet?"

I took my glass and joined her at the table. "That Truman interview was the high point for me. When will I ever exceed that, unless I uncover the political scandal of the century? I was raised on town newspapers. This is the work I should be doing."

"We're happy here, settled. And don't forget that you've worked and lived only in the North; you have no real experience of the South. Have you really thought this through?"

She was right about my being a northerner, but I've always considered myself adaptable. "I know more about the South than you credit," I said. "Look at the time I spent with your parents."

Abby waived that comment away. "Richmond is a college town. It's enlightened. We're talking about the real South, where you don't know how things work. You've never seen Jim Crow up close; it's not nice. You need to think very carefully about this. And do you really need the change? If you do, maybe there's something better for you nearer to D.C.?"

We both went silent. Abby looked away for a moment and then announced, "You really are a puzzle, aren't you? But..."

"But what?"

"Did you say Durham?" When I nodded, she said, "Chapel Hill is nearby, right?"

I missed her point completely.

"David, the University of North Carolina has one of the best English departments in the country. It's a progressive school and it would be a great place for my research."

I knew better than to speak. When Abby thought aloud, interesting ideas were often formulated.

"You may have struck the mother lode," she said. "UNC put out feelers to me a while ago. I told them it wasn't a good time, but I kept my options open. If you want to play Sir Lancelot and rescue the fair maiden in the guise of *The Durham Monitor,* I might just be persuaded to go with you. The children won't be so easy."

"How about if I talk Daisy into it and you take care of Louis and Lottie?" Daisy is our dog!

Abby couldn't help laughing. How like me to assume responsibility for the dog, leaving the children to her. We sat without speaking until she asked, "Are we awful parents? I mean, both of us are considering a huge upheaval, all for our own benefit, but we're not thinking about the children."

It was not unusual for Abby to amaze me, even after twenty-three years of marriage. She was a loving and supportive wife, true, but I sometimes forgot the depth of her ambitions as an academic. College life was a mystery to me, but Abby thrived on it. I had expected her to fight me. Instead, I found an ally.

We talked to Louis and Lottie that night. I explained the opportunity but much remained to be discussed with the bank. Abby told the children that if we decided to move, there might be big advantages for their futures in North Carolina. Chapel Hill not only had excellent high schools, but there would be easy entry to UNC. We would all visit Chapel Hill so they could see for themselves. We promised them we wouldn't move them in the middle of the school year and we would ask Gerry, Abby's sister, to look after them if Abby moved to Chapel Hill before school was out.

"Daddy and I will come back to Richmond every weekend until school is out," Abby told them. Judging by their expressions, they were not enthusiastic.

"Who do they remind you of?" I asked Abby when we were alone.

"I think they'll come around eventually," she said, but I knew she was trying hard to believe her own words.

All was not etched in stone. I still had to negotiate the deal with the bank. My trust levels were low, mainly because I was pretty certain Rayburn hadn't told me the whole story.

At our next meeting, I asked him to confirm he had indeed told me everything. He said he had. I agreed on a healthy fee just for looking over the proposal. There would be another up-front fee, far more sizeable, if I took the job. In exchange, I would take a nominal salary until the newspaper was profitable. Rayburn seemed amused at my commercial sense. When he first knew me years before, I'd had little. Times had changed.

My terms included additional funding to save the newspaper. Here Rayburn challenged me. "I can't throw good money after bad." I explained that it wasn't possible to re-engage two hundred people or more without a way to pay them. And there was the possibility that I'd need new equipment like a printing press. "These cost upwards of $250,000", I said. "I won't take the job on a shoestring. I'll have more than enough to worry about without money problems."

Rayburn was not pleased. "I can't be open-ended on funding, David."

"I'm not asking you for unlimited funds. Once I've made my initial appraisal, I'll let you know how much I think is needed. Then it's up to you to decide to fund it or not." I worked very hard to keep my voice steady and not sound like I was delivering an ultimatum, even though I was.

"What I will not do is negotiate a lesser sum than needed. If I start out with financial struggles, the deal won't work. You know it as well as I do."

It took patience on my part to get the deal I wanted. The bank had called its Note and now owned the newspaper outright. Rayburn agreed that if full repayment of the bank's loans were made, the newspaper would be sold to me for one dollar.

Rayburn also agreed that I would be in day to day control, without interference from the bank. Another major concession I finagled was freedom from any legal or financial responsibility if the newspaper rescue failed. The final term was the bank's debt would be repaid in one lump sum, in exchange for ownership. The last thing I wanted was to repay the bank bit by bit and find myself with both a problematic repayment schedule and cash flow problems.

At the end of the meeting, I lingered a bit, hoping John would explain the bank's relationship with Jeremiah Burns. He told me the bank had been trying to get into the North Carolina market for quite a while and tobacco was a safe bet. People smoked it, chewed it and snorted it. I probed as much as I could, but Rayburn wouldn't let me bring the conversation around to Burns. I left the bank with a signed agreement and a head filled with questions.

Chapter 3.

Two days later, I drove to Durham and set myself up in a local hotel. That first night, in a secluded area of its lobby, I met with acting *Monitor* editor, Joshua Frost. In his early forties, he was married with three young children. As fair haired and handsome as he was, I knew that his bald patch and early-stage paunch would soon change his looks. Josh had been the newspaper's chief crime reporter, but he had been forced to become editor when staff cuts took hold. He was pessimistic about the newspaper's survival, yet assured me he was in 'to the bitter end.'

The following morning, I went to the newspaper's offices and called a meeting in the large, open plan room, where the reporters worked. I stood on a desk, looking down on a couple of dozen people or so. The atmosphere was tense.

"Good morning," I began. "I'm David Driscoll. As you know, this paper is now owned by The First Bank of Richmond. The bank has engaged me to determine if there's a viable business here. I want you to know that there is only one question for me. Do we have a newspaper? I ask this as a journalist, not a businessman. My credentials include being a political columnist and editor for *The New York Standard*. For more than a decade, I was the owner and editor-in-chief of *The St. Luke Bugle* and have recently been a columnist for *The Washington Mirror*. I learned my trade from Sam Perkins of *The Culpepper Post*. For those of you who knew this business from the olden days, you'll agree Sam was a newspaper legend."

I saw glances exchanged, concerns far from assuaged. This was not going to be an easy sell, convincing this group that their futures might not include job hunting and possible foreclosures on their homes. I took a deep breath and continued.

"I've given myself seven days to decide if this newspaper can be saved. If any of you think it cannot, I'd like you to leave now. I won't have nay-sayers on my staff." No one moved. "Good. You need to know that if we go ahead, you will lose sleep, work twice as hard and you may well grow to dislike me intensely, but if we all give it a try, I will get no more sleep than any of you and I will work without a salary until the bank is repaid in full. By then, I expect to have some two hundred people working here again and you will be part of an enterprise that will make all of us proud. Questions?"

No hands went up. I wasn't surprised. These people were leaderless, defeated and stunned. I saw no smiles, no animation. I was concerned that not even one person stood out from the group. All the stuffing had been knocked out of them.

Josh escorted me out and walked me to the paper's library. I needed to read back issues and get a flavor of this paper. "Starting tomorrow," I told him, "I want to meet everyone individually."

I spent the rest of the day getting a handle on the newspaper's good times and bad. Years of back issues informed me that, prior to Burns' ownership, *The Monitor* had been an impressive newspaper, whether reporting on town, city, county, state, D.C. or world news. Coverage was supported by excellent photography, which was important for highlighting stories. There was a page for state politics called 'Under the Dome', as well as extensive news out of The Triangle, as Raleigh, Durham and Chapel Hill were known. There was the usual leader page which, until Burns' ownership, was written by editors who were schooled in fair and balanced reporting.

There was also a daily North Carolina poem, as well as standard pages for obituaries and society news. Most editions had three or four pages dedicated to sports and another to funny pages.

There was comprehensive commentary on commodity prices, especially tobacco as well as other agricultural news. The classified ads comprised two or three pages, with double that on Sundays.

Like pretty well all Southern newspapers, this one was pro-Democrat, but I detected something different from other newspapers where I had worked. There was no news coverage for Negro readers or coloreds as they call them down here, yet the crime pages were awash with stories of rapes, murders and other serious crimes. The paper reported that the culprits were mostly Negroes attacking whites. However, in the case of lynchings, this was reversed. Those reports were sometimes accompanied by 'art.'

As a business, there were serious problems. A forty-page edition newspaper had been reduced to a mere eight pages and advertisements were now limited to less than half a page. How had this been allowed to happen?

While addressing the team, I had detected embers in the eyes of Josh and one or two others - embers where I assumed passion had once burned - but even those signs couldn't mask how demoralized people had become. I wondered if they were up for a fight.

After a thorough evaluation, I knew that current advertising revenues would never support the expense of the business. The answer was a personnel overhaul, coupled with a strong marketing push, engaging local business and industry. However, if I expected advertising revenues to improve sufficiently to make the newspaper solvent, I'd have to get our daily circulation back to a minimum of 85,000. At the moment, it was less than 20,000.

The next challenge would be to revamp the print shop. Good people worked hard there against terrible odds, but there were too many printer-workers for a 40 page paper, let alone one of eight pages. All the men worried about their jobs and for good reason. After a meeting with the foreman and a top-to-bottom inspection of the equipment, I was certain that the printing press was fit to produce a much more substantial newspaper. Not having to invest in a new press was a big relief.

By the end of my fourth day in Durham, it was clear to me that if I was to take this task on, and if *The Monitor* was to survive, I would need the very best senior management, equal to my team at *The Bugle*. In addition to Peter Garibaldi, my former second-in-command, the paper thrived under Henrietta Carson, who handled marketing, advertising, and sales. Henrietta was a wunderkind, with a deep understanding of the newspaper business. The third member of the team, Emily Venn, had been with me the longest. As head of finance, she was responsible for every facet of *The Bugle's* costs and expenses. It was her expertise that had made me a wealthy man. I'm no money genius, so Emily was a boon. She had been with me from my first day running *The Bugle*. What she didn't know about the financial side of a newspaper wasn't worth knowing.

In the spring of 1946, when I was looking to make changes in my working life, I asked Emily, Peter and Henrietta if they'd like to buy *The Bugle*. It was Emily who told me that such a purchase was beyond their means. I explained that I wasn't looking for a windfall.

"You three have been responsible for my success," I told her, "and it's payback time." I asked her to meet with Peter and Henrietta and give me a figure that was fair. "Tell me how long you need to repay me and add a reasonable rate of interest for the money that remains outstanding. I'll be fine with this."

Soon we agreed terms. I would accept five hundred thousand dollars for my shares. Payments would be spread over ten years. As for the rate of interest, we'd go with whatever the Federal Reserve was charging banks. My attorneys tried to insist on provisions about security for my loan. I trusted Peter, Henrietta and Emily completely. I dispensed with that requirement.

On my fifth night in Durham, I telephoned Peter. It took only a little time to negotiate a deal for their help. Knowing that Peter, Emily and Henrietta would come to Durham and stay a month was the encouragement I needed. If the four of us couldn't save *The Monitor*, no one could. The plan was for them all to come for a one month period, followed one at a time for a further month over the ensuing six months. The fee I would pay them would be $50,000.

I called Abby at the end of the first week and explained my plan to bring in my old team. She gave her blessings to my decision to save *The Monitor*. I told John Rayburn I would accept the task but that everything had to be in writing. In particular, the bank would have to accept liability for the $50,000 management fee and pay it up front.

Three days later, with contracts signed and the challenge before me, I was off to the races. My St. Luke team arrived in Durham, assuring me that they had capable deputies in St. Luke and there was always the telephone if problems arose at *The Bugle*.

It wasn't long before Emily determined that I would need a minimum $400,000 for working capital. We inflated the figures to $550,000 to cover unexpected expenses and I presented this to John Rayburn. He settled at $525,000. I'd decided to leave the day-to-day management tasks, including hiring of staff, to my team. My role would be to either approve or disapprove recommendations.

I was determined from the get-go that Peter would not only re-hire as many of *The Monitor* local staff as possible, but also hire women and Negroes of both genders. *The Monitor* would be a progressive employer. When I presented the new hiring policy to the employees, I was met with immediate resistance. These were Southerners, almost exclusively white men not accustomed to working side-by-side with women and coloreds. I dealt with this impasse as if I were Abe Lincoln. In a famous Civil War debate with his cabinet about the war's conduct, all members bar Lincoln responded with 'nay' when a vote was taken. Lincoln announced, "The ayes have it," making it clear he was in charge. When the subject of employing colored and female staff arose, I told senior staff, "On almost every occasion, I'll take your views into account, but not this one. *The Monitor* has to be progressive, which means we'll hire the best people for the job, regardless of race or gender. There is no room for anything else on a newspaper I run."

At the end of the first week, I surprised my inner circle when I left Durham on Friday afternoon. My family was in Richmond and that was where I needed to be. I returned to Durham early on the following Monday. After an eight o'clock meeting with Peter, Emily and Henrietta, followed by an editor's meeting with Josh and his team, I made my way to the print shop to meet Harlan Street. Harlan had been a clerk in the advertising department, but had been put in charge of supplies under the Burns stewardship.

"Have you the inventory for me, Harlan?"

"Here it is, Mr. Driscoll." He handed me some sheets of paper.

I looked at the contents for a minute. "Has it been checked? Is it right?"

Harlan nodded, but seemed nervous. I could understand why. I told him, "Even if we're printing 200,000 copies twice a day, there would be enough newsprint to keep us going for over a year."

I saw misery cross his face. "You're in charge here, Harlan, so please explain to me how this happened." It took him several moments before he responded. "I was forced into doing this, Mr. Driscoll. When I told Mr Burns we had far too much in supplies, he insisted that such an important newspaper had to be properly supplied. And he made me pay full price to our suppliers. I told him I could negotiate, but he said that we'd get better service if we did not haggle. You see how my hands were tied. I have children to feed and I wasn't going to risk my job by arguing with the boss."

I calmed down. "Go through the inventory with Miss Venn. She'll decide what we don't need. She will know how to sell those supplies back." I could see Harlan's fear subsiding. "You seem to know what you're talking about," I said. "For now, I'd like you to stay in charge of supplies. If you decide you want to go back to the advertising department, no one is going to fire you."

At that moment, my new intern, Clayton Bates, rushed into the print shop.

"Mistah Driscoll, you have to come. Now!"

"Whoa, Clayton, where's the fire? What's up?"

"It's *Mistah* Burns. He's in your office and he told me to get you...pronto."

"Pronto?" I repeated, feeling my anger rise.

"Clayton, you go back and tell Mr. Burns I'm busy, that I'll be back presently and whether he waits or not is a matter of supreme indifference to me."

Clayton stared at me with fear in his eyes. "I can't say that to him."

I needed to calm down and be realistic about this situation. How could I send a young Negro to deliver a caustic message to one of Durham's 'good ol' boys'?

"Okay. Tell Mr. Burns that I'll be with him as soon as I'm free. Explain that it might be a while. Offer him a drink." When I saw Clayton's uncertainty, I put my hand on his shoulder. "I know you're new to life in this newspaper," I said, "but Jeremiah Burns is no better than you."

Twenty minutes later, I walked into my office to find a man in his mid-sixties sitting at my desk chair. He was of medium height and slim build. He had a good head of hair for a man of his age, probably early sixties, and his eyes matched the dark walnut of my desk. His aquiline nose and thin lips gave him a mean-spirited look. I glanced at his suit and thought 'sartorial splendour.' His cane, sporting a carved ivory handle, added the word 'dandy' to my silent description. He stood and we shook hands.

"My name is Driscoll," I said. "How can I help you?"

"Ah, yes, Mr. Driscoll. Good to make your acquaintance. I'm Jeremiah Burns." His smile came close to a sneer. "I used to own this pile, as I'm sure you know. You've piqued my curiosity, hence my visit which I trust is not at an inconvenient time."

I did not invite Burns to sit. "I'm busy. Make this quick"

"That's not the way we Southerners do things. We take our time. It's gentlemanly."

"Very well, we'll go southern. But I am rather busy this morning. It would have been gentlemanly had you made an appointment rather than crashing in. Now, what is it that you want?"

As if responding to an invitation, Burns moved round my desk and sat in another chair. "I do have some questions," he continued. "Let's start with why a Midwesterner would take on this Southern burden? What is there to rescue in this dying monolith and where would you start?"

I could feel a slow burn rising. To ease my temper, I sat in my chair. I leaned back, steepled my fingers and looked Burns in the eye.

"Mr. Burns, I hope I'm not being too blunt for a man of your Southern sensibilities, but what I choose to do and my reasons for those choices is none of your business." When Burns continued to stare at me, face devoid of expression, I went further. "Since you're here, perhaps you can explain why you went out of your way to ruin this fine newspaper? Do you not care about what it stood for, not to mention the employees who have lost their jobs?"

"These are good questions, very good, exactly what I would expect," he drawled. Was this a version of Southern charm? If so, it was falling flatter than the proverbial pancake. "I'll be willin' to answer all your questions but our discussions should happen elsewhere," said Burns. "Come meet with me. Mrs. Burns and I would be delighted to have you as our guest for dinner in our home, 'Silver Leaf.' Shall we say Friday night?"

I waited for what I hoped was an uncomfortable time for Burns before I responded.

"I'm busy, Mr. Burns. I'm not available on Fridays. And time is pressing. Please excuse me but this meeting is over."

Burns stood. "Would lunchtime on Thursday be better?" His eyes twinkled, as if he was a playing a game that he intended to win. "I forgot, you need to be in Richmond on Fridays."

How was he so well informed? Who at *The Monitor* was talking? This discussion might go on indefinitely if I was not careful and I needed to work. What was the harm in accepting the lunch invitation? I have to confess I was intrigued by Burns and was curious to see where and how he lived. I agreed to meet with him on Thursday at 12.30 pm.

"Will you please excuse me? I'll show you out," I continued as I moved Burns out of my office.

I called Abby that night and we shared the events of the day. When she heard about lunch with Burns, she took on that protective voice she sometimes uses. That's when I realized that Burns had run rings around me.

"Take care, newspaperman," she warned. "And use a long spoon when you eat with this particular devil."

Chapter 4.

I have seen large houses in my time. The old Brady mansion in St. Luke is as impressive as the mansions in Newport News. However, I was unprepared for Silver Leaf. Jeremiah Burns' plantation, some ten miles outside Durham, covered more than 600,000 acres of prime North Carolina farmland. It was both a farm, with a range for prize livestock and an agricultural spread with fields of rice, corn and wheat. There was a vast tobacco plantation. The estate boasted a village with shops, an orphanage, a school and a post office. A child stepped out of one of the cabin-sized buildings and I realized that these were homes for the workers. As I drove through, I passed what I later discovered was a retirement home. As much as I did not warm to Burns, his environs were beyond impressive.

The road leading to the mansion was guarded by a white painted, five-bar steel gate. At the sentry box, I gave my name to the guard and the gate opened electronically. I drove more than two miles until the mansion appeared at the top of a hillock at the far end of a wide circular drive. I parked my Cadillac close to the house and sat for a moment.

From what I could see, the main house must have been close to forty thousand square feet of living space. It was mostly on one level, except for a second-storey addition that was the size of a large home. Later, I learned that this was the Burns' private quarters, off limits to all.

As I climbed out of the car, I noticed another building, separate from the house and almost out of sight, which proved to be the servants' quarters.

The front door to the mansion was massive of carved oak. I rang the bell, which was answered by a liveried servant. He reminded me of the old drawings of flamboyantly costumed slave servants from pre-Civil War times.

Before I could be announced, Burns appeared at the door. He was accompanied by a man of similar age and build, dressed in the style of the nineteenth century. The man wore a charcoal gray frock coat and matching britches that were tucked into black leather boots. His jacket was set off by a burgundy vest, white frilled shirt and black-string bow tie. He carried a Stetson hat and a whip. Had I walked into a time warp? Were we back in the colonial days of the old South?

Burns came forward and shook my hand vigorously. "Let me introduce you to Jackson Murphy, our plantation manager." As Murphy and I shook hands, he fixed me with a steely gaze. His left eye was scarred above and below and he had other small facial scars. Did this man fight people or animals? Had he been wounded in duels?

Burns turned to Murphy. "We'll talk again tomorrow." With that, Murphy left. Burns led me along a thick-carpeted corridor into a large room where oak bookshelves filled three of the walls. There were leather armchairs, matching sofas and glass-topped side tables, located every few yards. The fourth side was almost entirely glass, diamond-shaped leaded lights. The room, a library, overlooked a tailored garden with lawns running down to a river in the distance. It was a magnificent prospect.

"Might I introduce you to our local drink, a mint julep?" Burns asked. "I assume a julep has familiarity."

"Some." Alex Porter, my late father-in-law, prided himself as an expert cocktail maker, but I wanted to keep this information to myself. My instinct was to protect details of my private life.

"While you're here, you should sample the best the South has to offer." Burns passed me a glass filled with a light brown liquid with a mint leaf immersed. As he poured a glass for himself, he said, "I know it is treachery, but I use Kentucky bourbon. Here's mud in your eye." He lifted his glass and winked. "And in yours," was my weak response.

The drink was good, refreshing and strong. I reminded myself to drink conservatively. Burns led me to an armchair overlooking the garden and sat opposite me. He looked at me for a while and I returned his stare.

"Formality can be overdone. May I call you David?"

"Certainly."

He nodded. "My friends call me Jez." He took a slow sip, savoring his drink. "I'll come to the point. You interest me. You're an outsider, what some might have called a carpetbagger in days gone by. That's a rarity in this state these days. North Carolina is known for its insularity, its closed society. So, I ask myself, why would someone from the Midwest and an inhabitant of New York City and Washington D.C. want to try to join in our life?"

He paused long enough for me to respond, but I remained silent. If he wanted to play games, I was willing to go along. I let the insulting carpetbagger remark slip by.

"I've had you checked out. You enjoy quite a journalistic reputation and I'm not surprised the bank hired you. But why would a man of your abilities take on a lost cause like *The Monitor*?"

"Mr. Burns, I'm sure your investigators will have told you my wife is from the Commonwealth of Virginia, hence Southern life is not totally unknown to me. As for *The Monitor,* time will tell. Now, I have questions for you."

Burns nodded, and I decided to start with something easy. "Where does the name Silver Leaf come from?"

When Burns smiled, it was without the cynicism I'd seen before. "It's a type of tobacco leaf found and grown only on this plantation. In season, the tip of the leaf gleams silver in the early morning sunshine, almost as brightly as Lou."

As if on cue, the door to the library opened and a woman entered. She appeared to be twenty years younger than Burns and an inch or two shorter. Slender, with an almost boyish figure, she eschewed the flowing locks of so many Southern women and wore her hair short in a page boy style. Even her outfit was unusual. In this world of crinolines and lace, she wore navy blue trousers with a white leather belt, a white blouse and two-tone shoes to match. I saw no jewelry, except her wedding rings, which included a very large diamond. Nothing seemed to hurry her, whether in movement or speech. Lou Burns was one of those women totally in control of herself, her surroundings and the people around her.

"David, may I introduce my wife, Louise-Beth Burns."

She approached me, smiled and said, "Charmed to meet you, Mr. Driscoll." I felt both inspected and judged. "How are you enjoyin' Durham?" she asked, switching on Southern charm. She addressed her husband. "I do believe luncheon is ready to be served. Shall we?"

My mind went back more than twenty years to a dinner at the Brady Mansion and being checked out by Connie Brady, then the owner of *The Bugle*. She, too, was the epitome of good manners, with steel at her core. I knew I needed to be on my guard with Louise-Beth Burns, as well as her husband.

Lunch was taken in a cozy dining room overlooking another manicured landscape. Before food was served, this was time for small talk, something at which I never excelled.

We dined on pork chops, baked potatoes and salad, followed by apple pie à la mode. I limited myself to one glass of wine and listened carefully to recommendations for restaurants, points of interests and neighborhoods that would suit my family's needs. I explained that I would be house-hunting somewhere in Chapel Hill and mentioned Abby's joining the college's English faculty.

"Lou is a trustee of UNC; I'm sure she'll help in any way possible," remarked Burns, as if it was the Burns family's right to run the college. I expressed my thanks, not mentioning that Abby wouldn't need help. I resisted the impulse to tell Burns that my wife was a real catch for Chapel Hill.

It was clear to me that Jeremiah and Lou were extremely influential and powerful people in these parts. Having met them, I could also see that there was tenderness and affection between them. After we finished eating, Lou excused herself and Burns took me into a conservatory, where he opened a cedar humidor, offered me a large cigar and took one for himself.

"Burns and Murphy Special Number One," he said. "Best in the world. You can't buy these anywhere. They're made just for me and my friends."

He took mine back and, with expertise, used a gold cutter to slice one end and then trim the other. He gave me back my cigar and repeated the exercise for himself. After lighting a match, he lit my cigar and had me puff. Then he did the same for himself. With the ritual completed, he drew slowly on his cigar until it burned scarlet. I followed his example. Burns rang a bell and a servant entered. "Coffee for two." We sat back into the armchairs, puffing on our cigars.

"Would you care for a cognac?"

"Coffee will be fine, thank you." I needed to keep a clear head. The servant returned, served our coffees and left.

Burns looked at me. "I know you have questions."

"Indeed I do, Mr. Burns."

"Jez, please."

"To start, why did you want to destroy *The Monitor* and cheat the bank?"

"Interesting beginning, straight to the point. Cheat is a little strong. I thought journalists kept an open mind." When I said nothing, he sighed and then continued. "The short answer is biblical, an eye for an eye. There's a lot to explain. Before I get to why things happened the way they did, are we off the record?" I nodded my confirmation.

Burns explained how, after the Civil War, his father partnered with a neighbor, Leland Murphy, to form Burns and Murphy. They focused on cigar production from their home-grown tobacco. I learned that Burns' mother died when Jez was young and he left school to work for his father, who then married Etta-Fay Gordon, a wealthy woman. He used her money to expand the business and improve their living quarters from one grubby room to a three bedroom home with inside plumbing. Etta-May and his father had two children together.

"My Dad died when I was eighteen. I found myself as head of the household. I never cared for Leland Murphy but Dad liked him, even though he drank away a lot of the profits. After Dad's funeral, I made a tough decision. Within a year, I bought Leland Murphy out. Etta-May financed me.

"I went to Durham and bought some land where I built a factory. In those days, cigarettes were expensive to make and not popular. I had plans to sell cigarettes to the masses.

"I believed if I could produce them well and cheaply, they would soon become favored and I would make a fortune into the bargain. I invested in the new Bonsack cigarette machines and took on people to work them. I also employed all kinds of engineers and technicians to improve cigarette manufacture and production."

"What is a Bonsack machine?" I asked.

"Actually, there are two machines. Both mass produce cigarettes. You feed tobacco in one end of the first machine and rolled cigarettes appear at the other end, with filters already attached. Then you feed the rolled cigarettes into the second machine and they come out in packs of twenty and then cartons holding ten packs."

"Sounds like simplicity itself."

"That was more than forty years ago. I had a big problem. How do you persuade the public to change their smoking habits and buy cigarettes? Not easy, but I had a lot of faith in myself in those days."

"I'm told you're regarded as a marketing genius." The moment I spoke those words, I saw his expression change. Was it modesty or simply a quiet acknowledgement of his gifts?

"So they say," he finally replied, reverting to a Carolina drawl. "I'm proud of what I developed, but I confess I had good help. I brought in New York people, experts in advertising, to design a campaign. We changed the name of our cigarettes from B & M to Holborns, followed by New Holborns and Gordons.

"I hired huge billboard sites in Times Square, New York and downtown in Boston, Chicago, Los Angeles and other big cities. We used radio, newspapers and magazines to advertise our cigarettes. We got a heck of a lot of publicity. Etta-Fay blew a gasket when she saw what it all was costing.

"Look at us now. We have 22,000 employees in our Durham factories alone. We have offices in New York, Los Angeles, Boston, Dallas and Chicago, agencies in all other major US cities as well as Canada, South America, Europe, Africa, Australia and New Zealand. We have grown a world-wide business." Jez explained that his family held sixty-two percent of the B & M ordinary shares. I tried to do a mental calculation to value its worth. It was too big a number for me to work out.

I still wanted to know why Burns was so set on damaging First Bank. As his story unfolded, I began to understand what made Jeremiah Burns tick.

I wasn't surprised to learn that First Bank had been keen to get B & M business for years, but Burns was loyal to the local banks. His brother, Charlie, decided not to join him in the tobacco business. Charlie became a successful trader in stocks and shares, and First Bank tried to get to Jeremiah Burns through Charlie, offering Charlie very favorable loan terms. At first, Charlie's business thrived, but in October, 1929, the $700,000 First Bank had loaned was lost in the Wall Street crash.

I found this confusing. "That was nearly twenty years ago," I said. "What does it matter now?"

I saw anger rising again in Burns' face. "It was the Great Depression. First Bank hounded Charlie to repay the money. He was forced to declare bankruptcy. I offered to clear his debt, but he was too proud to accept my help."

Burns shifted his weight, as if giving himself more time to think about his response. "So proud," he added, "that he told me, 'Jez, if you pay off the bank, I'll never speak to you again.' And believe me, he meant it."

Burns went on to reveal that the bank continued to hound Charlie. An honorable man, he worked at low level jobs to try to clear his debt. With interest mounting, he made hardly a dent in the loan principal. Work and worry killed him.

"He passed seven years ago," said Burns, his face changing with intense anger. "As far as I am concerned, First Bank killed him. They might as well have lined him up against a wall and fired bullets at him." I could see Burns fighting to control himself.

"I wasn't aware of any of this," I said, feeling some of his pain.

"That's no surprise," Burns shot back. "Those bastards at First Bank would hardly tell you the truth, would they? You'll learn that in these parts, we have a tradition of revenge, getting our own back. Like I said, an eye for an eye. Now you know why I screwed the bank for twice what Charlie owed."

I understood the emotions behind his actions, but there was something else I needed to know. Burns sat down and smiled at me. "So now you know the truth, how else may I help you?"

"Why destroy *The Monitor*? Why damage the livelihoods of all those people?"

"Business is business," he replied. "Besides, some of those people have found other jobs. And the ones who haven't, they were probably no good at what they did. It's just business, David. You can't let sentiment get in the way."

"So the ends justify the means?" I said, with more than a hint of challenge in my voice.

"Exactly."

I chewed on that for a moment. "If I fail to rescue the newspaper, you win, but if I save it, you lose. Does that make you my enemy?"

Burns smiled. "First Bank is small potatoes. And if you'll forgive the mixed metaphor, I have other fish to fry."

He crossed the room and poured another cognac for himself from a decanter. Holding it up to me, I shook my head and he returned to his overstuffed armchair.

"The tobacco industry is a good, solid business, but price controls and other issues will affect it over the years. People like me, the ones who run the American business engine especially in the tobacco industry, we have to diversify."

I was curious about those 'other issues' he mentioned, but I didn't want to break into his explanation. I now knew I didn't like the man, but I found his views educational and certainly germane to the future of *The Monitor*.

"The federal government is weak," said Burns. "This is good because politicians make a mess of whatever they touch. Businessmen like me, the Rockefellers and the others and bankers like Warren Burgess, we're the ones who run the show. We keep America supplied with decent housing, affordable food and life's necessities." His mouth twisted into a scowl. "You think the federal government does this or gives a damn about it?"

As Burns talked, he predicted a shift in world power with America in the lead and a massive growth in US military spending. Using his business prowess, he had already invested heavily in munitions companies.

"I fully expect all these investments to be increasingly successful," he told me. "If you want to be ahead of the game," he said, pointing at me, "invest in the munitions industry now. I'll even tell you which corporations to put your money into."

"And if I don't?" I asked, not liking being told what to do.

"More fool you. You'll miss out on a bonanza that will last decades. Between Truman's doctrine, the creation of the United Nations and the new CIA, our military will be more and more in demand. Who do you think will provide the equipment needed to beat other nations, especially the Russians?"

I checked my watch. It was almost four o'clock and I needed to cut this short.

"I'm sorry, but I have to go," I told him. "Many thanks to you and Mrs. Burns for your hospitality." As we stood, I added, "You have a magnificent home."

Burns smiled and nodded his thanks. "Next time, I'll show you around the estate. And you must have a tour of our Durham factory. As your paper is writing about this town, you need to understand how the tobacco business works. And I bet you haven't been out in the countryside." I shook my head. "Try the Crystal Coast. Have some time down there with your family before the summer ends, but go early. By July, it's too hot and there are too many mosquitoes."

"I'll talk to my wife. Thanks."

"Use my place," Burns added. "It's small, but it's perfect for a vacation. Now, before you go," he said, his eyes twinkling, "you still haven't answered my question. Why save *The Monitor?*"

When I responded, my eyes twinkled back. "For the same reason you sell cigarettes. It's what I'm good at."

On the drive back to the city, I asked myself why Burns had been so open. True, he had told me little that could not be found in a good reference library, except for the Charlie Burns and First Bank business. I had to admit to myself that I was seeing him in a different light. He was a major player in American business.

I still needed to check the facts and I made a mental note to look into the Crystal Coast. However, if I took my family there, it would be on my terms. I was not about to accept his hospitality and find myself beholden to this shark. Nor would I put a penny into munitions stocks. Under no circumstances would I be tainted by associating with Jez Burns.

Chapter 5.

On Friday, I left Durham before lunchtime. I drove direct to First Bank to see John Rayburn. As soon as we were seated, I scrapped the pleasantries.

"You lied to me," I told him. "You knew why Burns took action against the bank. Why didn't you tell me the truth?"

When Rayburn replied, I wasn't sure if he was contrite or defensive. "Would you have taken the job if you knew the truth? Besides, I had nothing to do with that business with Charlie Burns. Believe it or not, I didn't even know about it until a few weeks ago."

I wanted to argue the point, but he didn't give me the chance. "I am appalled that we hounded Burns. Since I heard, I've made changes here so it can never happen again."

Was he telling the truth or merely placating me? If the latter, I didn't like being played.

"How can I trust you now? I have grounds to rescind our agreement. And to be honest, I'm thinking about it."

Rayburn seemed to be working hard to keep his expression bland. "I understand what you're saying, but I think you'll find our agreement is watertight."

"Not if it was based on misrepresentation. You told me a downright lie!"

John became contrite. "David, the bank needs your help. Can we get this behind us?"

I wanted to rip the agreement up there and then, but something stopped me. I didn't want to walk away from *The Monitor* and its people. In fact, what I'd learned made me all the more determined to save the newspaper and confound Jez Burns.

In my book, Burns was just as bad as Rayburn. Talk about a nest of vipers. I told Rayburn I'd think things over and left as abruptly as I had arrived. I was still hopping mad. Maybe Abby was right. I didn't know the South.

I returned home to find a smiling Abby. "Guess who called me?" she asked.

"Isn't this when I give you the opportunity to reply 'the President' or 'the Pope' or other select luminaries?"

She ignored me. "The head of English at UNC. He wants me to start right away. I'll be in Chapel Hill in early February and they have an apartment for us near the campus. Are you good with this?"

My smile answered that question. "Have you told the kids?" Without their endorsement, the transition could be rocky at best.

Abby had already asked Gerry to look after them during the week and we'd spend weekends with them.

"It's only for three months," she said. "I think it might be good for them. Who knows," she added, hope in her face, "maybe they'll learn to appreciate us?" We both giggled. We agreed that we'd not move them to Chapel Hill until the end of the school year. By then, we would have found a house. Abby gave me one of her winsome smiles and I waited for the grand finale. She didn't disappoint.

"We should give them a holiday when they arrive," she said. "And all sorts of treats which you will fund, starting with dinner tonight at The Devereux. Our table is booked."

Was there something I was picking up in her voice? Hesitation, perhaps? "Abby, sorry to repeat myself, but have you actually told them?"

Another smile, less winsome. "I thought we'd do this after dinner. You know, soften them up and then tell them at an ice cream parlor." She stared out the window for a moment. "To be honest, my conscience is bothering me. I need you to help me with this one."

How could I say no? Abby had taken the lion's share of child rearing. It was only fair that I step up and do my part.

The Devereux was a renowned Richmond eating place, one that the kids loved. It catered for all tastes and ages. We skipped dessert and went to the children's favorite ice cream parlor. The children were into their two scoops of vanilla and strawberry when I broke the news of their mother's impending departure. They seemed to take it well and I figured that was because they adored Aunt Gerry.

It wasn't until our plans were in place that I realized how difficult it was for Louis and Charlotte. They were very attached to their mother and they missed me, too. Over the coming weeks, they showed their child's side, clinging to us when we arrived for weekends and being stoic when we left them on Sunday nights.

As much as I wanted to focus on my children's needs, the ensuing weeks were so hectic at the newspaper and demanded pretty well all my attention and time. My *Bugle* team returned one by one from the beginning of February. Two weeks later, I helped Abby move to Chapel Hill.

Everything picked up speed when Peter Garibaldi arrived in Durham and took charge. He increased our workforce by nearly a hundred, many of them former *Monitor* staff. He also took on a new editor, Brutus Elliott, an old friend from college days. Brutus had a strong background in town newspapers.

Peter and I discussed Joshua Frost. We agreed that he wasn't cut out for editing, and as Joshua wanted to return to the crime beat, we made that change too.

The newspaper's content started to improve. However, during its downslide, competing newspapers had taken away many of our readers. We knew it was going to take a great effort to get them back. Henrietta Carson faced a formidable task in marketing and sales, but I didn't doubt that she was up to it. If we could double our advertising revenues and more, the paper might have a real shot at survival. During her month's stay, she went to work at full throttle. With ten days to go before she was due to leave, our circulation figures showed a slight improvement, rising to 31,000. I was pleased, but I knew higher numbers were needed.

Henrietta persuaded me to try something we had done at *The Bugle* when I took it over. Give readers free newspapers for a week. When I told John Rayburn, he wasn't happy but the terms of our deal didn't give him a veto. The bank would have to carry the cost. I had to smile. A little bit of payback.

The plan worked. By the time Henrietta returned to St. Luke, our daily circulation was more than 37,000 and advertisers were starting to come back in serious numbers.

Henrietta hired Luther Hoyt to take charge of the advertising department. "Luther's got the potential to be as good as me. Not better, mind you," was her parting shot. I found Luther a bit cold, but Henrietta knew her business.

My newspaper experience told me we needed a scoop, something to attract readers, an exclusive that had a chance of being syndicated nationally. If we found that story, our circulation could double. I talked things over with Abby one night.

"You have a great story. Why Burns shafted *The Monitor* and First Bank."

"I can't use it. I agreed that what Burns told me was off the record."

"I know but can't you get it verified by a third party? Then you won't have broken your word."

"Theoretically, you'd be right but I don't operate that way and the only body that can verify the story is First Bank. Rayburn won't admit to something on the record that would put his bank in such a bad light."

"It was just a thought."

"I know. A scoop won't just drop into our laps."

Good newspaper work can be like a criminal investigation. It takes sleuthing, going door to door asking questions, digging deep and never giving up.

It helped that I had Abby to talk with at night. She was very busy, setting up lectures and seminars, meeting colleagues and students and settling into college life, but she always found time to listen. Some nights, we both came home late and exhausted, but our lives were full again, meaningful. We felt guilty about the children and the distance between us, but mid-week telephone calls and weekend visits helped ease our discomfort. Aunt Gerry assured us things were fine. Yet both of us worried about the day when there might be a reckoning from our offspring. We pushed that aside and kept working.

*****

Durham's business was tobacco and B & M was one of the tobacco corporations in the area. Two of the other 'Big Four' were also based in Durham. I felt strongly that I should find out more about a business that sustained not just the city, but buttressed the economy of the state.

I called Jeremiah Burns and told him I wanted to accept his invitation to visit his factory. "Come tomorrow," he said. "I'll be here. How's nine o'clock? We can have a bite afterwards." I told him that worked fine. "And dress in layers," he added. "It'll be cold outside, but the factories are both heated and air conditioned. Expect to be here for the whole morning."

I asked myself why a tour would take so long. I assumed that producing cigarettes wasn't that dissimilar to producing a newspaper. I could give a tour of *The Monitor* in thirty minutes, twenty if pushed.

I presented myself at B & M at nine o'clock sharp. Burns met me and took me into his office. After being in his home, I expected something palatial, but I had misjudged the man. His office was small and functional. He must have noticed my surprise because he said, "I don't need a huge office to remind others how important I am."

Before I could respond, he launched into a description of the manufacturing process. "What is important is consistency," he said. "When people light up a New Holborn or a Gordons, it has to taste like it did last week, last year, even ten years ago. This isn't easy."

The door opened and a woman peeked in. "I'm truly sorry, Mr. Burns. I told Emma Jane you were busy, but she insists on talking with you right now. What shall I do?"

Burns turned to me. "Sorry, it's my sister." To his secretary he said, "Let's find out the latest disaster."

The phone call was put through. Burns spoke. "Emma Jane, I'm real busy here. What is so important?"

I could hear the conversation because his sister had a very loud voice. She told him that her son, Beau, had been arrested by the police, he was going to be charged and could go to jail for five years. "You gotta help him!" she yelled.

No matter how important we might be, I thought, we're never too important to have a family crisis. This sounded like a doozy.

Burns sighed. "What's my nephew done this time?" She said Beau was being charged with lending money in breach of the usury laws. Burns exhaled loudly.

"Okay, Emma Jane, I'll make some calls. I'll get to the station precinct as soon as I can."

Burns put the phone down and turned back to me. "My apologies. I have a wayward nephew who refuses to listen to good advice. Hopefully, I'll be back to see you for lunch."

I made a mental note to talk with Joshua Frost about Beau. Was there a story here?

Burns called his secretary and delivered curt orders. "Have Earl come up here," he told her. "And get Bush Pollard on the phone. Tell him to meet me at the Pound Street precinct straight away." He hung up and exclaimed, "Hell! I don't need this today."

I assumed that Bush Pollard was one of Burns' lawyers. Earl Hunt arrived promptly. He was B & M's head foreman. As the number one man on the factory floor, his word there was law.

"Busy day, Mr. Burns. What can I do for you?"

Burns introduced us and we shook hands. "David here is the editor of *The Monitor*. He has expressed a wish to understand what we do here. I'd consider it a personal favor if you'd show him round." Turning to me, he added, "Hope to see you after the tour."

I could tell Earl was up to his ears in work, but the boss would get what he wanted. He always did.

Chapter 6.

Earl Hunt led the way outside and headed towards one of the many factory blocks on the B & M site. As we walked, I studied the man. He was short and sinewy, balding and with no memorable features. 'Nondescript' suited him well, yet there was an inner strength about him, not a man to dismiss.

He stopped outside Building 7. "Apologies for being abrupt," he said with a pleasant drawl. "It's a busy day. Give me a minute to delegate some things and we'll start again." While I waited, I saw the unmistakable figure of Jackson Murphy, the Silver Leaf plantation manager. Dressed in modern clothing - no fancy 19th century costumes today - he was twirling car keys on his finger. He hardly glanced at me and went about his business as if I wasn't there.

Earl returned and we continued into the building. "You might think making a pack of cigarettes is simple," he said. "Trust me, it's not." I followed him through a door leading into a hallway. "If you get confused, feel free to ask me any questions."

"My knowledge is limited to knowing some people who buy a pack and light up a cigarette."

"You're on virgin ground, eh?" he replied, smiling.

I was warming to him and it struck me that this tour might be interesting at several levels. I'd certainly learn about the cigarette manufacturing process and I might get more insight into Jeremiah Burns.

Earl explained how cigarettes were once rolled by hand and how the modern process began right here in Durham, in the 1880s.

"James Bonsack invented a machine to make cigarettes," Earl explained. "It turned out 100,000 a day, per machine. By hand, the maximum was three hundred a day per worker. The prototype machine was improved and daily capacity rose to 300,000. Bonsack also developed a machine that made the packs holding the cigarettes and the cartons holding the packs."

As we walked around the building, my education continued. I learned that growers sell their tobacco at auctions, which are held throughout the harvesting season. B & M could not grow anywhere near enough tobacco to meet the demand. Thus a lot of product was bought from other plantations at auction.

We entered a factory. Earl pointed out a cavernous area where tobacco arrived from the auction house. I noticed that all the workers were Negroes but their supervisor was white.

"The clerk checks the tobacco lot tag. If he finds any errors, the tobacco is sent back to the auction house. Otherwise, it's logged in and taken by elevator to be blended and dried." As he spoke, we climbed stairs to the top floor and crossed another large space. I saw several conveyors that ran the entire length of the building. Each carried sticks extending down one side and had tobacco piled nearby. As the chain moved, women hung handfuls of tobacco on the sticks. Again, I noticed that in this factory every worker was Negro. What were the reasons for their segregation? Maybe a silly question, knowing the ways of the South. What were these workers paid? Was it the same as their white counterparts?

Earl's response to my questions was straightforward. "We observe the law."

Earl returned to an explanation of the process. "When the sticks arrived at the other end of the conveyor, women remove them and place them on large wooden racks mounted on wheels. These are rolled to re-drying machines."

Earl mentioned the process was repeated in many factories on the B & M site. As Earl continued his lesson, it dawned on me that the manufacturing process was far more complicated than I'd imagined. I was shown how the passage of tobacco through a three-chamber re-drying machine takes about an hour and precision is vital. After the tobacco is processed, it is compressed and subjected to a stemming process, where the woody part of the stem is stripped from the leaf. All compressed tobacco is then transferred to a warehouse for aging.

I was taken aback by the heavy heat, uncomfortable conditions and the lack of ventilation. Everything was very clean, but only because workers swept and dusted continually. When Earl informed me that ventilation wasn't good for processing, it struck me that this was a place where tobacco took eminence over people.

Negro workers seemed to hold no positions of authority and they were segregated from the whites. I am sensitive to atmospheres. Most of the workers I saw looked sullen and defeated. Lincoln might have freed the slaves but not in B & M.

We entered another building where the tobacco was placed in piles and arranged on an automatic spreader, which emptied onto a conveyor. Earl pointed to another similar-looking conveyor which had Turkish Leaf tobacco and we watched the two conveyors combine and blend the tobacco. "After the tobacco is re-inspected for foreign materials, it's taken to the bulking room, where it settles into its final state before cutting and shredding."

Earl introduced me to Ray-Henry Jefferson, a large Negro supervising the cutting process. Earl was called away and I asked Ray-Henry if he would talk to me about conditions in the plant.

"It's no secret there's unrest here," he said, looking around to make sure we were not overheard.

"We've been asking for better wages and conditions, but it's been two years and we've got nothing. There was a union guy, Ed Butler, who was helping us, but he's gone."

I asked where and received an odd look. "You call yourself a newspaperman? He was murdered last October, his family, too."

The expression on my face conveyed my surprise. "Can we meet privately?"

Ray-Henry paused for a moment. "It's dangerous; I'll let you know."

I appreciated his willingness to even consider it. For a Negro in this town to share information with any white, much less a newspaperman, would take courage.

Earl returned and got back to business. He pointed out how the cut and shredded tobacco fell onto a conveyor, delivering it to more drying and cooling cylinders. I didn't need to look to know they were operated by Negro employees. I saw how tobacco went into spreaders and was dropped into tubs for delivery to operators, who eventually turned the product into cigarettes.

As Earl led me out of the building, I asked, "Do whites work here?"

"Sure there do. They do the same jobs in other buildings. It's the law," he said. "Separate, but equal. Like I told you, at B & M, we observe the law."

"Are they equals, like equal pay?" I asked.

"Can't say. You'll have to find that out from someone else."

I took the reply as a 'no', but realized there was no future in this line of questioning. After two hours or so at the plant, Earl led me to the final manufacturing area: numerous four-storey brick buildings, each one as large as a city block. They were well-lit and air conditioned for climate, humidity and dust control.

Cigarette-making machines, CMMs, were in a line, military-style. Tobacco went in one end, wrapped cigarettes with filters and brand names stamped on them came out the other and taken to other machines.

I watched the final stages of the process, putting cigarettes into packs, wrapping each with cellophane and then packing them into a carton box, sealed and ready for shipment. Interestingly, this part of the operation was handled by women only. "Their fingers are nimble," Earl explained.

Earl took me aside to a quieter area. "Mr. Driscoll, what you won't understand is the precision timing needed for the total process to work. Today, we are making packs of New Holborns. In a week's time, a pack may be smoked anywhere in the USA. It has to taste just like it did today and weeks and even years ago. It's all about consistency. Mr. Burns is at the forefront; he devised the entire production line and the process. He spends his time making sure our customers are happy with what they buy. He's a tobacco genius."

I thanked Earl for his time, we shook hands and I asked him to direct me back to Jeremiah Burns' office. I was impressed by the production process, but tension among the workers was palpable. I felt resentment and not just among the Negro workers. Was this an omen of impending trouble at the plant? Was there a story here? I needed to ask more questions of my staff. After all, B & M was a major employer, so it made sense that it would be under my paper's spotlight.

Whatever the situation, Jez Burns had earned my grudging respect for his business acumen. Like Truman, he was a man in total control.

Chapter 7.

I returned to the administration building. A woman from the accounts office approached me.

"Hello, Mr. Driscoll," she said. "I'm Dolly Peel. You're the new boss at *The Monitor,* aren't you?"

"I am," I told her, not sure if I should be flattered or concerned.

"I recognized you from a picture in the paper," she said cheerfully. "I just wanted to shake your hand."

As she did so, a piece of paper was pressed into my palm. She left quickly, without looking back. When I was sure no one was watching, I unfolded the note. *Please talk with me. It's important. Come to 17, Aspen Road, Durham, tonight at 7:30 if you can. Make sure no one knows you're coming and you're not followed.*

I slipped the paper into my pocket and made my way to Burns' office. He had not returned. His secretary gave his apologies. "Please tell Mr. Burns how much I'd enjoyed the tour. "I'll be in touch," I added.

Back at my office, I met with Joshua Frost and explained that I had a few things we needed to discuss. The first topic was Beau Beaufort.

"Do you mean Jeremiah Burns' nephew?"

"That's the one. The Durham Police just arrested him."

My crime editor's eyebrows shot up. "Why? What for?"

"I'm not sure, but I gather he's been lending money illegally. Is this a big deal in North Carolina?"

Josh thought this over for a long beat. "I think it carries a maximum sentence of five years. I'll get onto it. My contacts have told me nothing, so Burns has probably hushed it up already."

"There's something else. Does the name Edgar Butler mean anything to you?"

This time, Josh had the answer. "He was a colored, worked for the tobacco union. There was a grisly murder last year; Butler, his wife and their two children were murdered in a KKK-style operation. The killers were found at a roadhouse that same night. They had been murdered too."

"Would you get into this as well? I'd like to know everything the police know. Are there any suspects?" Josh shook his head.

"Why not?"

"It's the same old story, boss: whites killing coloreds. No brownie points and no votes for the Chief of Police there. Anyway, the likely killers were killed themselves."

I tried to smile at his cynicism, but neither of us found it funny.

"Who by and why?"

Josh just shrugged

"Okay. I want to know about labor relations at B & M? Who can talk to me? There seems to be a lot of resentment there, especially among the Negro work force."

"That's not going to be easy. I need to think that one over."

I told him to get back to me when he learned anything. Then I called Abby.

"Late night, I'm afraid. May I explain when I get home?" I knew that I was testing her patience, but I also knew that she would understand.

"Okay. I do have a lot of work to get through," she said.

I stayed in the office until dinner time and ended up driving to Mama Dips for fried chicken and collard greens. After I ate, I drove around until I was certain I wasn't being followed.

This was more for Mrs. Peel's benefit than mine. If she wanted to tell me something, she was more likely to spill the beans if she was happy her instructions had been followed. At 7:30, I knocked on her door and she let me in.

"Where's your car?" she asked.

"Up the next street, a good two hundred yards from here."

She peered behind me, as if expecting Jeremiah Burns himself to appear. "Are you sure you weren't followed?"

"I've done this before, Mrs. Peel. We're okay."

She seemed to relax a little. Dolly Peel was probably in her mid-sixties, a petite blonde with a withered face. However, in her day I was willing to bet that she would have been called a looker.

"Would you like coffee?" she asked. Five minutes later, we were seated together, hot mugs warming our hands.

"How can I help you, Mrs. Peel?"

"It's Dolly," she said, showing signs of a smile. "I work in payroll at B & M. Some time ago, maybe last September, I met a tobacco union colored, Edgar Butler. He said he'd been talking to B & M colored workers who were unhappy about a lot of things, including a compulsory deduction from workers' pay as a form of healthcare insurance. Most coloreds had seventy-five cents deducted each week. Mr. Butler discovered that B & M employed only one doctor and two nurses, at a total cost of $150 per week. That costs B & M $7,500 a year. However, take 15,000 colored workers, multiply by seventy-five cents and you have $11,250 per week. Where does the excess go? Is it retained in cash by B & M? Mr. Butler knew I was sympathetic towards the coloreds and he wanted to know what happened to that surplus money."

"Did you know any of this before Mr. Butler approached you?"

"I've been working in payroll for forty years," she said. "I don't have documented evidence, but I believe the surplus goes direct to Jeremiah Burns. If you've got a head for numbers, we're talking around $575,000 a year, all untaxed."

I wondered how she could possibly know what Burns declared to the IRS.

"There's more," she said. "Mr. Butler talked with many colored workers at the factory and they trusted him. He'd worked at B & M before he joined the union. Not only did workers sign statements about this scam, but I provided him with payroll details showing healthcare deductions. After he was murdered, the police said they found no papers at his home. So tell me, where have they gone? Were they all burned in the fire?"

"Who else knows of this scam, apart from you?" She shrugged, so I asked her why she was sharing this information with me.

She hesitated, then replied softly. "I have a score to settle with Mr. High-and-Mighty Burns. Forty or so years ago, he nearly killed me. Afterwards, I couldn't have kids."

I didn't know what to say. How true was any of this? Why had Dolly waited until now before saying anything? I know revenge is a dish best served cold, but this one was frozen solid. I needed another viewpoint. I thanked Dolly and promised, "If there's a story, we'll publish it."

The next day, I called Emily Venn and repeated what Dolly had told me. Her immediate reaction was to find out what Burns and B & M had declared in their respective tax returns. She suggested I try to get a rundown of everything, including hospital costs, surgery and other expenses.

The following afternoon, my crime editor came into my office.

"Which do you want first?" Josh asked. "The Butler murders, Beau Beaufort or the B & M workforce?"

"What have you got on Butler?"

Josh exhaled loudly. "To be honest, nothing. The Butler family lived a mile or so outside of Durham in Oak Grove. It's a small place with no shops, no services, not even electricity. Residents are colored families who work in Durham.

One night last October, soon after Butler arrived home, three men arrived in a truck at his place. They set fire to a cross outside the house to scare the neighbors. Two men went inside and shot the Butler family dead. Their final act was to set fire to the home, as well as Butler's car. All the men wore sheets and hoods, but the neighbors could see they were whites from their hands."

Josh went on to explain how later that night, the police stopped at a roadhouse and found a waitress and three men dead. There was a truck outside and sheets and hoods were found inside it. The tire marks matched those outside Butler's house. The dead men were never identified and there were no missing persons' reports matching their descriptions. "The bullets that killed the Butlers did not match those that killed the men," Josh concluded.

I thought about this for a moment. "Were any papers rescued from the Butler home?"

"I spoke with Buck," Josh said. When he saw my confusion, he added, "Buck LeGaillard, our Chief of Police. He says there was nothing to rescue. However, I know one of the clerks at his station and she tells me there was evidence that wasn't logged in."

"Work with Brandon on this one." I told him. At my request, Peter had hired Brandon Hanes, a young Negro whose first job had been a junior on a small Raleigh newspaper published for the colored community.

"Send him to Oak Grove to see what's there. Maybe one of the neighbors knew what Edgar Butler was working on. He should also go to the union and ask about B & M workers. Maybe he should talk to the workers, too."

Josh looked at me and I saw concern in his eyes. "Brandon's a reporter first, a Negro second," I told him, but my words didn't seem to convince him.

"I don't doubt Brandon's abilities as a journalist," said Josh, "but I do worry about his safety."

"We have much to learn before we move forward," I told him.

"Why the interest? What do you know that I don't?"

I smiled as I tried to appear confident. "Joshua, a yoke of oxen couldn't pull the cart hauling what I know and you don't!" Josh had the good grace to laugh. "Now, what about the B & M workforce?"

Josh shook his head. "I doubt anyone here will want to investigate. Burns made a very big and dark mark here at *The Monitor*. Our people are terrified of him."

I told him to leave this for another time. "What can you tell me about Beau Beaufort?"

The very mention of the wayward nephew's name caused Josh to smile brightly and with no small amount of glee.

"This one is interesting and not just because of the facts. What makes it so juicy is that the family is trying to hush it up. As you know, our boy is Jeremiah's nephew. Beau has quite a history for someone of his age of running get-rich-quick schemes that backfire. I believe Jeremiah has bailed him out more than once.

"Anyway," he went on, enjoying these revelations, "Beau formed The Big Mint Loan Corporation, raised money from investors and paid them interest at five percent per quarter. He then loaned the money at ten percent or more per week, usually in small sums of ten and twenty dollars at a time. Despite these paltry loans, the scheme attracted investors to the tune of nearly a million dollars. Three weeks ago, Big Mint's checks bounced and it was declared insolvent."

I wondered how many struggling people had been caught up in this racket. "I can see the ethical issues, but where's the crime?"

"Ah, this is where it gets intriguing," promised Josh. "It seems that Beau was warned repeatedly by the State Commissioner that he was practicing usury. In North Carolina, it's a crime to lend money without a license. Beau ignored the warnings and the State got him. If he's found guilty, he could well go to prison. Now," he went on, eyebrows raised, "get this. Bush Pollard is an old attorney friend of mine and he looks after some of the Burns family legal matters. We talked off the record and I learned that there's a meeting scheduled for tomorrow. All those investors who lost money are invited. My guess is that Jeremiah Burns will try to buy them off, in exchange for their agreement not to press for a prosecution."

"Is there a story here, Josh?"

This time, Josh spoke so loud it sounded like a bark. "Are you kidding? This is front page, David, above the fold!" He used his hands as a bracket and announced, 'Tobacco Baron Bails Out Wayward Nephew.'

"Great banner-line, but you got it off the record."

Josh sat back hard in the chair, thinking.

"Don't worry," I told him, "we can work this from both ends. Call the State Commissioner and get him to confirm or deny the story about Beau. I'll listen on the extension, but I want to do something else first."

I put in a call to Jeremiah Burns. When I had him on the line, I explained that I'd be publishing a story and wondered if he'd like to comment.

"So there's no misunderstanding, Mr. Burns," I added, "this conversation is on the record. Joshua Frost is listening in."

Burns was an old hand. He said nothing except, "I'm Mr. Burns now, am I?"

I set out the case against Beau, giving him the broad brush of the story we intended to publish.

"So, what do you want from me?" His voice had turned testy, suspicious.

"I'm telling you as a matter of courtesy," I explained. "You can give me your side of the story, if you want."

"Do you know your history, Mr. Driscoll? Consider me the Duke of Wellington." Before I could respond, the phone went dead.

"What the heck did he mean by that?" asked Josh.

"The Duke of Wellington famously told the London press to 'publish and be damned.' Write your story, Josh. No one else has it."

I figured the piece would cause a stir and I was right.

The Durham Monitor – February 23rd, 1948.
Jeremiah Burns Nephew Accused in Money-Lending Scam.

The name 'Burns' carries considerable weight in this city. Jeremiah Burns, major shareholder and chief executive of the Burns & Murphy Tobacco Company, is a mover and shaker in both Raleigh/Durham and this state. His corporation employs thousands of our residents. Everyone in North Carolina knows of Jeremiah Burns. Sadly, the good reputation earned by Mr. Jeremiah Burns may be sullied by the actions of his nephew, Beau Beaufort.

This newspaper has been told by an informed source that Jeremiah Burns is negotiating with investors to return their investments in Big Mint Corporation, an unlicensed lending vehicle run by Beau Burns, in exchange for their agreement not to press charges. Mr. Burns himself does not deny it. While family ties are important, Mr. Burns needs to remember that it is for The People, through the state's Justice Department, to decide whether a person should be prosecuted for a crime.

Undoubtedly, Jeremiah Burns has ample wealth to buy off the civil actions against his nephew, but the criminal implications are a separate issue. Mr. Burns should realize that no man is above the law and that his nephew must face criminal justice like any other citizen.

The story was a scoop, front page news for three days and our circulation rose to more than 60,000 in just one week. The newspaper was starting to look like it might be back in business. It had given Jeremiah Burns a well-deserved bloody nose.

Whether Burns was annoyed or not, he remained silent.

Beau's investors were paid off. For the moment, the nephew escaped the public humiliation of a trial and prison sentence.

"I can only guess what went on between Beau and his uncle," I told Abby.

"Are you worried that Burns will try something?" she asked. When I didn't respond, she added, "Like revenge?"

Why should I worry about revenge? I had freedom of the press on my side! But I forgot it's the quiet ones you have to watch.

Chapter 8.

The door to the room opened and a man in his sixties entered. He was of medium height, spry for someone of his age and he had dark hair speckled with grey. He smiled at the woman seated in a high-backed armchair.

"Good evening, my dear," he said. "How are you?"

She was dressed as if attending a cocktail party. Her off-the-shoulder black dress was stylish and made even more so by the stiletto-heeled shoes. Adding a final flare to her appearance was a hat, a black satin cloche with a veil folded away from her face. When the man motioned for her to rise, she complied.

He kissed her gently on her cheek and led her to the bed, where he removed her hat, turned her around and slowly unzipped the dress, holding her arm as she stepped out of it. As she stood there in a black lace bra and panties, he stripped to his underwear.

"Lie on the bed," he told her, picking up his jacket. From the inside pocket he removed a six-inch hunting knife. With one swift move, he slipped the blade under her bra, where it joined between her breasts. As if waiting for her to show signs of terror and then satisfied when her eyes widened with fear, he gave a tug to the knife.

Twenty minutes later, he dressed himself and left without a word. The woman was left on the bed, shaking and sobbing. Her face was bruised, as were her arms and legs. She stood and went into the bathroom, where she washed away the heavy makeup. The face staring back was not that of a woman but of a girl. She was twelve years old.

The man wanted a drink. He climbed into his car, adjusting the rear-view mirror to take an appreciative glance at the eyes staring back. "She's no longer of interest to me," he told his reflection. "Time to move her on."

BOOK TWO.
Spring, Summer and Fall, 1948.
Chapter 9.

The Durham Monitor - April 17th, 1948.
UNC Debate Challenges Plessy Ruling.

Last night, there was a debate at the University of North Carolina in Chapel Hill. The motion asked whether the 'equal but separate' doctrine of Plessy v Ferguson, a Supreme Court ruling back in 1896 about race, remained relevant in modern American society. However, there was a wider, unmentioned question, namely whether the treatment of the American colored people as second class citizens remained acceptable? The event was much anticipated and very well attended by renowned academics and journalists, both locally and from D.C., New York and Boston. A full report of the speeches can be read on the inside pages of today's edition.

Speaking for the motion was Professor Marrett Montgomery, an alumnus of UNC and a state Appellate Court judge. He based his case on tradition and status quo.

The argument for equal rights was made by another legal heavyweight, Chapel Hill Law School Professor, James Joseph (Jimmy-Joe) Burdett, also a practicing attorney. His forceful argument was that if we are not a nation of laws and equality, we are nothing.

Since the formation of the United States, men and women of color have suffered discrimination politically, economically and in every other conceivable way. The American Constitution gave no legal protection to colored people until the passing of the 13th and 14th Amendments.

The results of such discrimination were most forcibly expressed by Mr. Jefferson Smith of Madison, Mississippi. Part of Mr. Smith's trip to Chapel Hill was made in segregated rail cars where he travelled with other coloreds. He told how his grandchildren were being educated in a segregated high school that was starved of funding because it was situated in a poor district. He lives in a society where he must wash his clothes in a segregated laundry and where he cannot eat with whites in a public place.

Mr. Smith told the audience how his working life had been spent at Burns & Murphy where he, like all other colored workers, was paid significantly less than white workers doing the same job.

He also spoke about how he was forced to live in poverty through low wages and discrimination and that he had always been treated as second class by a company that knew riches beyond belief.

The few minutes accorded to Mr. Smith put paid to any arguments of equality which separatists might wish to use. With dignity and eloquence, he expressed the discrimination visited on him during the whole of his life.

In my short time in Durham as editor of this newspaper, I have found North Carolina to be a progressive Southern state. If the people of this state truly believe in American values of equality and justice, they should demand that their political representatives lead the South to seek to change its ways and prejudices. Our society should end discrimination based solely on the color of skin. This newspaper will support any legislator who puts his hat into the ring for this cause.

Chapter 10.

I met with my editorial staff every afternoon. This is when we discussed where things stood on current stories and investigations and what the content of the front and inside pages would be in the next day's edition. It was at this meeting a week or so after the Chapel Hill debate that I asked Josh where we stood on the Butler murder story.

He took a deep breath and exhaled loudly. "Nowhere, I'm sorry to say." He explained how Brandon Hanes had questioned Butler's neighbors, but got nothing. "The police have co-operated in their inimitable fashion," he said. "They showed Brandon the barest details of their investigation, so we can't accuse them of refusing to deal with the press."

"What's your assessment of this?" I asked, noticing what I thought was a sadness in his eyes, or was it defeat?

"I'm sure we have a racial problem here, as much as anything else," he said.

"Have you spoken with the Chief of Police yourself?"

"Buck LeGaillard and I have history. It's personal and it happened a few years ago. That's all I'll say. We don't have much of a working relationship."

I knew better than to press Josh, especially in front of the team. However, if history could get in the way of performing his job, it would have to be discussed.

"How have you survived as a crime editor in this town without the help of the police chief?"

"There are other cops who don't like Buck," said Josh. "And they help me. This time, Buck has cut off our access."

After the meeting, I mulled over the problem. I knew someone who could help, but I didn't know how things stood between Jez Burns and me after the stories about his nephew. There was only one way to find out. It took some time to get through, but I was patient.

"Well, well, our esteemed editor of *The Monitor*. What do you want?" Burns asked, his voice coming through the telephone like acid.

"First," I said, "would you tell me if we're on speaking terms?"

Burns sighed audibly. Was this derision? "Ah, yes, the Beau situation. You must know I'm not a man who harbors grudges, unless you're a bank. In a way, your stories actually helped."

"I'm listening," I said, curious to hear this interpretation.

"Beau's wings have been clipped by the exposure and he's doing some proper work. He's also behaving himself for a change. Probably won't last long, but he's out of my hair for now. Mind you, there's still a criminal trial for him to face." After a pause, he added, "So how can I help the fourth estate?"

I was relieved by his explanation and also by the fact that I didn't have to watch my back. "I need to get the Chief of Police to cooperate with my people, but he's stonewalling us on an investigation."

Burns laughed. "Getting' some real Southern hospitality, are you? It's best that I don't know what you're investigatin'. I need your assurance that it has nothin' to do with Beau or me." Burns' use of Southern drawl was his reminder that I was a stranger in his neck of the woods.

"I have no evidence to the contrary," I said, hoping this would satisfy him.

There was a pause. "In that case, I'll have a quiet word with Buck, suggest he speaks to you. He's his own man, so no promises."

"Fair enough," I replied. "Thank you. Now, what do you want in exchange?"

"I don't work that way, David. However," he quickly added, "Lou would like to meet your wife. We gather she has quite a reputation as an academic. Why didn't you mention it before? How about coming over for dinner on Monday night?"

My curiosity got the better of me. "Thank you. I'll have to check with Abby, but I expect it will be fine. I'll confirm."

"Oh, and by the way," Burns added, "we dress for dinner. Please be here for 7.30."

*****

The next day, Buck LeGaillard called and invited me to meet with him. That afternoon, I sat across from the Chief of Police in his untidy office, replete with police paraphernalia and memorabilia. Seated at his steel desk, LeGaillard was an imposing figure. Not so tall, but a big man, maybe two hundred and forty pounds and solid. He was bald, his neck short and his biceps bulging from a short-sleeved shirt. Not someone to mess with.

"Well, Mister Driscoll, uhh, how might ah help you?"

I wasn't fooled by the slow, good-ol'-boy southern drawl. This was a man to be approached with caution. At the same time, the last thing I wanted was for him to think I was intimidated. I chose the direct approach.

"I'm a blunt man, Chief. I want to know why you're stonewalling my reporters on our investigation of the Butler murders."

I saw the slightest change to his face: narrowing of eyes, compression of lips. "You're refusing to show my people statements and documents obtained from the scene of these awful crimes and you've provided no information whatsoever about the roadhouse killings. As a newspaperman, I have to ask, what are you hiding?"

With all my accusations on the table, I waited for his response. LeGaillard leaned forward, elbows on the desk and stared hard at me for a moment.

"Well, Mister Driscoll, ah guess that's blunt enough. Perhaps you ain't aware, being from up North, we have somethin' in this state called due process."

I started to protest, but he held up a beefy hand to silence me. "This is an on-goin' investigation," he said, "and providin' the information you seek could prejudice a future prosecution."

"That's an interesting interpretation of the law," I said with as much irony as I could muster. "Perhaps you could direct me to the statute that prevents you from disclosing the information? Because, sir, I think you'll find that our First Amendment rights trump anything you've got. So," I said, giving him a little smile, "I repeat my question. What do you have to hide? Or should I ask: Who are you protecting?"

LeGaillard stood so quickly, hands clenched into fists, I half expected him to strike me. Instead, he announced, "If you think I'm withholdin' information or protectin' someone, get a court order."

Burns had told me LeGaillard was his own man. I changed my tack. "Chief, I believe you are running for re-election next year."

"So?"

"Would it help you to have *The Monitor's* endorsement?"

He sat down hard, his eyes never leaving my face. "You offerin' me a bribe?"

I tried to look appropriately shocked. "Good lord, no! I may not know much about the South, but I know politics. You've won twice before, but you face a serious challenge this time around. Being an independent, you have to raise your own finances.

"An endorsement from an important local newspaper will give you a boost. Now," I added, bringing the point home, "if I believe your department is refusing to cooperate with the fourth estate for no good reason, I'll not be inclined to have my newspaper back you."

"So, it's not a bribe, Mr. Driscoll. Instead, you're blackmailin' me."

"Chief, you're plain wrong. If you're the best man for the job, you'll get *The Monitor's* endorsement regardless."

LeGaillard stared at me for what felt like a long time. "Send a reporter tomorrow and ah'll see what ah can do, but don't send that Joshua Frost and don't send your nigger reporter neither."

I decided to let that comment go this time. "One more thing: Chief, can you tell me why your people are no nearer to solving nine murders today than they were six months ago?"

"Mister Driscoll, five of those murders, the waitress, the cook and the three guys, took place off my patch or, as you would say, outside my jurisdiction. The murder of the Butler family was almost certainly committed by the men who were killed that night. We've uncovered no clues, at least not yet. Are you suggesting ah'm sittin' on my hands?"

My sixth sense, experienced by many of us in the newspaper business, came into play. Was LeGaillard anxious, even scared? "Let's say that I'm getting a strong impression that in these parts, the murder of a colored family doesn't count as much as the murder of whites. I hope I'm mistaken. Good day, Chief."

With that, I stood and walked out.

The following day, I informed my team that I'd decided to involve myself directly in the Butler case. I had to tell Josh that LeGaillard made it clear he wouldn't deal with Josh.

It was even more difficult to accept that the police chief wouldn't give Brandon Hanes the time of day. "I'll check out the police investigation of the Butler story," I told them. "Josh, you and Brandon can look into everything else and write the story if we get any evidence. Incidentally," I paused before adding, "it's high time Brandon started to meet with the tobacco union people, as well as the colored B & M factory workers."

I explained that Brandon needed to proceed with caution and to see workers outside the gates of the factory. "If he can meet in their homes, fine, as long as it's out of the gaze of any white workers." The last thing I wanted was trouble for my staff. "Are we agreed?" I asked everyone. I wasn't surprised when members of my editorial staff fought my involvement with the Butler case.

"You're the editor-in-chief," said Brutus. "You can't do that job impartially and be an investigator, too. This is a mistake."

"Why don't we see how things progress?" I suggested. What I didn't add was that long ago I discovered an instinct for unearthing unsavory truths. My decision to overrule the staff, at least for the time being, was based on more than a gut feeling. Later, I made a list of the questions I needed to have answered. Number one on that list: What is LeGaillard worried about?

Chapter 11.

Monday came and I arrived from the office late in the afternoon. Abby hadn't returned from Chapel Hill. I showered, and readied myself for a night at Silver Leaf. I was having the usual difficulty with my bow tie when she walked in.

"Here, let me do that," she said.

I didn't object. Abby's father had taught her well when it came to tying bow ties. She looked admiringly at her handiwork and then at me. "You scrub up well, Mr. Driscoll. Sometimes, I think you're prettier than I am."

"Never! Abby, you have thirty minutes. I'll wait downstairs."

Just over half an hour later, I heard Abby walking down the stairs. I looked up and my chin nearly dropped to the floor. The first time I saw Abby, I fell for her. She was the prettiest girl I had ever seen. Now, all these years later, she was a beautiful woman. On this night, however, she gave full meaning to the word *glamorous*. I could hardly breathe.

"You like my new dress?" she teased, knowing full well the effect it was having.

"I would charge through a herd of angry buffalo just to hold your hand. You look fantastic."

With her hair up, her long neck was so graceful. Her shoulders were bare and the dress, the color a rich silver-grey, fell to three-quarter length. There were sequins on the bodice and the dress fitted like a glove, showing her shapely legs. As I zipped her up, I took the opportunity to kiss her shoulder.

"I really hope you like it," she whispered.

"Words, my darling, cannot do the dress or you justice."

"Good," she said with a laugh. "Because it cost a fortune. I'm hoping it's my birthday present."

Without a word, I strolled into my study, unlocked a desk drawer and pulled out a black velvet box. I returned to Abby and handed it to her.

"Happy birthday, darling."

Abby opened the box and gasped. With what seemed like reverence, she removed the pearl necklace and matching earrings, gazed at them for a long moment and then looked up with tears in her eyes. "David, they're gorgeous, I love them. Shall I wear them tonight?"

I smiled. "Here, let me help you."

I secured the clasp of the necklace and waited while she slipped on the earrings. I took a step back and said, "Perfection!" I reminded myself how much I loved her. We'd had our ups and downs over the years, but I could not imagine life without Abby. After a long hug, we left the house. As we drove towards Silver Leaf, I thought to myself that Jez Burns might be one of the wealthiest men in the South, but he would never know the joy I felt being married to Abby.

There was traffic heading out of town, so we arrived at Silver Leaf fashionably late. Drinks were being served in the conservatory adjoining the library. Burns, an effusive host, came over to greet us and I noticed his eyebrows rise as he appraised Abby. Abby caught his look, but appeared unaffected. Burns turned his attention to the other guests and made introductions.

Among those present were Robert E. Lee Dixon and his wife, Mary Beth. Dixon was a professor at UNC, but I knew nothing about him. He was a little over five feet tall, bald and overweight. I guessed he was in his fifties. He was nervy and his eyes seemed to twitch. He smoked a cigarette as he shook hands. There was ash on the lapels of his tux. I got the impression that he was a man under pressure.

Dixon's wife wore an old-fashioned long, black dress which looked like it had been designed in the thirties. She was plain and mousy, the antithesis of Abby.

Next, Burns introduced us to James Burdett, who I remembered from the Chapel Hill debate. In contrast to Dixon, Burdett oozed confidence. At the debate, I had only seen him from a distance. Close up, he exuded conscious charm. I detected the danger of a viper.

"Everyone calls me Jimmy-Joe. Nice to meet you both."

Burns guided us to a couple standing nearby. "May I also introduce Max Gardner and his lovely wife, Sally Jean? As I'm sure you know, Max is a big wheel in this state's Democratic Party. People, this is David and Abby Driscoll. David's the new editor at *The Monitor* and his beautiful wife is a member of the English faculty at UNC."

I knew Max Gardner by reputation. He was the chairman of the North Carolina Democratic Committee. He held no elected political office, but he was the acknowledged boss of the Shelby machine, the outfit that controlled politics in the state. A man of medium height, he had a swarthy complexion and rheumy eyes that he fixated on me when he shook my hand. I estimated he was in his fifties. He looked very fit for a man of his age. His wife, Sally Ann, who I later discovered was Mrs. Gardner number three, was probably twenty years younger, a stunning redhead in the style of the Hollywood star, Susan Hayward.

We shook hands with several more guests and exchanged greetings, when Jez took my arm. "Our other guests, the esteemed junior US senator for this state and his new wife, are a little late, but I'm sure they'll be here soon."

"Who's he talking about?" Abby whispered to me.

"Billy August, Junior. A young man making his way in the Senate. He got married a month back. I don't know much about him and nothing about his new wife."

Abby indicated she would converse with Mary Beth Lee, who seemed out of her depth. I was left with the men.

"Did you enjoy our little debate last week, Mr. Driscoll?" asked Burdett.

"Call me David. Indeed I did. You argued very forcefully."

"Don't believe all you hear," he said and then winked at me.

Before I could respond, the door to the conservatory flew opened and in swept Louise Burns, accompanied by Senator and Mrs. August. Billy August was the youngest man in the room by several years. In his mid-thirties, he was trim and fit. Perhaps an inch over six feet, he wore his jet black hair long. With piercing blue eyes and a ruggedly handsome face, he cut a dramatic figure. His wife was petite, blonde, very pretty and giggly. I'm sure I wasn't alone in noticing that their clothing was in disarray. I reminded myself that they were newlyweds, so all could be forgiven.

Louise Burns announced, "I'm glad you're all here and I'm sorry to have kept y'all waiting. Has everyone a drink? Jez, are you being a good host?"

Jez rushed over to his wife's side. "Of course I am, darlin'. The mint juleps are flowing and everyone's happy as could be." He took his wife's hand and guided her to Abby and me.

"Now Lou, you know everybody except Abby Driscoll here, David's wife. Abby, may I present my wife, Louise Beth Burns?" He said this with pride.

"Everyone calls me Lou," she announced.

Abby and Lou started to converse, while assessing each other. Lou was wearing a tailored white evening suit. I had not expected to see her in trousers, but a woman with her figure and looks could carry off anything.

I turned my attention to the men, who were talking about how the federal government wanted to interfere in the businesses of all states and North Carolina in particular. Among the erudite men in the group, it was Jez Burns held court.

"How can we, as American businessmen and leaders, employ people and grow the economy with government on our backs? I understand the need for regulation in wartime, but we won that war almost three years ago! So, can anyone tell me why we still we have a prices and incomes policy? Why in the hell should some pencil pusher in Washington dictate the price of my cigarettes? Jimmy-Joe," he said, turning to Burdett, "you're the legal eagle. Why don't you and your lawyer brothers do something about this?"

I heard that last comment as more accusation than a question. All eyes turned to Burdett.

"Don't blow a gasket, Jez," he said. "All of us are in the same boat." I wondered how a lawyer who taught college and had a successful private practice could be affected by prices and incomes restrictions. "We have an election in a few months," Burdett continued. "Dewey and the Republicans will change everything. Truman and his party don't have a prayer. Just look at the polls," he added with enthusiasm. "Good times are a-comin'."

I asked myself, how could such a view prevail in a Democratic state? I guessed this was politics, Southern style. I reminded myself the state was Democratic in name only.

Burns stared at the attorney for a long moment.

"I should hope so," he replied. "That so-called Southerner," he added, referring to Truman, "has been in the White House three years too long. And he gets more luxurious benefits than a king."

"And you don't?" mocked Burdett, his voice suggesting that he was unwilling to be dominated by his host. "Come on, Jez, it's Congress who decides what the President gets. From what I hear, Truman's a pretty modest guy."

When Burns laughed, it sounded like a derisive snort. "Yeah? Well, he's got a lot to be modest about."

"Jez," coaxed Billy August, using the convincing voice he perfected during his run for the Senate, "he's not that bad. And he is a Democrat, after all."

I noticed that Max Gardner refrained from comment, despite being the most powerful Democrat among this group. I could have mentioned my interview with Truman, but it occurred to me that name-dropping, especially by a newcomer, would not sit well with this group. Instead, I turned to Robert E. Lee Dixon.

"Might I ask where you fit into this group?" I asked. "Are you Jez Burns' physician?"

Dixon pressed a hand against his chest, as if controlling himself. "Oh, no!" he smiled, "I'm in medical research. I'm a professor at Chapel Hill. I'm also a member of the Burns and Murphy Health Board."

There were a dozen questions I wanted to throw at him, but I had to go carefully. This man could hold the answers to accusations I'd heard about the health care of B & M workers. "How interesting," I said, keeping my voice friendly. "I'm new here, so could you please explain what the Health Board does?"

"It oversees the health of the B & M employees. Jez is a progressive in this area, as you might know, and he does what he can to provide a safe working environment.

"I also advise on health research issues which might be related to the tobacco industry."

'Like cancer and heart disease,' I thought, but kept it to myself. Before I could speak, we were interrupted by Lou's announcement that dinner was served.

We entered the dining room where Lou directed us to our seats. I sat to her right, opposite Jimmy-Joe Burdett. Abby was seated next to Burns. The Dixons, Gardners, Augusts and others were in the middle.

"Now, Jez," announced Lou, "no more business or politics till later, please. I know our old friends are used to you, but we must show our polite side to our new friends." She smiled first at Abby and then me. "We thought we'd have a Southern dinner in your honor. Now, I know that barbeque is the state food," she said, making a face when she said *barbeque*, "but I wanted to do something different."

"When my wife gets a bee in her bonnet," laughed Burns, "there's no point disputin' her."

Lou threw a look at Jez, a cross between annoyance and affection. "To start, we're having fried green tomatoes. Then to follow, it's suckling pig with all the trimmings. Now, I know that fried chicken would be expected, but trust me, our chef does a great hog dish. I'll leave dessert as a surprise. Oh, yes, we serve California wines. We love them and I do hope this will be a treat for y'all."

"Sounds delicious," said Abby. "Reminds me of home. Did you know I'm a Southerner?"

"I'd heard that," said Jez Burns, "but I understand that David captured you and dragged you up to Yankee-land."

Abby smiled. "And I have lived a life of shame and despondency ever since."

As the evening progressed, the conversation remained light. Once again, Burns surprised me with his relaxed, easy side. Lou beamed throughout dinner and even the Dixons seemed to lose their nervousness. The guests questioned Abby and me about our exploration of their state and were shocked to find that we had seen very little. Our excuses of work and weekend travels were dismissed, numerous suggestions were made and soon we had lists of trips to the west and the mountainous as well as the Inner and Outer Banks to the east.

A servant entered and whispered to Lou. She rose, giving her excuses and that she would return momentarily. I turned to Burdett and asked if he lived close by.

"Well, yes and no," he said. "I'm Jez's neighbor to the east, but Silver Leaf is a big spread, so it's an eight-mile drive to get here."

I had no idea the Burns estate was so vast. "That's quite a distance," I agreed. "Have you lived there long?"

"It's not my ancestral home, if that's what you mean. I bought the place about twenty years ago."

As interested as I was, my real curiosity centered on the debate. I asked if we could discuss it. "You made a magnificent case," I told him.

He nodded, clearly pleased. "Thank you," he said. "If you look at the language of the Constitution alone, there is a strong case for desegregation, but it's not that simple. There are many issues to consider."

"Such as?" I asked, and noticed that conversation around the table had gone suddenly quiet.

"Shall we leave this as an after-dinner topic?" Burns chimed in. I assumed Lou would not approve of this discussion at table.

At that moment, Lou returned. "I apologize for my absence. There's an issue at the orphanage that needed my attention. Now," Lou said, smiling at her guests, "are we ready for dessert? I've been looking forward to this all day. Our chef has mastered the dish."

"You have a Southern chef?" Abby asked.

"Oh, no. On one of our European trips, Jez and I found Maurice in a hotel restaurant in Cannes and we grabbed him. He's been with us for years. Luckily for us, he's made himself a master of Southern cuisine."

The dessert was brought in and displayed with fanfare. It was a peach cobbler with home-made maple ice cream. Abby's mother had been a marvelous cook and had made wonderful cobbler puddings, but one bite of this and I had to admit that Lou was absolutely right. It was like no other cobbler I'd ever tasted. The peaches were juicy and tart, baked in a Graham cracker crust, which was light and had a hint of semi-sweet biscuit. The ice cream was not sugary and was the perfect complement to the peach. In all, the combination was pure ambrosia. I could see from everyone's faces that this dessert was a hit.

When everyone was finished eating and that overall luster of satisfaction settled over the room, Lou announced, "Ladies, shall we?"

With that, the women stood and left the room. Moments later, on cue, servants arrived with bottles of bourbon and cognac, as well as pots of coffee.

"Old world and new," said Burns, pointing to the bottles. "There are some European traditions I really enjoy, like sipping cognac after dinner." He pointed to one of the bottles. "This cognac's special, a Delamain. And for those of you who like to drink American-style, we have George T. Stagg Kentucky Straight." There were appreciative murmurs as we indicated our preferences.

Burdett turned to me and began to speak, as if the conversation had never been interrupted. "You want to know why I'm opposed to desegregation." I tried not to look as if I'd been caught off-guard and gave him my full attention. "We have a way of life in the South and that includes traditions, beliefs and links with the past. What we do and think, well, we've grown up with these customs, we're comfortable with them. You like motor cars, I believe."

I nodded. "Yes, they are a bit of a passion."

Burdett nodded. "So how would you feel if you were told, regardless of what you could afford, that you cannot have your choice of make and model? Or worse, you cannot have an automobile at all. What would you say?"

I had no idea where this was going. "I'd say it was a gross interference with my freedoms, not to say a breach of my First Amendment rights."

"Indeed." Burdett looked around and saw that he had everyone's attention. "For years we've had people who don't live here, but they tell us what we should or should not be doing with our coloreds." Tipping his head in emphasis, he added, "We've obeyed the law. We've kept things separate and as equal as has been reasonably possible."

I felt pressure. I was the newcomer and needed to fit in. "Doesn't that depend how *reasonable* is defined," I responded. "Take our host's factory in Durham. Do coloreds have equality there?" How many coloreds work in management?"

Burns quickly interceded. "Now you two, don't be going hammer and tongs at each other. Surely we can agree that there are two sides to this debate and we won't solve things tonight." With that, he rose and walked to the sideboard, where he lifted a humidor and brought it to the table.

"Gentlemen, may I cut you each a B & M Number One Special?"

Soon there were large cigars being smoked, as cognacs and bourbon were being sipped. We all sat back and enjoyed these luxuries and it was several minutes before Burns spoke again.

"David, you're a new friend and won't know how things work in these parts. We Southerners work together, one backing the other. It's what we do."

Burns looked directly at me. The silence made me uncomfortable, but I wasn't going to be the one to break it. "There are other gentlemen who are both friends and advisers," Burns finally said, "but they're not here tonight. I'd like to introduce them to you and I'm hoping you might like to join our group."

A strange feeling crept into me. Was I being recruited? If I became part of their group, would I be expected to suppress my professional voice?

"Jez, in what way could I help you? I'm just a journalist."

Burns leered. I thought of a wolf going in for the kill. "You're being rather modest, aren't you?" he said. "You know your way around Washington and you know the real players there. I'm a bit of a fish out of water in D.C. and there's a limit to what Billy here can do. You could give me pointers, advise me."

All sorts of questions flashed through my mind. Was Burns in trouble with the federal government? Unlikely. Surely, he had plenty of help in our nation's capital. What did he really want from me? I decided I didn't want to know.

"You flatter me. My connections in Washington aren't that good and I wouldn't want you to think they were. As you know, we journalists are an independent breed and I don't know of any editors who act in a kind of advisory capacity." Actually I did, but I sure as hell wasn't going to play ball with Jez Burns.

Max Gardner, Mr. Politics in these parts, looked hard at me. "Your connections were good enough to get you that interview with Truman. Perhaps, Mr. Driscoll, you're being too modest."

There was some kind of power game being played here and clearly I was the target. "I was fortunate to get the interview," I said. "Right place, right time. I am no Washington insider and I certainly don't want Jez or any of you to get the wrong impression."

Burns may have thought a row was brewing. I didn't know Gardner, but he did. "It was just a thought, David." With that, he stood and the others followed. "My watch tells me it's time to join the ladies, so bring your drinks and we'll have more coffee on the terrace. It's a lovely night."

When we stepped outside and joined the ladies, Abby gave me a look which said both *'thank heavens you're here'* and *'where the hell have you been*?' Burns apologized to Lou for keeping her waiting, although she seemed untroubled by our absence. We all chatted for a while until I explained that I had an early start in the morning.

"Lou, Jez," I added, "it has been a wonderful evening. Thank you very much." Abby added her thanks, we said our goodbyes and we were shown out. When we were outside the electric gates, I stopped the car and asked Abby if I could put the top down. We both understood that fresh air was needed at several levels.

"What an odd evening," she said, pulling the pins from her hair and letting it flow onto her shoulders.

"*Odd* is the word," I said, touching her face. She looked so lovely that it was hard to keep my hands off her. We kissed and I thought how special it was that we were still in love, after all these years.

"We'd better go before I get us arrested."

Abby giggled. "Where's your courage?"

"I left it back there at Silver Leaf." When she gave me a questioning look, I said, "I just turned down an offer from our host. He'll be gunning for me, I expect. I'll tell you all when we get home."

I put my foot to the accelerator and we were home in twenty minutes. In our bedroom, I unzipped Abby's dress and watched admiringly as she undressed.

"Do you really want to talk tonight?" She knew only too well how to be seductive.

"Yes, I want to talk," I answered and then paused for effect. "However, tomorrow morning will do."

Chapter 12.

The next morning, I called my secretary and told her I'd be late. Abby wasn't teaching until noon, so we decided to have a family breakfast. Although more than half the family was missing, this would be remedied soon. In less than a month, Louis and Charlotte would join us, with our dog Daisy. Abby prepared fried eggs, bacon, biscuits, fresh orange juice and coffee "Pity you don't like grits," she remarked. I made a face that brought on the giggles. With breakfast on the table, Abby said, "You seem disturbed by last night."

"Where to start? Apart from wanting to show off their home," I asked, "why were we invited?"

"Maybe it's because we're new and they're curious," said Abby, smearing butter on her biscuit.

"Why have us meet people who are said to be trusted friends and tied to Burns in ways I don't understand?"

"To flex his muscles and win you over to his side?"

I thought about this for a moment. "He knew enough about me to know I'd never lobby for him. And when he hinted in the strongest way that I would be taken care of financially..."

"I'll play devil's advocate," said Abby. "Jimmy-Joe Burdett is his neighbor. We know that he's an expert corporate lawyer, so it makes sense that he could play an important role in B & M and reject any role of lackey."

"We don't actually know he's one of Burns' lawyers, but go on."

"As for Billy August and Max Gardner, they're both important politicians. Burns owns a huge business, so it'd be expected that he'd have close ties to political movers and shakers. As for Dixon...I'm not sure."

She took a mouthful of eggs and chewed slowly before announcing, "Let me find out more about Dixon through college. If B & M indeed has a health advisory committee and if he's just one of the members, maybe you're seeing things that aren't there."

"All good points." I started to eat and then stopped. "Tell me, did Dixon's wife finally lighten up? She seemed too scared to say anything."

"She became even quieter. Mind you, Lou did most of the talking. She also made a few barbed comments to Mrs. August. In a polite way," she added, eyes sparkling with mischief, "she told Julie that it was unladylike and ill-mannered to have sex and arrive late for dinner!"

I wasn't sure how to respond, but Abby was clearly enjoying both the gaffe and our hostess's response to it.

"I'm curious about that call Lou took during dinner," Abby said. "Some emergency at the orphanage? I don't buy it. I asked Lou if I could visit the orphanage but she blew me off to begin with. She said visitors weren't generally welcome because the children got upset but she would call me to try and fix a date."

She added, her face suddenly serious, "I don't have a good feeling about these people. And our hostess has an infernal cheek. She found a moment to take me aside to admonish me. Our conversation was brief and Lou intended it to be hurtful:

> 'Here in the South, the wives of important men do not have their own careers. They support their men by running a home and taking care of the children. If you want to fit in here, you should resign your position at UNC, find a large house, take on servants and live the life of a Southern lady.'
> 'And if I disagree with what you say?'

'Regard for your husband in these parts will be less than it should be and doors will not necessarily open for him.'

'Indeed. I think you know I am a Southerner, raised in the Commonwealth of Virginia? In Richmond, women are not objectified in the way you suggest. But thank you for marking my card.'

'I see. Well, Jez and I only want to help. Shall we return to the other guests?'

"So, husband dear, the choice is yours. Shall I defy the leaders of Durham society and keep my position at UNC or would you like me to be the mistress of your house?"

"Will you come with crinoline, cotillions and curled blonde hair?"

"Naturally."

"In that case, I think I'd prefer to keep you as you are. I really don't want a big house and servants and I like the Abby I've got."

We sipped our coffee, laughing and enjoying the moment. I appreciated the chirping of birds and a light breeze through the trees.

"I did discover a few things about the men," I told Abby. "Burdett, it seems, is actually a segregationist, a white supremacist, despite his stance in the UNC debate. Burns hates the federal government and wants it to stop interfering with his business. By comparison, Gardner is the voice of reason. I believe he sees himself as equal to Burns, although I doubt that Burns agrees. August was chatty, pleased with himself, whereas Dixon said virtually nothing. Burns hinted that he paid Dixon enough money to support unspecified vices."

"In other words," said Abby, "none of these men have much in the way of redeeming features. Good thing we've done our social duty and don't have to go back, at least not for quite a while."

"If at all! Now I'm wondering if there was anything good about the evening."

"What about the cobbler? And I really do love my pearl necklace and earrings! Thank you."

I laughed and squeezed Abby's hand. "I don't have to leave for a while," she added. "Want me to model them again for you?"

I rose quickly from the table. "I'd like nothing better," I announced and we headed upstairs.

*****

When I arrived at the office with a smile on my face, Josh remarked, "Someone is in a good mood."

"Just a lovely day," I said. "Give me a few minutes and then let's talk."

I placed a call to Peter Garibaldi. After we exchanged pleasantries, I got to the point.

"I need to find a private eye in Durham. There seems to be a lot of dirt to dig into here."

"Why don't you ask your staff for a recommendation?"

"Two reasons. I don't want anyone here to know what I'm looking into, since I don't really know myself. And I can't be certain that everyone on my staff is trustworthy. I'm pretty sure there's a mole passing information to the former owner. The last thing I want is for anything to get back to the people I'm investigating."

"Fair enough," he said. "Leave it with me."

Two nights later, Peter called me at home to say he'd found someone. "Her name is Patti Lou Gains. Her office is in Raleigh."

When I asked how he'd found her, he said, "no names, David, but I have friends in low places. She comes highly recommended."

"What's her story?"

"Her father came from Boone in the Appalachians and was widowed young. He raised Patti in Raleigh on his own. He was a private eye. Patti worked for him until he died about eight years ago and she runs the business now. I'm told she's a straight shooter, reliable and good at her job."

We chatted for a while, which made me realize how much I missed Peter. I called Patti Gains and made an appointment for later that day. I parked a distance away from her building, not wanting anyone to know about this visit. I climbed to the second floor, knocked and entered. A middle aged woman was seated at the only desk in a sparsely furnished room.

"I'm David Driscoll," I said. "I'm here to see Miss Gains."

"You're looking at her."

Patti Gains was not an attractive woman, dressed in dumpy clothes and without make-up. When she smiled, it was more a glare. She led me into another room, where there were two tables covered with stacks of files.

"My filing system isn't classic," she said, clearing another stack of papers off a chair pushed next to an old desk, "but it works for me. Now, Mr. Driscoll, what can I do for you?"

I sat down. I appreciated her business-like attitude. For some reason, I took an instant liking to the woman. It was soon clear that this was not reciprocated. She preferred the direct approach, so I pushed aside pleasantries.

"Cards on the table, Miss Gains. I'm the new editor at *The Monitor*. We're looking at a number of stories where there are hints of wrongdoing."

"And where exactly do I fit in?" Ms Gains was not happy.

"I want a private investigator to look into a few situations for us."

She nodded, lips pursed. "So, I'll back up a kind of investigative reporting thing, is that it? You want me to muckrake for the muckrakers."

The expression 'hitting the nail on the head' came to mind, but I needed to play this carefully. "I wouldn't put it quite like that," I said. "I'm new down here and I don't know who on my *Monitor* team I can trust. I'm told that you're trustworthy, hence this meeting."

She pulled out a legal pad and took a pen from the desk. "Who are the people you want me to find out about?"

She wrote as I spoke. "Jeremiah Burns is at the top of the list and a few of his colleagues and advisers. Also, Chief LeGaillard and how he's connected to Burns."

She tapped the pen against the desktop. "In other words, you want me to help a Yankee by digging into our good ol' boy stuff, is that about right?" Before I could answer, she continued. "Of course you do. Let's get dumb Patti to dig up the dirt, probably wreck her business while she's doing it, but that doesn't matter, does it? Oh, and then you'll take all the credit if I find anything."

I stayed calm. "No, that's not it at all. Maybe it's best if we stop now." I stood to leave, then turned back. Trying very hard to keep my voice calm, I said, "At least show me the respect of finding out about me before you dismiss me and my ways of doing business." I held my ground, unsure how she'd take this rebuke.

She raised both hands, as if surrendering. "Maybe I was a little hasty, Mr. Driscoll. Give me a little time to check you out. If you're on the up and up, we'll talk again."

I gave her my card and asked her to call as soon as she'd decided. "And please call me at home," I added. "The number is on the back."

I arrived home to an empty house. Nearly six o'clock, it was still in the eighties and humid. I showered and changed into a T-shirt and shorts, then set about fixing dinner.

Despite the heat, I decided on baked potatoes and steaks. I turned on the oven, wrapped potatoes in foil, took two Kansas strip steaks from the fridge and started to make a salad. A few minutes later, Abby arrived.

"Good evening, chef," she breezed. "Before you say anything, I have to tell you that I know more than you do."

"Ah, Abigail Einstein, as I live and breathe. Of course you know more than I. After all, you are a fully paid-up member of the Flat Earth Society."

"Mock me, my friend, and I shall not only disrespect your cooking, but I will also not impart said information about one Robert E. Lee Dixon."

I kissed her. "To disrespect my cooking, most would say, is a kindness, but even I can't ruin a baked potato, can I? As for Mr. Dixon, it's a topic of conversation for dinner, which will be ready in about thirty minutes."

Fifteen minutes later, Abby bounded down the stairs, also dressed in T-shirt and shorts. "The outfit looks better on you," I said.

Eventually, we ate. Abby heaped praise on my culinary abilities, probably out of surprise. I don't kid myself about my skills in the kitchen. "So, tell me about friend Dixon."

"I can't tell you much about him professionally - he's medical and there's not much contact between medicine and the arts - but I can tell you that he's renowned for something else. Does *Assault* mean anything to you?"

"He attacked someone?"

Abby laughed. "No, it's the name of a racehorse. Everyone knows about the Triple Crown and that any horse that wins even one of these classic races becomes very valuable. Two years ago," she continued, "Assault won all three of them, a feat that is beyond rare. Our Robert Dixon won a lot of money when he wagered and won on all those races. A kind of three-race trifecta."

"How much did he bet?" I asked.

Abby shrugged. "I've heard it wasn't chump change."

"So he won big?"

"Nobody knows for sure, but some believe he cleaned up the best part of twenty-five thousand dollars."

I starteed to throw questions at Abby, but she stopped me.

"There's something else you should know," she said. "Dixon was found the day after The Belmont at six in the morning, sleeping it off in one of the campus ponds! How anyone can sleep lying in shallow water is beyond me."

"Or would want to."

"The point is, our Professor is a gambler, an addict. I've heard that his winnings went right back to the bookies. I've also heard that he's always short of cash."

I chewed this over for several moments. "So are you saying Burns knows about Dixon's betting weakness and that he keeps Dixon funded while Dixon does what Burns tells him?" I gave Abby a big smile. "And if so, dear wife, this is what we journalists call inspired instinct."

Abby laughed. "And that, my dear husband, is what the rest of the human race calls speculation. David, you can't possibly reach a conclusion like that."

"About...?"

"Burns effectively blackmailing Dixon."

"Of course I can't, but I reckon it's the sort of thing Burns would do. Anyway, thank you."

I told her about Patti Gains. "If she comes back to me, I'll have another ball-breaker on my hands."

"Oh, really!"

"I've got stories bubbling away, but nothing to print yet. I need better research. But the good news is that our circulation is holding pretty firm in the sixty thousands."

We cleared the dinner table and washed the dishes. I suggested we walk to the local ice cream parlor. There is something quintessentially American about ice cream parlors. All those flavors, all those toppings and the sweet aromas. For me it's intoxicating. I have to confess that Abby and I indulged to excess, but why not? Our children were arriving soon, so we wouldn't be able to behave like teenagers for much longer.

*****

At the editors' meeting the next day, I raised the question of a link between tobacco and poor health. After a brief discussion, it was decided to have one of the interns do some research and report to me. Twenty minutes later, Molly Nolan entered my office.

"Mr. Elliott says you have a task for me." The young woman was in her early twenties, well-dressed and confident.

"It's Molly isn't it? Good to meet you. I want you to check out whether the medical profession sees a connection between cigarette smoking and poor health. In Raleigh/Durham or Winston Salem, this would not be a popular investigation. Big Tobacco is responsible for tens of thousands of jobs, not to mention huge profits for the shareholders, but the public deserves to know what risks it takes by smoking. However, you must be careful."

"Any suggestions where I start?"

"There's a library at Duke, which I gather is your alma mater. See what medical journal back issues they have. Look at the major newspapers like *The New York Times,* starting from the early 1940s or even further back if you think you might uncover anything. I don't know about Duke, but UNC has a prestigious medical school; its library should be well stocked. However, if you speak to people, make sure you keep things general and do not tell anyone what you're actually looking for. Your cover story can be Advances in Medicine since the Great War."

Molly nodded. "If my suspicions are right," I continued, "and if they can be proved, we'll have a great deal of local opposition and a heap of trouble." I tapped my watch. "Now is a good time to start. Check in with me every few days and let me know what you find. And I repeat, be careful."

Molly made a good start and uncovered some interesting stuff. As early as 1912, an article in *Harpers Weekly* alleged that people were being poisoned by nicotine. She also discovered that in 1915, *The Scientific American* was reporting on the adverse effect of tobacco on the heart. I called Molly into my office to go over her findings. Any doubts I might have had about her research abilities were quickly resolved.

"After the end of the Great War," she told me, "American medical opinion on the health impacts of smoking was sharply divided. I found a 1923 *American Journal of Public Health* article saying that school records indicated the intellectual work of a student declined when he began to smoke. I found a very worrying study by a Dr. Roffe. In the 1930s, he developed a technique that distilled residues in burning tobacco. From this came his hypothesis that tobacco tars cause cancer."

"You say a hypothesis." We had to be very careful here, treading on the hands that fed thousands of local mouths.

"Yes, that's the problem. In 1937, Dr. James Walsh conducted a study and concluded that smoking was making previously rare ailments common. He also wrote that nature was reaching a limit where the introduction of foreign substances into the human system was harmful."

She went on to explain how the study was not proof beyond a reasonable doubt. "A few years ago, researchers at the Mayo Clinic found evidence that smoking tended to constrict blood vessels and increase heart rate and blood pressure. But they were unable to link such conditions to any definite cause," she added.

"So as of today, there's no conclusive proof?"

Molly nodded and then launched into more research findings. "There's an article in the *NEA Journal* which states that lung cancer cases in America have tripled over the past three decades. It's entitled *Cigarette Smoking Causes Lung Cancer* and it's given me the incentive to quit smoking."

"Good for you!" I told her. "Is there anything on the other side of the argument?"

"Indeed there is," she said with an emphatic nod. "For example, a 1934 *Hygeia* article - that's the AMA magazine for the general public - states that smoking by mothers was probably not an important factor on infant mortality. There have been numerous studies, very possibly funded by the tobacco industry, that smoking is the norm for adult Americans and is not harmful. You might recall last year's Reynolds advertising campaign, boasting, *More Doctors choose Camels than any other cigarette*. It's against the interests of the tobacco industry to allow their products to be linked to illness. For me, this explains the storm of pro-tobacco advertising."

"Sounds about right."

"There is a wider issue you might not have considered," said Molly. She had my full attention. "Let's say there's conclusive evidence that smoking is bad for our health. If that's the case, what action should the federal government take?" I waited for her to explain, anticipating that it would be well thought out.

"That would make it a serious public health issue, one that the government would need to address. Should people be allowed to smoke? But what right does our government have to regulate personal behavior?"

I thought this over for a moment. "Are you saying there is a state's rights issue, and that it's for individual states to determine the extent to which its citizens need protection?"

"I think it goes further," she said. "Does the government, whether federal or state, have the right to intervene in a scientific dispute?"

"And your answer?"

Molly grinned at me. "Better brains than mine are needed to resolve that question. I guess the equivalent was Prohibition. Drinking in large quantities was bad for the drinker and his family but government interference failed."

"You argued the case well. Have you taken law courses?"

"No, but I prepared for today."

"You did a good job, thank you."

She stood to leave, but turned back. "If the story progresses, may I work on it?"

"We'll see, Molly, but so far, good job."

*****

That afternoon, Brandon Hanes and Brutus Elliott came to see me. They felt it was time I was brought up to speed on Brandon's investigations.

"Brandon," said Elliott, "tell David what you've discovered." I looked at Brandon and nodded.

"A while ago," said Brandon, "the Local 31 tobacco union executives wanted the colored B & M workers to strike for better pay and working conditions. The Tobacco Workers Union muckymucks at head office refused to support any strike action."

"Did you find anything about Edgar Butler?" I asked.

Brandon shifted his weight, taking his time before responding. It struck me that, as one of the few Negro reporters in the area, he must have felt an enormous responsibility to be more prepared than his white counterparts.

"Hundreds of colored workers spoke with Butler about the absence of medical care, despite money taken from their pay every month. Butler took their pay slips with him, but they were probably destroyed when the Butler home was set on fire. From my talks with the colored workers at B & M, as well as some union people at Local 31, the TWU bosses in Maryland might have been bought off by B & M. It surely sounds like bribes and payoffs are involved, but I've got no evidence."

I wanted to say that everyone in this part of the world seemed to have a hand in someone else's pocket, but I held my tongue. "What did Butler ask the Negro workers?"

"He wanted to know exactly what job they did, how long they had worked at B & M, what their pay was and what deductions were being made from their wages."

"And did you get any statements from them? Did you seen any of those pay slips or anything like this?" Brandon Hanes shook his head.

"But I do have a list of names of the workers I spoke with, their job descriptions and notes of the conversations. The Local 31 representatives refused to talk to me on the record, but I have fairly meticulous notes of our meetings. After Butler was killed, the B & M investigation was closed down by 31. Their explanation was that they didn't want to risk the lives of anyone else."

"Did you speak with LeGaillard?"

Brandon looked askance. "Depends how you define 'speak.' Our meeting wasn't exactly long or productive and it sure wasn't friendly." I waited while he seemed to be sorting through his thoughts.

"As it turned out," said Brandon, "all the Chief told me, I could have found out by reading any newspaper. I asked to see the police files and the evidence collected from the scene of the crime, but the Chief refused. He said the on-going investigation might be compromised and any case brought by the state could be prejudiced."

I shared a long moment of frustration with my reporter. "Did you challenge him?" I asked and immediately regretted it. Brandon could easily interpret that question as distrust on my part. "There's no law that I know of that gives the police such protection," I added.

He gave me a look. "Of course I challenged, him. I'm not that green, Mr. Driscoll. As you can imagine, my attitude didn't go down well. The Chief told me that niggers who came into his station were usually locked up and that they weren't allowed to be uppity, to give him lip. He suggested I get out of his station before I found myself on a charge."

I felt my anger rise and worked hard to control it. "With what would he have charged you?" I asked, running through possibilities in my head. Brandon's face shifted and I almost expected him to laugh.

"Wasting police time," he said.

I took a breath and told myself to stay calm. There was only one way to handle this. I told Josh and Brandon to stay where they were and asked my secretary get LeGaillard on the phone. When the call came in, Josh and Brandon listened on an extension phone.

"Chief," I said, my eyes on the two men seated nearby, "I thought we had an understanding that you were going to cooperate with my paper."

There was a long pause before LeGaillard responded. "And I thought, Mr. Driscoll, you were sendin' a reporter. Did you send a nigger kid to wreck my election chances or just to embarrass me?"

Brandon shook his head, but said nothing. I tried to imagine how he felt, hearing himself demeaned like this. "Chief, under what law do you work? Where is it written that a Negro reporter cannot work in this town? By what law do you block a legitimate line of questioning by the press? And what protections of a defendant would have been violated? Where I come from, we call bullshit by its name and we also know what racial prejudice looks like."

"Well, Mr. Editor, it seems our deal couldn't last one meetin'. I was elected to do a job and my job doesn't include panderin' to niggers and helpin' them write stories about nothing."

"Tell you what, Chief. I'm coming down to your place now and I'm bringing my reporter. If you refuse to show me the evidence we're permitted to see by law, I'll take the problem to a judge. And if the judge refuses to follow the law, I'll take it to appeal, all the way to the Supreme Court if I have to. You might want to read the First Amendment to the Constitution before I get there."

I heard LeGaillard exhale. He took a beat. I waited. Finally, I heard, "Okay, okay, I'll show you the stuff I have, but just you, not that reporter of yours."

I had him and he knew it. "No deal, Chief. When are you going to realize that times are changing? Negroes have exactly the same rights as whites. Jim Crow is not law here. It's a dark blot on the South's landscape. So it's both of us or nothing and you know what might happen in your race for office if you screw around with me."

There was a long silence. "Okay, both of you. Give me an hour. I'll have the evidence ready."

Josh looked at me with respect. Brandon just blinked. I looked at both of them, asking, "Who is going to say 'not bad for Yankee help'? Brandon, come back in forty-five minutes; we'll go give the bastard a coronary."

At the police station, we were shown into LeGaillard's office. No pleasantries were exchanged, no words spoken and many eyes followed us. On a table were piles of charred papers. "I assumed you didn't want to see the personal effects, clothes, kids' toys and the like. If you do, they're in a warehouse. I'll stay here while you look, if you don't mind."

"Is this it, Chief? Nothing else?"

"That's it. There was a heck of a fire and nothing to fight it with. The house just burned to a cinder."

"Okay. Brandon, start looking."

Brandon approached the pile of charred documents. LeGaillard turned to me. "You know that this meetin' will get out. I'll be tarred and feathered for helpin' a nigger. My chances of re-election will be in smoke like those papers."

I was unable to conjure up any sympathy for the man. "We have a deal, Chief. *The Monitor* will be right behind you, now you've done the right thing. You can't tell me every white in this city is racially opposed to Negroes. That's just not so. And remember that no one can see what goes on in the voting booth."

I joined Brandon and we sifted through the papers. There was not much legible, certainly no pay slips that were any help. After twenty minutes, we gave up. I thanked the Chief and shook his hand. "We have a deal. You'll find I keep my word."

Back in the office, I told Brandon to keep talking with B & M workers. On my way home, I delivered a note to Dolly Peel's home, asking her to let me have copies of the payroll slips that Butler might have obtained. The next night, she called me to tell me it would take a few days and that she wanted fifty dollars for her trouble. I didn't like the woman, but I didn't argue. The evidence would be worth the cost.

I needed to see Robert E Lee Dixon. It had to be casual. Dixon would clam up if I made it formal. That Thursday, there was an end-of-year professors' shindig, hosted by the School of Medicine and there was a good chance that Dixon would be there. Abby and I arrived at the gathering and I was relieved to see Dixon, a bottle of beer in hand. His complexion was flushed, his eyes were bloodshot. From the look of quiet desperation on his wife's face, I guessed he had been drinking for quite some time and was feeling no pain.

It was one of those delicious North Carolina summer evenings, not overly hot, low humidity and a pleasant breeze. "Good evening, Professor Dixon," I greeted him, not sure he was sober enough to recognize me. "I'm not used to these occasions, but I like to support Abby."

Dixon stared at me for a moment. He seemed confused. "How are you, sir?" he offered. I resisted mentioning that, unlike him, I was sober. We made small talk. There was no point in engaging him in serious conversation. This would have to wait. I found Abby and told her that for me, the night was a waste of time.

"Abigail, I have been remiss. I should teach you the game of poker. There's a hand known as a busted flush, when you hold four cards of the same suit but the fifth card is another suit. Meaning the hand is a waste of time and effort."

"Ah, got it," she said. "That's why I play solitaire, a game for innocents."

She left me to talk with her colleagues and I found a few people for conversation. They were complaining about a grant made to a colleague, which made me think yet again that I would never understand college politics.

The next morning, I telephoned Dixon. "Good to see you last night, Professor."

"Did we see each other last night?" he asked. "I have to confess, the ache in my head tells me I may have had one or two too many."

"I plan to be on campus later today," I told him, "and I'd appreciate a little of your time."

When he asked why, I explained that I was seeking his views of local issues and the like. He told me he was free around 2:30 and we agreed to meet at his office.

Dixon saw me on time. We chatted about local issues, problems of research funding and college politics. He was very forthcoming, including the information that he and Burns had been friends since his twenties when he first came to Chapel Hill.

Finally, I got around to the topic I really wanted to discuss, namely the adverse effects of smoking. Molly Nolan had found more evidence. A draft American Medical Association report had linked smoking to lung cancer and heart disease, but the report had somehow been suppressed by members of the US Congress. I asked Dixon if he was aware of this study. Dixon blanched. He paused before asking, "What's the source?"

"The American Medical Association."

"I am not aware of any published AMA report."

That was a clever answer as the report had remained unpublished, but I doubted his honesty. "The publication appears to have been spiked," I said. "My researcher didn't know why, but we're guessing it was due to pressure from the tobacco industry. In your medical opinion," I went on, "is there a link between smoking and cancer and heart disease?"

Dixon seemed to pale, and a sheen of sweat appeared on his face. He failed to look me in the eye when he responded. "I am not involved in academic research of this nature," he said. "Of course, I've heard opinions over many years about a possible link, but I've never seen empirical evidence to support the theory."

"Could you possibly be a little biased? I mean, you sit on a health committee for Burns and Murphy, don't you?"

Dixon stood, making a play of checking his watch. "I'm sorry Mr. Driscoll, but I've run out of time."

I left the campus, musing about the lengths to which Dixon might go to do Burns' bidding. And I thought I knew why. For a man with Dixon's weaknesses, money is a strong persuader.

Chapter 13.

Nicholas Anslow, my old boss and editor of *The Washington Mirror,* called the night of my meeting with Dixon. "I thought you'd like to hear some Beltway gossip." How like Nick to get right to the point.

"Oh, how I love political gossip," I said. "That's the stuff we don't print, right?"

Nick laughed. "Mock me, my friend, but this one might have legs. If so, they're walking right into your backyard."

"Okay, you have my interest, shoot."

"You know that the Senate War Investigation Committee did not disband after the War." Before I could acknowledge this, he rushed forward. "It continued investigating deals between companies supplying Uncle Sam and the Defense Department. You might remember that your good friend, also known as the President of the United States, did quite a bit of work in that area."

"I'd say! He saved the taxpayers tens of millions."

"Yes, well it seems that a number of North Carolina corporations have been supplying a bunch of munitions and stuff to the US Army and there's word that members of a Senate sub-committee have had their eyebrows raised over some of these deals. Does the name Billy August Junior mean anything to you?"

"Sure. He's the junior US senator for the state. I met him recently at a dinner. I didn't take to him much."

"Judging by his politics, I'm not surprised," said Nick.

"Jeremiah Burns, the B & M guy, had a dinner party. Abby and I were invited. August insisted on telling me his life story. It must have taken all of five minutes.

"Mind you," I added, "I don't suppose it would take much longer for us to tell ours, but he seemed to think I couldn't live without knowing. He might be quite a physical specimen, but he's also smart enough to know that he wasn't blessed in the brains department. According to him, he was one hell of a high school quarterback and it got him into Duke. When he got injured, he focused on academics and joined the Democratic Party. The Shelby political party machine recognized his potential and groomed him well. He won his Senate seat a year or so ago."

"The Shelby machine?"

"It's led by Max Gardner, who I also met at that dinner. The Shelby machine is the dominating force in North Carolina and Gardner is the boss. What gets to me is that the machine represents the interests of big business, including people like Burns, but ignores the working Joe. There seems to be hardly anyone in North Carolina politics who champions the downtrodden. Men like Billy August advance through the favour of those in power."

"So you're saying that he's in the machine's pocket."

"Very definitely. So what's the skinny on him?"

"Your man August got appointed to that War Munitions Oversight Committee, which oversees all military contracts under thirty million dollars. However, it seems that the junior senator may have exceeded his powers and lobbied for corporations supposedly linked to Burns, or so the rumor goes. Most of them don't even sell munitions; they sell uniforms, helmets, boots and personal equipment like water bottles.

"Here's where it gets suspect. One of those corporations sold howitzers and the Army contract was for fifty thousand of them. When they malfunctioned with regularity, the committee wanted to investigate the contract, but they couldn't. August put an anonymous hold on the investigation."

I sat for a moment, the phone pressed to my ear, trying to comprehend the significance of what Nick just revealed. How would he know the hold was anonymous?

"Nick, are you saying that August froze the inquiry just like that?"

"I'm saying that he tried to. The committee chair became suspicious and discovered what August was doing. I might add that the chairman's a good ol' boy from Alabama, but he wasn't going to let southern kinship get in the way of doing his job."

"I'm guessing that there's plenty of competition between Alabama and North Carolina," I replied.

"Agreed and the scuttlebutt says there was a heated meeting between the chairman and August. August was told to lift the hold or be sacked from the committee. August did what he had to do and now he's in deep trouble because it looks like the corporation supplying the howitzers paid him to make sure their contract wasn't cancelled. If this can be proved, the committee will turn over its findings to the Justice Department and the ambitious senator may find himself in federal prison."

I could already imagine the scandal brewing behind closed doors. Abby came into the room, just as I was asking, "What do you suggest I do?" She made as if to leave, but I gestured for her to wait. She had excellent instincts when it came to judging human behaviour and I was curious about her read of Billy August.

Nick suggested I do the leg work and we'd share the story, but this wasn't an option for me. This had to be a *Monitor* story. However, I said I would syndicate it and pay 10% of the profits to his paper. "You've got plenty in D.C. to keep you going," I said, "and you don't need this story too."

"That's gratitude for you! I discover the good stuff and you take the deal!"

I laughed. "Come on, Nick, you've only got a whiff of a story. You know if there's anything in this, I'll get the skinny locally, something you can't do."

He eventually agreed to my terms, which reminded me why I liked him. Nick knew reality when it hit him in the face. We said our good-byes. I suggested to Abby that we sit on the veranda.

"So, how is our Nicholas?" she asked.

"Our Nicholas may have dropped quite a story into my lap. If I can get the evidence, my circulation problems may well be solved." I related the conversation to Abby. "Do you remember my telling you about the private investigator I met a few days ago, Patti-Lou Gains? Maybe she can help."

Abby gave me a strange look. "David, think for just a minute. Who's the best person you know at getting to the bottom of money stories?"

"Emily Venn?"

"Of course, Emily."

The next morning, I made some calls. Peter Garibaldi wasn't happy about Emily taking time away to help me, even with the promise of equal billing on the story and a 10% share of all syndication rights. However, Emily was keen to help. I wondered if she was a little bored with life at *The Bugle* and wanted an adventure.

I had spent enough time in D.C. to have made some useful contacts. Ken Royall, the War Secretary and Forrest Donnell, the senior Senator from Missouri, were former drinking companions. They were happy to give me contacts at the War Munitions Oversight Committee and the War Department, all of whom would be willing to give off-the-record information to Emily. I called Emily, told her what I wanted to know and asked her to stay in touch when she got to Washington.

My next call was to Patti-Lou Gains, but from a pay phone. I was still worried I might have a spy on my staff.

"Miss Gains, something has come up. I need to know if you and I are going to do business."

"I was going to call you," she said. "I've checked you out. As long as you pay my fees, we have a deal."

I told her I'd be at her office within the hour. When we sat together, it took only minutes to agree her terms, seventy dollars a day, plus expenses and a retainer of $500. I outlined what I needed her to do.

"First and foremost," I said, "I want as much information as possible on Jeremiah Burns." As I spoke, she took notes. "In particular, I want to find out about his investments in the munitions business."

I explained the concerns of linking tobacco to health issues and asked her to look into the affairs of Robert E. Lee Dixon that related to B & M and health issues. I told her about Billy August and the tip I had received. I explained that I would use my D.C. contacts to see what I could discover.

"I'll share all of that information with you," I added, wanting to reinforce that I trusted her discretion. I asked her to check the August story from this end.

I wanted information about Jackson Murphy and what he did for Burns. I explained the role of Emily Venn and my hope they would work together, if and when. Patti accepted what I said with one or two questions.

When I returned to the office, Brutus Elliott and Joshua Frost were waiting for me. Both of them were grinning, like children hiding a secret. "What's so damn funny?" I demanded, failing at my attempt to sound gruff.

"Beau Beaufort's criminal trial ended this morning," said Josh. "The jury took thirty minutes to convict him and the judge gave him three years."

I ran this through my head, trying to imagine Jez Burns' reaction to someone in his family finally getting nailed.

"Burns was in court with his sister, Emma-Jane," said Brutus. "She made quite a scene. In fact, she screamed at her brother. I quote, 'Fix the appeal now and get that bastard Driscoll.' Any comments, boss?"

I wanted to say how sorry I was to have missed the performance. Instead, I said, "Just write the story and leave out the gossip. Three years, eh?" I added, "Any bets on how much time he'll actually do?"

Elliott and Frost left shaking their heads.

Chapter 14.

Billy August Junior entered the exclusive Captains' Room at the Duke University Alumni Club. The room was reserved for only the most elevated of Duke's alumni and prominent North Carolina citizens. A steward stood behind the bar and nodded when August ordered a mint julep. Ten minutes later, Jeremiah Burns entered and took a seat with him.

"Billy," he said, his voice cold. "I can do without this today. My nephew has just been sent down for three years. I assume this isn't a social call. What do you want?"

"Jez, take it easy." He nodded towards the steward. "Have a drink."

Burns motioned the man away. "Just get to it."

August paused a long beat, as if trying to remind Burns that a US senator was the one in charge. "I'm grateful to you for helping me get elected to the Senate."

Burns closed his hands into fists, as if trying to control his temper. "When I said get to it, I didn't mean more bullshit."

Billy took a deep breath and held up both hands, as if in surrender. "You need to know that I'm being investigated in D.C. It's that howitzer contract. Remember how you told me to make sure the contract wasn't cancelled? I did my best for you, Jez, but everything's coming out. I'm worried that the way those other contracts were done might be investigated too." He leaned closer to Burns, anxiety etched in his face. "I don't know what to do. You've got to help me."

Burns edged away, creating distance between them.

"For God's sake, Billy, pull yourself together. These contracts you're yammering about, I may have investments in those corporations, but I don't run them. And I sure as hell don't make executive decisions. You know this perfectly well, so don't go trying to lay this manure at my door."

August's eyes widened, as if he just realized he would be left holding this bag of worms. "Jez, we were…what're you saying?"

Burns gave August a sinister smile, taunting the man. "Billy, you're a United States Senator. You wield enormous power. Surely you can figure out solutions by yourself."

Before August could respond, Burn pointed a finger at him, holding it inches from his face. "Just to be clear, Senator, do not even think of getting me personally involved. This is nothing to do with me. So one move in that direction and…"

With that, Burns stood and strode out of the room without a backward look.

Chapter 15.

The next morning, Brandon Hanes was waiting for me in my office. "I'm finally making headway with police evidence," he said. "Those charred papers from Butler's house weren't totally illegible. I managed to decipher fragments of pay slips relating to B & M medical cost deductions." He went on to tell me that he'd talked privately with several B & M colored employees and that these deductions were still being made.

"What's shocked me," he said, "is that there's only one nurse on site to help those workers when they're injured, never a doctor. He has to be called in if things look serious. So, what are these people paying for?"

I ran that over in my mind. Was this an issue of segregation? Or, plain and simple, a scam designed to line peoples' pockets?

"Here's another line of enquiry for us," I told him. "I'll get more written evidence for you soon. Just keep digging, but be very careful not to alert anyone in B & M management about what you're doing."

After Brandon left my office, I called in Brutus Elliott and Joshua Frost. I told them, "You need to know that I'll be gone for a few days. Abby and I are picking up Louis and Charlotte and we are taking a short holiday. Once I know where we're staying, I'll call in with a phone number."

When I asked them to use the number only in an emergency, they agreed. I explained Molly Nolan was making headway in her research on the health issues and had left me a memo which I found interesting.

"To summarize, The American Cancer Society has just published a paper alleging a link between cigarette smoking and both cancer and heart disease."

I let the allegation sink in. "This isn't the first time this allegation's been made, but their study is supported by research academics from Harvard and Yale, as well as scientists in Chicago and Los Angeles.

"While I'm gone, give Molly whatever support she needs. I am particularly interested in how manufacturers deal with these allegations. But," I added, pointing my finger at them so there could be no doubt as to my concern, "do not let her go anywhere near B & M. Do you understand? She is to take no risks."

When I was given assurances by both men, I told them to prepare drafts of stories for me to approve on my return. "Let's be clear, don't run them until I get back. I want to be sure we are right."

I instructed Brutus to keep a watch on Robert E. Lee Dixon. "I have a hunch he's involved in all sorts of things for Burns. That means he'll be under pressure to refute the Cancer Society's allegations."

I hesitated a moment, forming a thought in my mind that I wanted the men to consider. We were stepping into a minefield and I made no attempt to disguise my concern.

"I want to run a theory past you both," I said, looking pointedly at them. "Would you agree that it's unlikely that the Butlers were murdered by the KKK?"

Both men nodded. "So, if it wasn't the Klan, who had an interest in murdering the Butlers? Or, more accurately, who wanted Edgar Butler dead? What was he doing that put him at risk?

I paused to give them time to think.

"We know he was talking to Negro B & M workers at the plant and we also know that he had evidence that would blow the cover off a healthcare insurance scam.

"What we don't have is proof that Burns has done anything illegal. Was the company deducting medical expenses from Negro workers and pocketing the cash? Did Butler discover something that frightened the B & M people? And finally," I added, after taking a very deep breath, "is it too far-fetched to suggest that Burns or his people were engaged in these murders?"

My team knew that the people who killed the Butlers were themselves murdered hours later and we all agreed that it was no coincidence. Was Jeremiah Burns ruthless enough to have so many people killed to cover up a financial scandal, especially one from which he could buy his way out? I wondered if, perhaps, one of his henchmen got his orders wrong.

Josh looked at me with astonishment. "I would call that a hunch at best. Where is there any evidence? What I mean is, Burns is a fearsome businessman, but he has never been involved personally in acts of violence, so far as I know." The look on Josh's face confused me. Was it incredulity or fear? "He's not a murderer, David," Josh continued. "Certainly there have been stories that Jackson Murphy is his enforcer and that Murphy can be ruthless when it comes to keeping the coloreds on the Burns plantation in check. Did you see those scars on Murphy's face?"

"I must admit to wondering about them," I replied.

"He got them dueling. Dueling with swords! Can you believe it?"

I could see that my argument would need some heft.

"Please don't dismiss the theory yet," I said. "I hate to say it, but I'm getting a clear impression that there's something rotten in this part of the world. Teddy Roosevelt called these types of investigations muckraking. I'm sorry to say there seems to be a lot of muck to uncover in this town."

I gave each man a meaningful look. "And I want *The Monitor* to expose the muck. You won't be carrying this alone. We'll talk more when I get back."

Josh left shaking his head, not liking what he'd heard. I talked over some business stuff with Brutus, gathered a few things and made my way home.

*****

The next day, Abby and I left early for Richmond. We stayed overnight, mainly because we understood that Gerry's farewell to the children would be sad. Abby's sister loved Louis and Charlotte very much, but it was time for the Driscolls and Daisy to resume family life.

We were back in Chapel Hill in time for dinner and stayed there on Sunday, settling Louis and Charlotte into their new bedrooms and Daisy into her new quarters. We showed them around town, this time concentrating on activities for teenagers. Sutton's Drug Store and its soda fountain got a high approval rating.

On Monday morning, we left for the Crystal Coast, where the Atlantic Ocean washes up on the coastline of North Carolina's Inner and Outer Banks. I had researched the area and accepted Jez Burns' advice that Beaufort was a good destination.

After a six-hour journey, which included lunch at Doug's Diner, Pulled Pork our Speciality, we arrived at Beaufort's Inlet Inn, a B & B where I had booked a large family room.

There was neither a swimming pool nor a beach but I chartered a sailing boat with outboard motors and a skipper. The boat was equipped with the kind of gear which would let us have cook-outs for lunch and dinner, should we want to anchor.

During our week in Beaufort, Abby and I focused on re-acquainting ourselves with our children. Charlotte had not changed and we thought her typical of fifteen year-old girls. For her, getting through the day was an exercise in optimism and fun. She had no idea what she wanted to do with her life, but, at her age, why should she? We were both confident that she would find something to fire her interests.

Louis, on the other hand, was different. Two years older than Charlotte, he was far quieter, shy and introverted. What concerned us was his apparent lack of belief that we cared for him. Not for the first time since my children were born, I worried that I had wasted the opportunity to be a good father.

Over the days in Beaufort, Louis eased up on himself. He struck up a friendship with our skipper, George, a thirty-something local, a man happy with his lot in life. George taught us the rudiments of sailing. Abby and I weren't that interested, but the children were fascinated. Before the end of the week, both had taken the helm with George navigating.

It was at dusk on our second evening when we sailed into Taylors Creek, about a mile out from the docking slot in Beaufort. Quietly, but with urgency in his voice, George called for Louis to drop anchor. The boat bobbed on the tide, a nature reserve called Carrot Island close by.

George directed our attention toward the island. Very soon, a pony appeared and then another. Soon, at least fifty ponies were drinking from the creek. George explained they were wild ponies and that no human had ever made contact with them. What an amazing sight it was. We stayed moored for an hour or so, watching and enjoying nature at work. We returned to Beaufort in the dark.

For reasons I can't fathom, the incident seemed to change Louis. He became more like the delightful boy I had known years before. That night, he and I spoke properly for the first time since we'd collected him from Richmond.

"Great day, Dad, and a great holiday," he enthused. "We have to come back!"

I told him I agreed, but it couldn't be in the summer. "You know this area is called the Mosquito Coast, don't you?"

Louis laughed. "You're not scared of a little mosquito, are you?"

"For sure I am!" I said. "Anyone who grows up in the Midwest knows that when there are thousands of these horrors buzzing around, they're worthy of respect." I explained how, when I was his age, my summers were hell because of the mosquito swarms. "I don't fancy re-living the bloody mosquito experience," I said. "Don't you remember them when we lived in St. Luke?" When Louis laughed again, I said, "I guess Richmond mosquitoes are more refined!"

I suggested we leave the women on their own that night and have a beer. Louis was astonished.

"Dad, I'm under age; we'll get into trouble."

"You look like you're twenty-one," I said. "I'll vouch for you. You can't tell me you've never had a brew."

Later, we took our leave of Abby and Charlotte and walked along Front Street. We found a bar that seemed tame and no one objected when I ordered two beers. When they were poured, we headed for a booth. We settled in and enjoyed a slow sip of our drinks. It was the first time we'd done 'a man thing' together and I wanted both of us to savor the moment.

"Your grades were good this year," I told him. "When we last spoke about your future, you wanted a career in medicine."

"Grandma and Grandpa were happy as doctors, weren't they? And they did really good work. I'd like to do the same."

"You know we'll support you, whatever you want to do. Have you thought about college and med school yet?"

"I've thought about it, but I don't think you'll like my thinking."

"Why on earth not?"

"I want to go to Stanford."

"That's near San Francisco, isn't it? What's wrong with Harvard, Yale, Penn, even UNC?"

"Nothing, Dad, but Stanford's very highly rated and I need to get some distance, find somewhere new and make it on my own. You did this when you were just a little older than me and look what Mom's achieved. You're hard acts to follow. I know it will be expensive, but you've taught me to go for the best."

"Good point. I'm not saying yes and I'm not saying no. I need to think and talk to Mom. Stanford is a long way away."

As medical school comes after four years as an undergraduate, there would be time to consider Louis' proposal. No need to make a federal case of it.

"Let's have another beer."

By the time we returned to the Inn, both of us were a little worse for wear. Abby was in bed, reading. One look at her slightly inebriated husband and she laughed, tut-tutted and bade me goodnight. When I dropped my toothbrush in the bathroom sink, I heard her giggle.

We awoke to discover that the weather had turned. This didn't stop the children from wanting to sail, but Abby and I decided to stay ashore.

We ate lunch at the harbor and I told Abby about Louis' choice of schools. She looked concerned, but we knew that while decisions weren't in stone, Louis was old enough to know his own mind.

We talked at length about Jeremiah Burns. I revealed to Abby what had been unearthed and what was being investigated.

"This man is haunting me," I said. "What sort of a man is he? Is he cheating employees of hard-earned wages and then making it even worse by not declaring on his taxes the amount he skims? Is he the hardest of employers? Is he involved in murder?"

I pushed food around my plate, wanting to talk more, but also wondering if I was putting Abby in any danger by sharing with her.

"He may have ignored health warnings about the dangers of smoking cigarettes, which means putting lives at risk. And is he also supplying weapons that don't work and kit that is sub-standard without a care for our soldiers?"

"I wish I could give you answers," Abby replied, reaching across the table and placing her hand on mine.

"I need to find out the real Jeremiah Burns," I continued. "What kind of man is he, running a virtual monopoly for himself? Is he a monster, someone who no ethical society should tolerate?"

Abby stayed calm. "You'll work it out, David, you always do. And I know you won't publish anything unless you have clear proof, but please use your reporters to dig up the facts. That's their job; don't do it for them. Oh, I forgot to tell you, I've called Louise Burns once or twice to visit the orphanage. She called me back just before we left for Richmond. I have a date to visit next month."

I suggested to Abby that she be careful in her conversations with Mrs. Burns. There was already more than enough grief from her and her husband.

Two days later, we drove back to Chapel Hill. Louis and Charlotte seemed to have changed. Abby and I both saw them as more relaxed and happy. It was my hope that our children didn't consider us, particularly me, such awful parents after all.

*****

Within an hour of arriving back in Durham, I learned of developments in the army contracts investigation. Patti-Lou had liaised with Emily Venn and their report made for fascinating reading.

There were five corporations involved. Four had contracts with the military and each had a potential connection to Jez Burns. Those four were registered in North Carolina. Three were contracted to supply uniforms, helmets, boots and personal equipment. It was the fourth corporation on the list that was by far the most significant: it supplied howitzers, that small, deadly cannon known for its accuracy. Patti had obtained the names of the corporations, purchase order numbers and the like. The fifth corporation appeared to be a holding company registered in Delaware. It held the shares of the four trading corporations, hence another potential connection to Burns.

The four trading corporations, it seemed, were middlemen, brokers in the transactions. Patti was checking whether this might be a breach of army regulations, which apparently required contractors to be manufacturers, unless prior approval for sub-contractors had been obtained from the Army. She wrote that she was continuing her enquiries. I mimed a thank you for her good work and kept reading.

She had nothing solid on Jeremiah Burns or Jackson Murphy, but she would let me know if and when she had anything worthwhile. I remembered our last conversation, when she told me that Southerners kept things tight, meaning they don't want to talk about other people. This was going to be a tough nut for her to crack.

I had almost finished reading the report when I received a call from Dolly Peel. She had the documents I wanted. I agreed to come to her home that night. She was quick to remind me of her terms. "Make sure you bring my dollars," she demanded, as if I would forget. What a piece of work she was!

When I arrived at *The Monitor*, I asked Brandon to come into my office. Before he could get comfortable, I told him to draft his story on the B & M medical expenses scam.

"Let me have it before the end of day," I said. "You can assume that you'll have documented evidence needed by then."

His raised eyebrows told me he questioned my timeline. However, by five o'clock, the story was on my desk. It was a solid read.

I called Henry Atkins, an old friend in the Treasury Department in D.C. I put the facts of the B & M medical expenses story to him in detail and asked if he would check them out. He agreed to have the matter looked into.

That night, I went to Dolly Peel's home. She handed me a thick stack of fully itemized papers. A brief glance told me I had the documents needed to prove that B & M had fleeced their employees. Not only could I prove deductions from workers' salaries, but there was an itemized list of medical expenses, medical employees' salaries, payments to hospitals and more.

And everything was listed year by year, since the start of the War. Either Burns himself or B & M was pocketing over $500,000 annually, all at the expense of those loyal workers who struggled to put food on their tables. Dolly had more than earned her fee.

"Where's my money?" she demanded.

I handed her an envelope containing ten five-dollar bills. She opened it, counted the cash and nodded without a thank you.

We were walking towards the door when I stopped. "There is something else, if you want to help," I said. "Do you know anything about Burns' involvement in corporations selling munitions and equipment to the military?"

Dolly said nothing for a while, staring at me. Eventually, she said, "I might. Why?"

I felt my heart pound unusually fast. "I'm interested in finding out what our friend Burns is up to in his dealings with the armed forces."

She gazed out the window, into the dark street illuminated by a dim light. "Yes, I'm aware of these deals," she finally said. "This is a risky area for me. I can cover my tracks on the medical stuff, but getting copies of the documents you're asking for could be traced back to me. I need time to think."

Normally, I'd have offered a large sum of money for the information, but something told me not to. Instead, I told her that I understood and she should take her time.

A week after I had spoken with my Treasury friend, Henry Atkins, he called to say that something was going on that he didn't like.

"Any investigation the Feds start will be still-born," he said. "It seems that the North Carolina legislators have blocked any action by Treasury, yelling Tenth Amendment rights and it's an election year. The President needs North Carolina's Electoral College votes," he explained. "Looks like States' rights trump the taxpayers or, to be more accurate, the Shelby machine had come to the aid of Jez Burns."

We talked for a while longer about how the Constitution was used and abused by the rich and powerful. As the conversation was coming to a close, I said, "I know I don't need to ask this, Henry, but can I take it as gospel that you won't divulge my involvement? I'd prefer to keep off the Burns radar for as long as I can."

He gave me his word. We agreed to have lunch when I was next in D.C.

I had no one at *The Monitor* whom I trusted sufficiently, so I called Patti-Lou. In short order, she gave me a lesson in politics, Southern style and how Yankees like me weren't high in a popularity contest, especially when running a newspaper.

"You may be editor-in-chief of Durham's foremost newspaper," she said, "but in this town, you're barely tolerated." She also warned about the dangers of bringing federal tax agents into the state's business. She laid out the grim facts; no punches pulled. "You, Mr. Driscoll, are a stranger in a strange land."

Back at my office, my secretary handed me a note that Jeremiah Burns wanted to meet up over lunch the next day. I wondered what Burns had up his very expensive sleeve.

*****

The Confederate is a Durham restaurant that's more like a members' club. The general public isn't actually refused entry, but the maitre'd would often find the place fully booked when the diner was not a good ol' boy.

I arrived on time and found Burns waiting for me. He didn't offer me a drink and I could see that he wasn't in a cheerful mood. What was rattling his cage? I'd never known him to be impolite, so I girded myself and asked the waiter for a bourbon and branch. Before the drink arrived, the attack was launched.

"Mr. Driscoll," he began. Such formality was hardly a positive sign, "I'm very disappointed by your newspaper's coverage of my nephew's trial."

The waiter placed the drink in front of me. I took a sip.

"How so?"

"There was neither a report of his defense, nor of his good public record."

I tried hard not to laugh at Burns. "What defense? What good public record?"

When Burns said nothing, I forged ahead. "I challenge you to tell me how the trial was not reported in every detail. There was neither gossip nor innuendo in our reporting. In fact, Mr Burns," I continued, with emphasis on his name, "*The Monitor* told the story exactly as it was revealed in court. I might add, I was quite the gentleman when I didn't react to your sister's outburst against me."

Burns sat back and studied my face for a moment. "I do not see things the way you do."

I was tempted to express my relief over that, but held back. Instead, I backed up my side.

"Then let's look at Beau's so-called good public record. First, he's been involved in any number of scams. Be honest, how many times have you bailed him out? The most you can say is that this is the first offence for which he's been convicted. Second, what work has he done to benefit the public at large? My bet is you've done more this morning than he's done in his entire life."

Burns seemed to struggle to suppress a smile, but then soon became serious again. "Perhaps you make a point," he said. I was hoping issues were resolved, but the man was far from finished.

"Listen, Driscoll, I know you put the feds onto me, investigating my tax affairs and I don't appreciate it. I'm warning you now. Stop this witch hunt of me and my business interests."

I doubted there was any way that Burns knew I'd set an inquiry in motion. The only people who knew were Henry Atkins and me. This was a time for denial, denial, denial.

"Burns, I have no idea what you're talking about. How could I possibly persuade the US government to do anything? I'm just a journalist."

"In this part of the world, sir, we call a liar a skunk and you're smelling pretty rank to me. So I repeat: I'm warning you now to drop your investigations into my affairs. We Southerners don't appreciate our ways being questioned by carpetbaggers. Back in 1865, people like you came to this state and pushed us around, stole our land and houses, told us how to handle our affairs, raped our women and got our coloreds all uppity. It took us a while, but eventually we regained control and kicked the carpetbaggers out. And now here you sit, thinking you're Mr High-and-Mighty because you run a newspaper."

He leaned forward, until his face was inches from mine. I could smell his expensive cologne.

"People here don't like you and don't want you in these parts. Don't even think of taking me on, do you hear? We have our ways. Fail to respect them and it will end badly for you."

I confess that I was shocked at that last declaration. "Are you threatening me? Is that a threat to my family?" I was angry and wanted him to know it. I also wanted him to understand that one false step and I'd go after him.

"We must protect our own," was his chilling reply.

At that moment, a line was crossed. I was now the enemy of a very powerful and vindictive Jeremiah Burns. I put down my drink and stood. "I cannot stomach a drink with you, let alone lunch." Without another word, I walked out.

Chapter 16.

I like to think that I'm calm in a crisis, but I have to admit that Burns shook me to the core. I have come across powerful men before, men who savored the art of intimidation. This was years ago in St. Luke, when I was much younger and didn't have a family that might be at risk. Life was very different now in Durham and people I loved could be in danger. What were my options? I could ignore Burns. I'm not one to knuckle under. There was a lot at stake, but why did I need to take risks? After all, did I really have skin in the game to challenge Burns and his associates? I am a newspaper editor, not a warrior.

Abby's reaction astonished me. "Bring the children into your confidence. They're teenagers and deserve to be told. See what they have to say." So that was what I did and I was surprised by their maturity.

"Dad," said Louis, "what makes you think you should give in to Mr. Burns? Mom told Lottie and me what you did when the mob tried to take over in St. Luke and how you fought them. We both know what happened when Lottie was kidnapped. You've faced stuff like this before." Before I could respond, he held up a hand to silence me. Me, his father! "We know we have to be careful," he said, his face so serious, no longer the teenager, but a young man with intellect. "Mom knows it, too. Do you really think this jerk would try to do something to us?"

What my son said was true. Much depended on how close I was to getting Burns into serious trouble. There were a lot of things going on where bad publicity would damage him and make him come after me. Us.

"Exposing his wrongdoings is a different matter," I told Louis. "The closer I get, the greater the danger will be for all of us. I have to ask myself if it's worth it."

We talked into the night. Everyone agreed to be careful. At the same time, my children insisted that I should not be cowed by Burns' threats. Their concern for my safety and their insistence that I should not back down made me realize what fine adults they were becoming.

The discussion with Louis and Charlotte brought home to me how much I needed to tell someone in authority about these threats. But how could I use back channels to make Burns aware that I would not let him scare me off? I thought through my contacts and came up with the obvious choice, Henry Atkins. Who better than someone with clout in D.C.?

I called Henry the next morning, told him the tale and he agreed to help. A few days later, he told me that a senior man in the Justice Department had spoken with someone in the North Carolina Justice Department, which meant that Burns would soon hear that his threats were on the record. I knew he'd be furious, even enraged, but I felt that the family was safer.

In that same week, *The Monitor* started to publish stories about the medical expenses scam at B & M. Brandon had four or five stories ready, so we were able to keep the public's interest for quite a few days. In addition to Brandon's articles, I wrote an editorial intended to shake up a few old timers.

The Durham Monitor. June 14, 1948
Is Burns & Murphy Involved in a Medical Expenses Scam?

In today's newspaper, we are publishing a story concerning the Burns & Murphy practice of deducting contributions from its colored employees to cover potential medical expenses. The story lays out the facts, namely that the corporation deducts seventy-five cents each week from the pay of all its colored workers, purportedly to support the cost of medical expenses incurred for treating any worker injured on the job.

B & M claims the deduction is a form of necessary insurance because some of the work is dangerous and medical expenses are often high. However, evidence uncovered by our reporters has established that B & M employs only one doctor and two nurses, at a total cost of $7,500 a year, whereas 15,000 colored workers make enforced contributions totaling $585,000 a year.

We have asked B & M senior management to answer a number of questions, including what happens to the surplus funds and why three medical employees need to be funded by the workers, when the corporation could easily afford to pay. We have received no response.

> We enquired of the state's other Big Tobacco manufacturers, seeking to know if they adopted a similar health insurance scheme for their employees. They, too, have declined to answer.
>
> If a tobacco manufacturer actually paid for all hospital bills, drugs and follow-up medical expenses for its workers, then there is potential justification for the medical deduction from wages. Nevertheless, we would query the amount deducted. There is an important question that must be answered: Is Big Tobacco making a secret profit from its employees?
>
> It is hoped that our questions will receive a speedy and satisfactory reply.

The public's reaction was heartening. Letters to the newspaper expressed shock that hard-working and poorly rewarded people should have their salaries reduced. There was also sympathy for colored workers who were forced to exist in unacceptable working and living conditions. We published letters from our readers demonstrating the feeling that B & M's policy was unreasonable. My team asked senior B & M management to comment on the letters, but they refused. Two weeks later, we published stories about anti-trust and the unwillingness of the federal government to take the tobacco industry to task.

The main thrust was that manufacturers were taking advantage of the smoking public and, through the tobacco cartel, the retail price of cigarettes was kept artificially high. I was careful to ensure that the stories did not specifically criticize B & M. It was only fair that all North Carolina cigarette manufacturers came in for equal punishment! Unlike the response to the medical expenses scam, the manufacturers let *The Monitor* have it with both barrels. True to my creed, the newspaper printed their side of the story as well.

One important consequence of our exposés was a new public dialogue about the dangers of cigarette smoking. The debate was stoked even further when we introduced damning evidence from the American Cancer Society, amongst others. It was during this open dialogue that my staff experienced the full force of the backlash from the tobacco industry. One of their weapons was to run creative and convincing advertisements about the benefits of smoking, including the testimony of medical experts vouching for the safety of cigarettes. We were pilloried for scare-mongering.

Local tobacco workers also let us know they didn't appreciate their jobs being put in jeopardy. We fought back with the most convincing weapon – truth.

We published even more evidence of the dangers of smoking. I doubt that Burns could have expected this to happen in the heart of tobacco country.

The Monitor experienced a sudden, substantial increase in circulation. "More than 100,000 daily sales!" When I got the news, I rang Abby. I couldn't wait to tell her.

"So the paper's in the black?"

"Not quite! But it's heading that way," I enthused. We agreed to celebrate over dinner.

With the added circulation came increased advertising revenues. Our success was quickly noticed by the First Bank of Richmond and I received a call from John Rayburn.

"I'm in your area tomorrow, David. Can we meet? How's eleven o'clock?"

I could hardly say no. Rayburn arrived the next morning and got down to business.

"You're doing a great job," he told me. "And I think you're brave, taking on Burns and big tobacco. We both know he has a mean streak." He removed a file from his briefcase and examined a document. "I see from the latest figures that you're turning the newspaper around."

There was no need to comment on Burns and his behaviour, so I focused on the praise. "So you're pleased."

"Of course I am," he said. "However, the Bank is owed a very large sum and we'd like it repaid. I want us to agree a repayment schedule."

I stared at Rayburn in astonishment. We had an iron-clad deal that said otherwise. Was he shaking me down? I let my exasperation show.

"Oh, why am I not surprised? After all, you lied your head off about Burns. May I remind you," I told him, trying hard to control my wrath, "we have an agreement that the bank will be repaid in one lump sum and that will happen at the end of my time as editor-in-chief. There is nothing in our deal requiring installment repayments. I'm not finished here and I reject your demand. Would you like me to produce our agreement? What are you trying to pull, John? When I met you, you were straight. You seem to have gone crooked."

He shifted in his chair. He made a play of closing the folder and slipping it into his briefcase, as if nothing more need be said.

The drama wasn't lost on me. "I'm not trying to pull anything, David. I'm simply introducing some prudent business practice into our relationship. You have to understand that my Board is very unhappy about this debt."

It seemed to me that Rayburn was trying not to smile. Or was it a gloat? I wasn't sure, but it niggled at me.

"Of course they're unhappy," I said, "but aren't these the same careless, greedy people who got themselves into this mess with Burns? Listen to me carefully, John. This debt is not my responsibility. Thanks to me and my team, the bank has every prospect of being repaid in full in a few months' time. You can posture all you like, but I will not move away from the terms we agreed. What's more," I added, the tone of my voice leaving no doubt as to my anger, "I strongly suggest you keep your end of the bargain. If not, I may well end our relationship. I'm neither poor nor inexperienced. I understand law suits. Your actions could leave you in a heap of tar and feathers."

The sudden change on Rayburn's face told me that he knew that he was defeated.

"Steady on, David. No need to speak of going to court."

I stood and moved toward my office door. "John, we're done here. Just tell your Board that I keep to my bargains and I expect them to do likewise. What is it with you Southerners? Don't you know how to behave decently? Shall I get the dictionary out and read the definition of honesty?"

Without ceremony, I showed him out.

That night at home, I let rip to Abby. She replied that my annoyance had got the better of me. My meeting with John Rayburn was eight hours old and I was still hopping mad.

"How could he even consider changing the terms of the deal?" I asked, my voice leaving no doubt that an answer was neither expected nor appreciated. "Does he think I'm an idiot? What's happened to him over the years since I bought *The Bugle?* He was a straight-shooter then. My God, Abby, times have changed. Is anyone in the South honest?"

My dear wife took the flack with equanimity. She was used to my flying off the handle. As usual, she managed to calm me down by reminding me that business had changed a lot since *The Bugle* days. "The Great Depression is done and dusted," she said. "You know that banking is a competitive business and that Rayburn has a responsibility to his Board."

"So I should let him bully me into ignoring our deal?"

"I'm not saying that, David, and you know me better! What I'm saying is, try not to judge him too harshly." Abby suddenly smiled. "Mind you, had he tried this on with my father, he probably would've been horse-whipped."

I couldn't help laughing at the thought of my late father-in-law lashing the devil out of Rayburn's hide.

"Now you have that out of your system, I just want to remind you I have an appointment to visit the Silver Leaf orphanage tomorrow. So, if I'm not here tomorrow night, you'll know your pal Jez kidnapped me."

The next evening, Abby was at home before me. I was late and she and the children had eaten. "I'll sit with you while you have dinner," she said, as she produced a tasty looking chicken salad.

"So how was your visit?"

"Lou Burns wasn't there. Evidently, she'd been called to an emergency meeting at the University.

"I was shown round by the manager, Helen Grady. A pleasant lady, in her early fifties, I'd say. She gave me the 10 cent tour. They were busy, Helen told me, with thirty two children staying. They have a maximum of forty but Helen told me that was a push. Not enough staff, too crowded, that sort of thing. The children were lovely."

I gave Abby a look, as if asking, 'oh?'

"No, I'm not tempted. After the tour, Helen gave me a few minutes. She told me the children who are not adopted get to stay at the orphanage until they are thirteen. Then they are moved to an adolescent orphanage. When I asked Helen about the adoption process, she clammed up at first, claiming confidentiality but she opened up as she got more comfortable with me. Some orphans are moved locally and a few to the care of Professor James Burdett, who runs a Foundation that arranges adoptions with families out West. She was unwilling to talk details but it sounded very odd to me."

"Does it? I would not have expected her to disclose anything that would be confidential, such as arranging adoptions? Why do you think it sound fishy?"

"Helen's main beef was that state money for the children was inadequate to run the orphanage. What was left unsaid was that Mr. and Mrs. Burns didn't put enough money themselves into the place. If this is true, it's outrageous and odd. Why have an orphanage and starve it of funds?"

"But where is the evidence? Did the children look half starved, poorly dressed?"

"No, but I think there's a story here."

"Maybe, but you need to look at it from the positive as well as the negative. You know, local benefactors caring for orphaned children. I'll get someone to look into what you have if you like."

"When?"

"Wow, you have your dander up. I'll talk to Brutus and ask him to get things started. However, we have to be careful not to poke the bear with a stick. Burns has it in for me quite enough, thank you."

Chapter 17.

Autumn was approaching and we took another trip to the North Carolina coast shortly before school started. Abby was preoccupied with preparations for her teaching year, so she stayed ashore most days preparing her courses. Louis, Lottie and I had George teach us more about sailing, which gave us plenty of moments to laugh together. The evenings were spent en-famille, causing Abby and me to dream that our children might actually look back on these times with joy and pleasure.

Ten days after school started, Charlotte telephoned me at my office, something she never did.

"Are you okay?" I asked, imagining a disaster had befallen.

"You have to come home right now," she said, her voice bordering on panic. "Mom is lecturing and the college won't disturb her, but I need one of you at home. Please, Dad, right now!"

I tried to question her, but she was adamant that I drop everything. I was having a very busy day fighting the tobacco industry, so I didn't need a hysterical teenager. But Lottie was not prone to histrionics, so I dropped everything and left the building. By the time I got home, my reasoning had fallen apart and I was furious about my work day being interrupted. I even rehearsed what I might say and it wasn't going to be pretty. However, my resolve disappeared as soon as I walked into the house. My daughter was frightened, shaking and white as the proverbial sheet. I had never seen her like this. She ran to me in tears and hugged me with such strength that I could barely breathe.

"Lottie, darling, I'm here. What's happened?"

"It's Louis, he's very drunk. He keeps being sick. Someone, I don't know who, left a message for me at school and told me to go home straight away. I told my teacher and she said it was okay. I found Louis on the doorstep. I tried to reach Mom, but I was told she was teaching and couldn't be disturbed. Dad, he's in a terrible state!"

"Where is he?" I asked, disengaging from her arms.

"In the downstairs bathroom. He's thrown up all over himself; he's a real mess. Did I do the right thing?" Her eyes filled with tears again and she swiped them away with the sleeve of her blouse.

"Of course you did. Now, don't worry," I added. "You go inside and sit down, I'll take care of Louis. Also," I said, before she could walk away, "please call Mom's office and leave a message that she's to come home as soon as possible. Make sure you tell them it's an emergency. If you speak with her, tell her what happened just like you did with me."

I found Louis slumped over the toilet. The bathroom stank of vomit, which was everywhere. I called out to him and gave him a gentle shake, but he didn't open his eyes. That's when I ran into the kitchen and called for an ambulance. I know my son. This was not a drinking binge. Had Jeremiah Burns carried out his threat? Had Louis been poisoned?

Within ten minutes an ambulance arrived and the paramedics took no time to decide that Louis needed to be treated at the hospital. I went with Louis in the ambulance to Chapel Hill General. Lottie waited at home for Abby. I was shooed out of the Emergency Room and told to sit in the waiting area. I felt my temper rising again. As soon as my son was out of danger, I would get to the bottom of this. If it had anything to do with Burns, there would be hell to pay.

I was so wrapped up in my dark thoughts, I didn't notice Abby and Lottie arrive. It wasn't until they sat beside me that I felt their presence. Lottie's eyes were still red and Abby looked just as worried as she did the day Lottie had been kidnapped so many years ago. All I could do was shrug helplessly and then I felt my face wet with tears. Abby leaned into me and took my hands.

"No news, I'm afraid," I told her. "He's in the Emergency Room. They've promised to come out and talk to us as soon as there's something to say."

Twenty minutes later, a man in his forties, wearing dark green scrubs, joined us. "I'm Doctor Norton," he said. "I've been looking after your son. It's a bit complicated, but he seems to be suffering from alcoholic poisoning. Tests show a huge amount of alcohol in his system. We pumped his stomach and he should be fine in a day or so. We'll keep an eye on him overnight and see how he is in the morning. I have to ask, does Louis have a drinking problem?"

"Dr Norton," I replied, "I bought Louis his first beer a month ago. He's a diligent student, not a drinker."

The doctor listened, nodded and said, "We'll let Louis sleep it off, then we can talk with him in the morning. You can see him now if you like, but he'll be asleep for the rest of the night."

Throughout this exchange, Abby said nothing which was so out of character for her. She kissed me on my cheek. "After you and Charlotte have seen him, will you take her home, please? I don't know what there is for dinner, but if you're hungry, get a pizza or something. I'll stay here."

I nodded and tried to smile reassuringly. "I'll look in on him now."

I asked Lottie if she wanted to come in with me. She grabbed my hand and we went into the ER together. Louis had been cleaned up. He was sleeping soundly, looking as if nothing had happened. After a while, we left. There was nothing either of us could do.

We said our goodbyes to Abby and asked if she needed anything from home. She shook her head. "Call me whenever you want," I told her. "It doesn't matter what the time is." She nodded. I knew what was going through her mind, those feelings of guilt that she hadn't been there for her son when he needed her, but I had been there. She was not to blame. This was something we'd talk over. The thought of such a conversation was not to be relished because blame belonged somewhere else. I had an idea where but I had no evidence. Abby was a wonderful mother. I knew she'd blame herself. I felt for her, knowing too well what she was going through.

At home, I cleaned up the bathroom, getting angrier by the minute. Who had done this to Louis? Early the next morning, I called the hospital and was told that Louis was still asleep. I took Lottie to school and drove to be with Abby, who looked exhausted, shattered. However, Louis had woken up. He was alert and seemed to be almost his old self. He complained that his stomach felt tender, but he was ready to go home.

"Have you talked about what happened?" I asked Abby.

"I was just about to."

I sat on the edge of the hospital bed. "Louis, do you feel up to answering some questions?"

"I can try, Dad, but I don't remember much."

"I took you to school yesterday. Did you stay there?"

"No, the principal called me into his office before prayers and said that I'd been invited to a seminar for high school seniors at the UNC Medical School."

"Chapel Hill?" asked Abby, incredulously.

Louis nodded. "When the principal said you had agreed to it, I was pretty surprised, but a day off school is a day off school. They gave me directions how to get there and the name of a student to contact. So I went."

Something was off here and I needed to know what. "What happened when you got to Chapel Hill?"

"I found my contact, Martin Deans, where he said he'd be. We talked for a while, and he said the seminar would be led by a Professor Dixon. Martin is hoping to be one of Dixon's interns next semester. We went to the seminar and there were maybe fifty students there. Professor Dixon told lots of funny stories and he explained all sorts of opportunities for medical students."

"What I don't understand," said Abby, "is how alcohol is involved."

Louis took a deep breath and inhaled loudly, as if preparing himself for a long explanation. "At lunchtime, Martin said he knew a good place where we could get a drink and I went along with this. I assumed he meant a beer. The place was a cellar and there were only men there. Nobody challenged me about my age. Everyone was drinking. Martin put a glass in front of me and told me to knock it back in one go, so I did. It tasted awful, but it gave my stomach a warm feeling. I remember having a second. And that's it. The next thing I remember was seeing Mom this morning."

Abby and I exchanged glances. There was no need for Louis to know that he'd been set up. I squeezed his arm gently, to let him know we weren't angry.

"I may want to ask you other questions, but that's enough for now. Let's concentrate on getting you better." I stood and said, "Abby, I have some things to do. Will you stay here? I'll be back in an hour or so." I turned back to Louis. "Is this okay with you?"

They both nodded, so I walked to the nearest pay phone and called my office. I told Brutus Elliott that I wouldn't be in and he didn't ask for an explanation. He must have known by the tone of my voice that none would be forthcoming.

I made my way to Louis' high school, strode into the main office and demanded to see the principal, Mr. Hills, immediately. It took the secretary a split second to accept that I would not be deterred. I was ushered into his room, its walls lined with bookcases. Any spare wall space was taken up by photographs, many of which were classes from years gone by. Hills was seated behind his desk, with what I judged to be impatience in his face.

"What is the urgency, Mr. Driscoll?"

"My son ended up in the Emergency Room at Chapel Hill General yesterday. He was suffering from alcoholic poisoning. He told me that you sent him to UNC Medical School and that I had approved the trip."

"That's right."

"May I see the letter I supposedly signed?"

Hills walked to the outer office and returned, holding a letter. It was typed on *Monitor* letterhead, approving the excursion. And it was my signature. Someone had gone to a lot of trouble to bamboozle the principal.

I apologized to Mr. Hills, who uttered a few bromides about 'boys being boys' and 'not to worry,' but when he wondered out loud who might have done this, I decided to leave. I didn't want him to know my business and I certainly wasn't going to share my suspicions with him.

I drove to the medical school and made my way to Dixon's office, where I found him leafing through a medical magazine. He looked up and smiled. "What can I do for you, David?"

"Who is Martin Deans?"

"I beg your pardon?"

"Who is Martin Deans and where can I find him?"

"David, we have hundreds of people here, students, interns, hospital workers, colleagues. I have never heard of a Martin Deans. I'll check with my secretary. What's this about?"

"My son attended a seminar here yesterday."

"Ah yes, 'The Future of Medicine.' I'm pleased to say it was well attended. Did he enjoy it?"

"At lunchtime, he was lured into a drinking hole by one of your people, this Martin Deans, who poisoned Louis with alcohol. I'm going to get to the bottom of this and find out who did it and you're going to help me."

Dixon bristled. "I won't be bullied by anyone, including you! I'll find out what I can, but I know nothing about your son being here."

I told myself to calm down. "Robert, I'm sorry. I'm just so shocked by what has happened to Louis. I'd appreciate any help you can give."

Dixon seemed to accept this and his body relaxed. "I'll contact you if I find out anything," he replied, but his words went unheard.

I returned to the hospital, where I found Louis dressed and ready to leave. Dr Norton delivered a lecture about drinking, but I was sure my son had been the recipient of doped drinks, Mickey Finns. Within ten minutes of arriving home, Brutus called to say I was needed and it was urgent. Abby had everything in hand, so I left.

Jeremiah Burns was waiting for me in my secretary's office. "What the hell do you want?" was my greeting. "Ever heard of an appointment?"

"I thought we could use a little chat," he said, his voice just conciliatory enough to make me suspicious. "I was saddened by our last exchange, so I wanted to put things in better order."

"And how exactly do you propose to do that?" I demanded, wasting no energy on being the good guy.

Burns eyed me for a moment. "What's got your goat?"

"If you must know, my son spent last night at Chapel Hill General. Did you carry out your threat to harm my family? Have you come to gloat? Just get out of this office before I throw you out."

Burns rose, hands reaching out as if to calm me. "David, I assure you, whatever happened to your son had nothing to do with me. Is there anything I can do to help?"

"Yes, you can get your lying self out of here!"

Burns took a few steps towards the door, then turned back. "I'll leave, but before I go you need to hear what I came to say. It's time you faced the truth. Take a close look at those stories you're printing about me and see where they're headed. Like the workers' medical deductions you dislike so much. Your problem is that you have no connections in the Governor's mansion, whereas I do. I also have excellent relations with our state's U.S. senators and Congressmen. The facts of life are that the tax people of North Carolina will neither take any action against B & M nor me personally. This story is dead in the water. Shall I continue?"

I glared at Burns, too angry to speak.

"I'll take that as a yes," he said.

"Now, about the anti-trust bullshit. Do you really want to take on big tobacco? All of us in North Carolina are close to friendly federal and state legislators. We've blocked the US Justice Department before and we'll do it again, whenever we need. Only Truman has the power to unblock the investigation and he won't do that, not in an election year. He needs us Southern Democrats to win the White House."

I wanted to argue every point with him, but I was too drained from the Louis experience and I knew that, in too many ways, he was right.

"As for your investigation of contracts with the military," he went on, "I don't know where you're getting your information, but, as my friends in the oil business say, you've drilled into a dry well. Frankly, I'm surprised that a man of your knowledge and sophistication could be so naïve. This part of the world is ruled by the Shelby Machine. Do you really think Max Gardner would favor *The Monitor* over me?"

Burns stood and straightened his suit jacket. "I want to make it abundantly clear that you are out of your depth. You should never have taken me on and if your newspaper continues to print stories about me, you'll regret it. I'm sorry to hear about your son; it was not my doing. But let me be as clear as possible. If you continue this crusade against me and mine, there will be casualties and you will come off much worse than anyone else."

I could no longer hold my rage, which I unleashed without thought. "This is a nation of laws, Burns, and no matter how big you think you are, the law is above you. You think you hold all the cards? You don't, you feral bastard. I've met people like you, people who think they have so much power, they could do what they like. And for a while it may work, but eventually they all overreached themselves."

I felt my heart pounding, a light-headedness making me feel off-balance, but I couldn't stop. "And you, you're no different. I don't believe your denial; I think you were behind that foul trick on my son. And you still keep threatening me. Give me a straight answer. Are you threatening my wife and children?"

Burns could not conceal a smirk. "Asked and answered," he replied. I can't remember ever wanting to kill another human being until that moment.

"How can you live with yourself? You're a bully. You throw your weight around whenever you feel like it. You think you can control me by terrorizing my family? Trust me, you cannot. Now get out!"

Burns left and I sat for several minutes, trying to recover my composure. My place was with my family, so I told my secretary that I could be reached at home, but only if it was urgent.

That night, the children were back to normal. Louis had his head in a book and Lottie spent far too much time on the telephone chatting with friends. I wondered what it was about teenagers that helped them recover from adversity so quickly. By contrast, their parents felt like wrecks. When the children were in bed, I told Abby about Burns' visit.

"Abby, I'm really worried. If this man is prepared to damage our children's health to show his power, what else might he do to us? And the business with Louis seems to have taken no effort. Burns just clicks his fingers and his minions do his dirty work. I can't protect you and the children all the time. You all have to go to Richmond till this blows over."

Abby had hardly said a word since the Louis drama had unfolded, but now she let rip.

"Have to? It's bad enough that I put my career before the children," she said. "It's even worse that when they needed me yesterday, I didn't take the time. How could I have behaved this way? I'll feel guilty for the rest of my life. But," she added with real firmness, "what I won't do is let Jeremiah Bloody Burns or you dictate my life. No one's going to tell me where and how I live. We're a family and we'll stay together right here in Chapel Hill."

I hadn't seen my wife that angry or so determined for a very long time.

"Abby, darling, I don't think this is wise. Why put the children or you at greater risk? I've had the clearest message from Burns. If I don't stop my investigations, all of you are in danger. You have to leave."

To my surprise, Abby shouted her response. "No, damn it, I do not! And why should I take all the blame? Your whole life has been about putting your career ahead of your family. I've done it for just a few months and it's not working. This stops for me and it stops now." I thought of arguing the point, but she was so angry and determined to speak her mind.

"The children will come first, as they should. Will you change, David? I doubt it. And here's the proof. Telling me to move to Richmond with the children, just like that. You, of course, will stay here and remain in the firing line. Business as usual, isn't that right?"

"Be reasonable," I said. "I'm not blaming you for what happened to Louis. Yes, we've both put careers first, but who could've predicted what happened yesterday?"

I didn't want to raise my voice, but more than anything I needed to drive my point home.

"I don't know how else to say this," I finally said. "I repeat, you and the children are in danger. Of course I don't want you to leave town, but what choice is there? How can the three of you be safe until this blows over?"

I needed time to think things through more clearly. The altercation with Burns had happened only an hour earlier. I recognized by the set of Abby's jaw that she was not going to let this one go.

"If the children and I leave Chapel Hill, Burns wins," she said. "And what's worse, I lose, the children lose, and you lose too. My teaching post here might be terminated and our children's schooling goes to pot. This is such a big year for Louis and he needs both of us around. As for you and me, we would be apart yet again, at a time when the children and I need you most. It's a bad plan, David."

I understood her reasoning, but I was unwilling to give in on any issue that dealt with the safety of my family. I also felt guilty, being the one who chose to take Burns on. However, if he was making serious threats, it meant I was getting closer to his secrets.

"I'm going to talk to LeGaillard," I said. "If anything happens to one of us, at least he'll know about these threats."

Coming up with this idea made me feel better. Perhaps my family could stay together. The next day, I arranged to meet with the Chief of Police. Before I left to meet him, I received a call from Dr Norton. "Mr Driscoll, how is Louis doing?" Before I could reply, he continued. "We did a blood test and found traces of chloral hydrate. It is an incapacitating agent, a psychoactive drug. No wonder Louis was in such a bad state when I saw him. Fortunately, the drug has no lasting effect. I will write to you to confirm our findings, in case Louis needs proof he was drugged. I am sorry I thought he was drunk. Sadly, it's an easy mistake to make."

I thanked Norton, told Abby of the call and said goodbye. Then I left for Durham where I found LeGaillard seated in his office.

"What can the constabulary do for the esteemed editor?" he said. I detected mockery in his voice.

"What I am about to tell you is off the record," I said.

LeGaillard's manner changed to serious. "Mr Driscoll, the police can't do things off the record. If you allege a crime, I have to investigate. Just tell me the story and I'll see how my office can help."

I started with my first meetings with Jeremiah Burns and his story about why he wrecked *The Monitor*. I took the Chief through my disagreements with Burns, as well as some of the things I had discovered. Then I related the business with Louis. Finally, I told him about my last meeting with Burns and the threats he made. LeGaillard was all ears. He didn't ask questions, but he made notes. When I was finished, he looked me square in the eye.

"Do you promise that everythin' you just told me is the truth?"

"Absolutely," I said.

He put the pen down and clasped his hands in front of him. "So help me analyze this. There are no independent witnesses to your conversations with Burns. You have no evidence that will stand up in court, linking Burns to the assault on your son."

"The conversations between us took place in private, but he did threaten me and my family and Louis was hurt."

He leaned towards me, as if about to confide. "I realize this must be very distressful for you and your family, but I have nothin' that requires me to interview Mr Burns, let alone arrest him. I'm sorry, but that's the long and short of it."

I felt the muscles in my jaw begin to twitch.

"So, this is Southern justice? I might have known a Northerner would get the bum's rush." The moment I said those words, I wanted to take them back. Nothing would be accomplished with insults.

"I do not play politics with people's lives," said LeGaillard, anger in his voice. "You don't have sufficient evidence for me to do anythin' against Mr. Burns, period. But did I say I wouldn't help?" Before I could respond, he rushed forward. "My dealins with you tell me you're a straight-shooter and I believe what you're tellin' me. However, what you don't have is a link, somethin' to help me rattle Mr. Burns' chain. How would you feel about havin' some police protection, at least for a week or so? It may cost you a bit, since my budget is already stretched. I could provide two men to guard your home. They can also accompany you and the family when you go about your daily activities."

I didn't think this was a viable solution. Questions would be asked and people would wonder why a story of police protection for the editor and his family was not being reported in *The Monitor*.

"It's a kind offer," I said, "but not one I can accept. How about my telling Burns that I've reported his threats to you? Maybe that will make him think twice."

The man shook his head. "That's not how we do things here in Durham. However," he added, "I know Max Gardner quite well and I could get a message to him. In turn, he'll probably tell Burns to back off. The offer of protection is still there, if you change your mind."

Chapter 18.

Senator Seth Andrews arrived at his Capitol Hill office. Seniority gave him pride of place, which meant an elegant space on the third floor, his windows overlooking one of the Capitol's reflecting pools. Andrews was in his early sixties, a balding, grey-haired colossus, handsome and a voice with a drawl befitting the senior senator from South Carolina. He was admired for his sartorial tastes, specifically the Savile Row-styled suits that camouflaged his excess weight. He was serving his fourth term and was married to a woman half his age, of whom he said, "God created feminine pulchritude, bless Him."

People close to the Senator knew that within the facade of a courtly Southern gentleman beat a heart that sought intense power. When the new Congress convened, his fortunes would be on the rise. The patronage enjoyed by his state's rival, North Carolina, and the pork barrels of privilege they received at his state's expense, were sure to be slashed. By how much, no one could be certain, but it would depend on how Andrews played his hand. Whatever happened, his new role as chairman of the Senate War Investigations Committee would endow him with more influence than he had ever commanded.

Andrews spoke to an aide. "Tomorrow, I have to go to a meetin' at the DNC office in Raleigh. Some local, interstate business to resolve. Fix it so the editor of *The Durham Monitor* comes see me, would ya? David Driscoll is the man's name. Thank you kindly."

*****

I picked up the phone, listened, responded, "yes, of course," and hung up. I pulled on my jacket, strode to Josh's office.

"I've been called by Seth Andrews' people to see the Man at the DNC office in Raleigh. No idea why or when I'll be back."

"That is, if you survive!" said Josh, eyebrows raised.

By the time I met Senator Andrews, I had rehearsed my responses to several dozen anticipated and loaded questions, the most important having to do with *The Monitor* revelations about the underhanded politics and business practices of Jeremiah Burns.

I was shown into an office, where I found Andrews smiling so broadly, he resembled a shark going in for the kill.

"Hello, Senator," I said, offering a hand, "glad to meet you." Andrews shook it and motioned to me to sit.

"What can I do for you?" I asked.

"Mr. Driscoll," replied Andrews, laying on his drawl with a trowel, "so nice to make your acquaintance. I've been readin' your articles about our friend, Jeremiah Burns. I have to confess that you've tickled my funny bone. Your observations have been, shall we say, *interestin'*, even if they're somewhat hostile to some of us good ol' boys."

We talked about a few of the editorials and I worried that Andrews might deliver some poorly shrouded threats. Before he had the chance, an aide rushed in, whispered something to him and I was left in an empty room. When the Senator returned several minutes later, he apologized profusely for inconveniencing me and asked if we could continue our discussion over the weekend at his home, about thirty miles north of Charleston.

"Called back to D.C. for an unexpected vote," he explained, stuffing folders and assorted documents into a large attaché case. "I have to dash. So sorry. I believe the trip will be worth your while."

A few days later, I sat on the veranda of Senator Andrews' antebellum mansion.

Although it was fall, the air was still steamy and humid, but a massive ceiling fan made it bearable, as did the iced tea. His servant poured two glasses, held out a plate of lemon slices and waited for me to drop one into my drink.

"So, shall we talk a little business, Mr. Driscoll?" said my host, his southern drawl magically dropped. "You're fighting our man Burns on too many fronts."

"I run a newspaper, Senator. It's my responsibility to overlook nothing."

"That's as may be, but you have no hope with this tax evasion claim." He took a slow sip of his tea and studied me over the rim of the glass as he leaned back into his stuffed armchair. I could tell this man missed nothing. "The IRS will have its hands tied, there will be a fight about states' rights and the case will go nowhere. I might add that any attempt to get anti-trust off the ground won't work either."

"You say that with great confidence, Senator."

"There's a presidential election coming," Mr. Driscoll.

"Uh huh. Assuming you're right, I'd be interested to know why I'm here."

Andrews placed his glass on an ornate cast iron side table and looked hard at me. His chair seemed to have transformed itself from perch to throne. "I'm told you're politically astute. You seem to have been off target of late, so I'll put this down to your having been away from D.C. for too long. Now, come January, I'll be heading the War Investigations Committee. As you know, this gives me authority over many areas regarding the military and the defence budget. I'm considering naming myself to the War Munitions Oversight Committee as well."

I sat quietly, not quite sure where he was going with this.

"I gather you have evidence that corporations possibly controlled by our man Burns have been breaking our laws. I'm also told that there are allegations regarding these companies supplying sub-standard munitions and goods."

"The military budget is huge," I said, "and the amounts being made by the corporations from these contracts are miniscule in comparison." When I paused, I realized that Andrews wasn't jumping to Burns' defense. The narrowed eyes and creases in his brows told me that he was truly concerned and interested.

Andrews ceased to smile. "You're aware that military contract rules don't permit sub-contractors to supply goods and munitions without being approved by the military. I've learned you have evidence showing that sub-contractors were not approved. To me, that's a blatant breach of the rules."

I waited for him to continue.

"I know about the defective howitzers and that there's been a cover-up. I also know that one of my fellow Senators is up to his ears in mud. I intend to make his life hell. So," he added, exhaling as if relieved to have discussed this, "my aim is to stop these North Carolina bastards from screwing their government and the taxpayers."

I had a strong sense that there was more, things he was holding back. I sipped my iced tea. "You suggested that I'm politically naïve. Let's see if I can change your mind. Lately, South Carolina has been the poor relation of your northern neighbor. There have been too many pork barrels and boondoggles allocated to North Carolina. The Shelby machine and Burns wield enormous influence and it seems to extend into the federal government. My guess? You're hoping to tip the balance towards your state, give South Carolina a bigger slice of the pie."

Andrews studied me for a minute before speaking. "You may well think that, but you've only scratched the surface. From our infancy, this country has always faced corruption in the way business is done. North Carolina today? It's in the clutches of corrupt men and I'm determined to see the balance restored to the people."

"So your goals are predicated on fairness to all citizens?"

Andrews smiled again and for the first time it was open and honest. "My popularity will soar if I take on these corrupt people and beat them. I might mention," he said, "I'm very popular anyway!"

I laughed. I had anticipated that my information on the army contracts would be useful to Andrews and now I felt I could trust him.

"I guess you might warm to a little help from a newspaperman. This is what I have so far," I said, handing him a copy of the report prepared by Patti Lou Gains and Emily Venn. "I'm asking you to keep this confidential. If a story is likely to break, I trust you'll let *The Monitor* have the exclusive."

He took the papers and scanned them quickly. "I assure you," he said, taking on his senatorial voice. "I've made it a priority to keep friendly relations with members of the fourth estate, especially those who treat me fairly and with respect."

Chapter 19.

Despite his age, the man retained his vigour and strength. In shirtsleeves, with suspenders holding up his pants, he threw aside his pick and set to digging with a shovel. He had started more than an hour earlier, when there was enough moonlight to cast a glow over his work. It was now pitch black and the glimmer from a kerosene lamp was his only light. He didn't mind. For what he was doing, he needed to remain hidden from prying eyes.

Fifteen minutes later, the pit was deep enough. He walked a few yards to his truck, removed a sack from the trunk and dragged it to the pit, where he unceremoniously shoved it in. Jumping into the pit, he arranged the sack lengthways and assessed the depth of the hole. Satisfied with his work, he climbed out and shoveled earth onto the sack. Within half an hour, the work was completed. He would return in the morning to grass over the earthwork.

Back home, he stripped naked and stuffed the dirty clothing and mud-stained shoes into a sack. These would be burned. After a hot shower, he climbed into bed and for the first time that day, felt relaxed. It was over. No one would miss the boy, no one would care. Better than anything else, no one would suspect him.

BOOK THREE.
Winter, 1948 – 1949.
Chapter 20.

Fall brought a welcome relief from the heat of summer, but the winter months were proving harsh. I took Senator Andrews' advice to heart and accepted that nothing would be gained from chasing B & M over their apparent tax evasion or focusing on the virtual monopoly they had created. I took no comfort in spiking the stories, but my staff seemed to understand. As for those army contracts, I had to keep my powder dry until Senator Andrews took charge of the War Investigations Committee. If you grow up in America's Midwest, you get taught from an early age about the perils of poking a bear.

Abby wasn't impressed with my decisions. She didn't go so far as to accuse me of going soft, of acting like a weakling, a coward and shirking the responsibilities of a journalist, but she didn't remain silent.

"What would your old mentor say?" she chided. She was referring to the late Sam Perkins. This was not going to end well.

"Mercifully, darling, we'll never know," I said, "but I'm pretty sure he'd tell me not to write half-baked stories. And, like it or not," I added, more gravitas in my voice than intended, "I need to keep an eye on my family. This isn't St. Luke. Burns is powerful, dangerous, unpredictable and a law unto himself. Even if the LeGalliard accepted all my theories, he wouldn't be able to protect us if Burns was determined to do us harm."

I expected Abby to argue or insist that protecting the children was a responsibility shared by us. She's never been one of those wives who considers herself 'the little woman' in need of protection. However, this time she let it go.

I took the opportunity to tell Abby about my orphanage enquiries. "One of our reporters checked out the law," I told her. "Orphanages are regulated by the state through the Bureau of Children's Affairs. Welfare, health and education of orphans is a state responsibility but there aren't enough state and city orphanages, so quite a few are run by charities. The state pays a per capita sum each year to the private orphanages but it's not much.

"The trouble is that the regulations aren't enforced properly. The system breaks down when practical help is needed. The Bureau employs only three Inspectors of Orphanages for the whole of North Carolina. This seems totally inadequate."

"What about records, that sort of thing?"

"Good point. Orphanages are required to keep records but the information is minimal: name of child, birth date if known, date of arrival and date and destination of departure is all that is required."

"Is that all? Did you find anything out about Burdett?" asked Abby.

"I was coming to that. He runs the Raleigh Orphan Foundation, placing orphans in distant states out West with families who are childless. The Foundation complies with all state regulations. Burdett is its president. There are no other officers or employees. The Foundation is required to keep records similar to those kept by the orphanages. Interestingly, it is sufficient for the Foundation to state the destination of a departing child merely as city or town and state. No address is required under the rules. The reason given is that North Carolina cannot enforce regulations across state lines."

"This is preposterous." Abby's dander was up again. "There's no check on what happens to these children?"

"It seems not. I didn't leave it there. I asked that private investigator, Patti-Lou Gains, to look into things. She found a nurse who worked at Silver Leaf Orphanage for more than two years. This nurse left six months ago after asking Mrs. Burns about the children who were taken by Burdett. She was worried about what happened to them. Days later, she was given her marching orders. The reason given was that there were insufficient numbers of orphans to require her services."

"This sounds suspicious, or am I prejudiced?"

"There's more. Patti found a woman who worked as a cleaner for Burdett. The house is quite big but Burdett occupies just a few rooms. He sleeps downstairs and the upstairs is closed off. The cleaner was told not to bother with it. She told Patti that now and again she thought she heard noises coming from upstairs, a child crying but she was too scared to go and see."

"Anything else?"

"Patti said she had heard whispers but her investigation turned up nothing solid, just conjectures and rumor. Mind you, I asked her to avoid attracting Burns' attention. I don't like to think what Burns would do if he thought we were investigating Lou Beth."

"But what about the orphan children. Are some missing?"

"Abby, please. For the time being, this investigation has to go on the back burner. I have nothing solid. And Sam Perkins would tell you exactly the same if he was here."

"Will you promise me to keep an eye on this one?"

I said I would but I confessed it wouldn't be top of the list. Too little evidence, too many other things going on was my excuse. Abby didn't like it but she accepted my decision.

*****

There was plenty going on to keep the newspaper busy. The presidential election was a hot topic: Republican nominee, Thomas Dewey, was a handsome man who looked like a matinee idol. He'd earned quite a reputation as a crime fighter when serving as New York's District Attorney. On the national scene, he'd made his mark as Governor of New York. The polls had him well ahead of Truman. My people followed both candidates. We were the only newspaper in the region that recognized Truman's campaign had caught fire. He was stirring up big crowds and his policies made sense to a country still healing from a world war. Despite the polls saying that Dewey would be our next president, *The Monitor* predicted a Democratic win. Rival newspapers mocked us, but we held to our prediction. Two days after the election, we had the pleasure of printing that famous photograph of Truman holding up the front page of *The Chicago Sun-Times* with the headline, *Dewey Wins*! We made our critics eat crow!

Behind the scenes, Patti-Lou Gains was slowly gathering evidence about Burns and his interests. At one stage, she felt she was getting nowhere. "If you want me to stop, that would be fine," she said, but I asked her to keep digging and to stay in touch with Emily. I knew well how these kinds of investigations rarely hit pay-dirt quickly and there were always obstacles.

It was mid-November before the scales were tilted against Burns. It started with a telephone call from Buck LeGaillard, asking me to drop by his office. I settled into the chair across from him, wondering what he could possibly tell me that would be of interest.

"I wanted you to know there's been a development in the Butler case."

That got my attention.

"The men killed in the roadhouse have been identified as members of a gang that operates out of Atlanta. The police there have been looking for these men. Their families reported them missing a while ago."

I pulled out a notepad and pen. "Any thoughts, Chief, anything I can publish?"

"All I can do for now is release their names and where they lived. But there's no exclusive here since there's nothing yet to connect them to the Butler murders except circumstantial evidence. I'll send out a press release later today."

I put away the notepad, slipped the pen into my pocket and rose to leave.

"Not so fast," he said, prompting me to stay put. "I'm as certain as I can be that these men were brought in to kill Butler. But why? We know what he was working on? Did he find somethin' unknown to us that put him in danger? And how would the people who wanted him dead know who to contact in Atlanta?"

I knew that LeGaillard was thinking aloud, but these were good questions that required answers.

"And the people," he went on, "the ones who wanted the Atlanta boys dead, would they have the balls to eliminate the killers themselves? Or did they get someone to do it for them?"

I thought about this for a moment. "So you're thinking it was only Butler the killers were after."

LeGaillard nodded. "His wife and children were in the wrong place at the wrong time. Think about it," he added. "Would the killers know that he was a family man? Whether they did or not, they couldn't leave witnesses."

I waited for him to continue. Clearly, there was something on his mind.

"I've called you in because I need your help. I've been readin' your editorials. *The Monitor*'s been chasin' Burns and his people pretty hard, but it seems you've cooled things down for now. Not that I blame you," he added, looking directly into my eyes. "Jeremiah Burns can be one son of a bitch to fight."

"There are things I can tell you and things I can't," I replied, "but I can promise you that I'd never withhold anything that would hamper your investigations. My first thoughts? Burns is a dangerous man to cross. We haven't stopped our investigations of his empire, but we have reached some dead ends. The stories we have about Burns aren't ready for publication. We need better evidence. Just between you and me," I added, "I'm quite sure there's trouble coming soon at the B & M works. It might develop into a strike."

LeGaillard didn't appear surprised, but he remained silent.

"As for Edgar Butler," I said, "you know he uncovered a scam about deductions taken from wages to pay for health services. B & M made huge profits off the backs of their workers. It might not have been illegal, unless they conveniently forgot to declare the surplus for tax. We published the story, excluding allegations about tax fraud, but that was all we had. So far, the IRS has taken no action and the state tax authorities have ignored the matter. It's just politics, I know, but I find it hard to believe that Butler was murdered because of this. I'm wondering if whoever was told to shut Butler up may have exceeded his authority."

"So you're saying that Burns wanted Butler stopped, not necessarily murdered. An interesting thought. Any idea who would have been delegated to handle this?"

"Your guess is as good as mine," I said, "but it has to be someone who is totally loyal to Burns and terrified of him."

The Chief nodded again and asked me to describe the trouble brewing at B & M.

"Low wages, poor working conditions, for starters. Workers have been fighting for better pay and shorter working hours for a long time. I wouldn't be surprised if the atmosphere at the plant turns ugly. But if we're talking about the Butler investigation, I'd want to know who is harmed, apart from Burns, by disclosures of poor health practices?"

I returned to the office and asked Brandon to join me. I asked him to catch me up on the news at B & M. "Is there any movement by management?"

Over the months, Brandon had established a close relationship with some Negroes at B & M. He'd followed the build-up of worker discontent and kept tabs on the hot issues. The main problem centered on the company's refusal to increase the low wages paid, despite the government's recent elimination of price controls on cigarette sales, which resulted in substantial increases in profits but B & M had made no offers to workers. Poor work conditions, the long working day and, sometimes, night were also major elements in the dispute. Management had been dragging its feet in talks, probably hoping the problem would either go away or get deferred.

"The colored workers are paid less than whites for the same job," said Brandon. "And they live in the poorest housing. There's hardly enough money for food and rent, which means their families are forced to live on the breadline. And they're given the menial jobs. Dangerous ones, too. What kind of a life is that? They can barely eke out an existence."

When I asked Brandon what he thought would happen, his voice became animated.

"Many of them are talking strike. Their local union branch will support them, but bosses in the union head office are opposed.

"They, the Union, say they can't afford a strike, it'll get the workers nowhere and they might find themselves worse off than before. My guess is that Burns and his people have bought off the union bosses, but I have no evidence, let alone proof. However, I do have executives of Local 31 on record and they're telling me a strike will succeed."

I walked to the door of my office and asked Brutus to join us. I explained that I wanted Brandon to work closely with him on this story. "This is a real opportunity for you," I told Brandon. There was no need to mention the obvious. A Negro reporter with a by-line on a major story would make a lot of people pay attention.

As editor-in-chief, my life was filled with day to day responsibilities. One of these was to be sure talented reporters got a fair chance. With a veteran like Brutus supervising Brandon through his first big assignment, success could almost be guaranteed.

"Let's summarize our strategy," I told them. "We'll report the facts as they happen, so you need to be at the factory gates, if and when a strike starts," I told Brandon. "We'll need a photographer there. Brandon," I added, my voice heavy with authority, "do not enter the factory gates under any circumstances. Do nothing that contravenes the law. Keep talking with the workers and work closely with Brutus. Always follow his instructions. By the way, do either of you know the last time there was a strike at B & M?"

"I don't think there has ever been one," replied Brandon.

"Even better! Lousy jobs and poverty make interesting reading." Both men looked at me with discomfort, but they knew that I was right.

Three days later, the colored B & M workers went on strike. Three quarters of their work force put down their tools and walked out. They cited low pay, compared not only with white workers, but with colored workers at other tobacco plants. They listed unpleasant and dangerous working conditions in their complaints, as well as long working hours.

The Monitor supported the strikers. We stuck to the facts, set out the workers' claims fairly and quoted the Local 31 officials who said that they wanted to support their members, but had been prevented from doing so by their union chiefs. Our articles were supported by photographs showing the desperation in the strikers' eyes, as well as a photo spread on their dreadful living conditions.

I suggested to Brutus that he write a summary of the dispute as an editorial. I couldn't have done it better He covered all the salient points and left the readers with a real sense of where this paper stood regarding workers' rights.

The Durham Monitor. October 28, 1948
Fair Play at Burns & Murphy

Burns & Murphy supplies Americans with almost thirty-five percent of cigarettes smoked domestically. This makes it an important corporation, contributing not only a vital commodity but also to the prosperity of this city. B & M employs thousands of workers, which begs the question: If its workers are so unhappy, why have they not protested before? Why have they not taken strike action in support of their demands? What is this dispute really about?

This newspaper has investigated the facts and has uncovered some unsettling data. When we take the wages of the colored workers and subtract the deductions taken from their pay checks, the amount remaining puts every one of those workers at or below subsistence levels. Not only are they paid substantially less than their white B & M co-workers doing the same job, but they are also paid less than other cigarette manufacturers pay coloreds throughout this state. After paying rent, how do these people feed, let alone clothe, their families? We have printed our evidence elsewhere in this newspaper.

If B & M wishes to dispute our facts, space will be given for them to set out their side of the issue. However, this newspaper will first require B & M to produce documented evidence in support of their claims. They must also agree to a neutral party examining such evidence.

The law is clear. The Supreme Court ruling in Plessy v Ferguson sets an "equal but separate" test for whites and coloreds. Colored workers at the plant are indeed separated from white workers, but they are not treated equally, especially in terms of wages. On average, they earn slightly more than two-thirds the wages earned by whites for the same job. This is unfair and unjust, as well as unlawful.

> Reporters from this newspaper have visited the homes of colored B & M workers. Many of these homes have no running water, no electricity. This is no way for people in post-war America to be forced to live.
>
> What is the true definition of poverty? Poverty exists when an individual must plan how money is spent from day to day, rather than months ahead. The vast majority of colored workers at B & M fall into the former category. This alone is cause for *The Monitor* to support the colored workers in their strike action.

After the editorial appeared, I was worried that our coverage of the strike and support of the minority workers might result in a backlash from our readers, which would also cause a drop in circulation. Since advertising revenues keep a paper afloat, stating an unpopular belief can be risky. B & M had already stopped advertising with *The Monitor* months before, as soon as the anti-Burns campaign started. The other tobacco manufacturers followed suit. I wondered if this could be used as evidence of a cigarette manufacturers' cartel, but I kept that thought to myself. My discussions with people in D.C. convinced me that pursuing this line was hopeless.

The withdrawal of cigarette advertising revenue proved to be immaterial. New advertisers more than made up the gap. Circulation increased yet again, which told me that many people supported our stance on the strike. The letters I received as editor proved that a significant number of Raleigh/Durham citizens were sympathetic to the strike.

B & M had anticipated the strike and had built up a huge inventory. The trouble was that cigarettes can have a short shelf life and complaints were soon coming in from all over the country that the product was stale. Before B & M could deal with this, their white workers threatened strike action for better pay and conditions. The union representing white workers wanted to ensure that their members continued to receive a significantly higher salary than their Negro counterparts. Abby and I wondered what was going on in the B & M board room and the wrath visited by Jez Burns on his management team.

The Monitor ran daily stories about the strike, adding pictures demonstrating the plight of the strikers. We interviewed both colored and white workers, local trade people, politicians and anyone with a relevant opinion.

We did our best to publish all views, with an emphasis on fair and balanced reporting. Every time we approached B & M management for comments and interviews, we were rebuffed. We made sure that our readers knew about these refusals.

When the strike entered its second week, Brutus suggested we run an appeal for food and clothing to help the striking workers. We weren't sure it would work, especially in a Southern state.

"Are you talking donations of money?" I asked him.

"Money, yes," he said, "but more importantly food and clothing, all the things the colored strikers can't provide for their families when walking the line."

I wasn't sure this appeal would go anywhere, so I was very surprised and pleased when I had to add resources to deal with distribution of the truckloads of food and goods that poured in.

The story of the strike at B & M caught the eye of newspapers nationwide. From the second week, our stories were syndicated throughout the states.

The paper's bank balance increased. By the end of the third week, our stories had appeared in more than two hundred newspapers. However, despite everyone's efforts, there seemed to be no end in sight.

"It's a classic battle of wills," Abby said one night, over yet another nearly-midnight dinner. "Do you think the strikers will be able to hold on?"

"If the white workers strike," I said, "that may prove to be the last straw. I'm guessing that B & M will stand firm in its refusal to negotiate. Maybe the local union will defy instructions and support its Negro members."

At the beginning of the fourth week of the strike, Brutus wrote another editorial asking Burns to intervene personally to end the strike. He closed the piece with:

> "Mr. Burns, the people of this city know the solution to this strike is in your hands. *The Monito*r hopes you will listen to the protests and that common sense will prevail."

In response, B & M issued a press release, deploring the interference "by elements of the press in an industrial dispute." They claimed to have "incontrovertible evidence" that the local union had been infiltrated by communist elements and that the Communist Party of America was assisting the strikers.

"A pretty flimsy excuse for not negotiating," Josh announced during a staff meeting.

"Playing the communist card is brilliant," said Brutus. "Citizens might well believe all that conspiracy crap."

I approved publication of B & M's statement and asked Brutus for another editorial.

I suggested he comment on the point that B & M had ignored the big issue, namely the case for an increase in wages which was affordable.

The response of Local 31 to the communist allegation was quick and emphatic. It denied the accusation of communist infiltration and accused B & M of "red baiting." The next day, the U.S. Congress got involved. The House Un-American Activities Committee announced it had authorized a full investigation of Local 31. I decided to handle this one and got myself to D.C. as quickly as I could, accompanied by a senior political reporter. We did the rounds, but got little information. It was clear that the announcement of the investigation was half-baked. My guess was that to help both B & M and Burns, the Shelby machine had relayed its requirement to its U.S. congressional representatives "to get federal help."

The next day, *The Monitor* reported that action in Washington on the communist infiltration issue was significantly absent. More importantly, a day later, we reported the outbreak of deplorable violence at the plant.

The Durham Monitor. November 23rd, 1948.
<u>Violence at B & M Factory. Who is to Blame?</u>

Yesterday, violence broke out at the B & M factory in Durham. An eye witness told this newspaper: "More than fifty people were hurt. Twenty-two men who were protesting peacefully are now in the hospital, receiving treatment for their wounds."

A senior B & M manager was spotted, watching the scene. I heard a reporter call out to him, "Why have you done this? Why is such violence necessary?" His response was chilling: "An eye for an eye."

This newspaper has demonstrated a keen interest in the strike. Our reporters have been at the factory gates daily to witness events. What follows is the eye witness account of what took place yesterday, when a previously peaceful strike erupted into violence:

As usual, the morning started quietly. Striking pickets patrolled outside the factory gates, never interfering with those employees entering to work. Immediately inside the gates, company guards were at the ready. There was the usual exchange of banter between strikers and guards, but nothing more than words.

At 10.27 am, a Dodge pickup truck, carrying ten or eleven colored men, sped towards the factory gates, causing picketers to scatter and guards to retreat hastily. The truck smashed through the gates. The men riding on the truck wielded Billy clubs and other weapons and quickly set upon the guards, causing injury. A number of strikers on the picket line rushed in to protect those guards, receiving cuts and bruises themselves. The onslaught lasted less than five minutes, after which the attackers withdrew. Ambulances arrived and those guards with serious injuries were taken to the hospital.

At 11.18 am, the violence was renewed when guards at the factory gate, now four times the number from earlier, turned on the strikers. The guards used Billy clubs, batons, rifle butts and assorted weaponry. One of our reporters suffered a head injury which will require him to be hospitalized for several days. Numerous men on the picket line were also taken to the hospital."

The pickets were asked if they knew the identity of the colored attackers in the Dodge truck. None said they did. One reporter gave the license number of the Dodge to the police, but neither driver nor owner has been identified.

This newspaper deplores violence of any kind; we are calling for a police investigation to identify the men who attacked the factory and to uncover the perpetrators of the counter-attacks. Those who suspect the work of agent provocateurs will not be satisfied until a thorough investigation uncovers the entire story.

The article was accompanied by photographs, mostly revealing the violence meted out by the B & M guards. Some of the shots were horrific, showing armed guards standing above pickets, poised to strike blow after blow.

On the Sunday of the strike's fourth week, B & M suddenly called in representatives of both colored and white workers. The negotiations lasted almost three days before a settlement was hammered out.

Ray-Henry Jefferson told Brandon Hanes that B & M warned that if even one whisper of details of the negotiations appeared in the press, especially *The Monitor*, talks would end. On Wednesday night, an announcement was made to the press:

> "B & M Management announces that terms with its workers have been agreed. Colored workers will receive a 15% increase across the board. Likewise, white workers will receive a 10% increase. Commencing 1st January, 1949, all workers will receive one week's holiday pay annually. The contribution towards health costs will be reduced to 25 cents per week. Union recognition is not agreed."

So, that was that. Cigarette production resumed the following day and life gradually returned to normal. Or did it? How likely would it be for Chief LeGaillard to prosecute those who meted out the violence? I learned the answer very soon when the Chief cited evidential problems, despite the photographs we had provided.

Brandon met with B & M workers. Many of them, Negroes and whites, asked that he pass on to his editors their opinion that publicizing potential health issues caused by cigarette smoking was not helpful or wanted. They were worried for their jobs, no matter how paltry the wages. If the health issues were real and if people stopped smoking, where would that leave them and their families?

*****

I was increasingly uncomfortable with this North Carolina life. Abby and I had made friends in Chapel Hill, but they were more Abby's kind of people than mine. She was accustomed to Southern ways and customs, I was not.

And the longer I lived in the South, the less I wanted to adapt. What had happened with Louis still stirred my discontent and matters did not improve.

A few days after the strike ended, a note was pushed under our front door. When I opened it, I felt a sense of dread. *You have cost me greatly. You will pay.* It wasn't signed, and I was certain that Burns had not written it himself, but I was equally sure he had someone write and deliver it. After I showed it to Abby, I began the conversation I'd been mulling over for some time.

"Are you happy in Chapel Hill?" I asked her, while pouring a biting Cabernet into two glasses.

I felt her eyes on me, as if trying to second guess the meaning of that question. "Yes," she said, "on the whole. Why?"

I handed her a glass and took a long drink. "I know that I've said so before, but I don't think North Carolina is the place for me." Abby sipped her wine, but said nothing. "I don't like the way things are done here."

"The newspaper's doing well and you seem to have few problems with your staff. You're balancing your life," she went on. "We're building friendships here and the children are settled."

"I know you are making friends," I said, "but I'm not. Yes, I like some of the people at the paper, but I am their boss, not their friend."

"Are you sure this isn't just Jez Burns yanking your chain?"

One thing about Abby, she doesn't pull punches. And sometimes her assessment of a problem, her perceptions, are dead-on. But not this time.

"I can't put my finger on it," I said, "but I've said for a while there's something rotten in this place and I thought you felt it too."

Before she could respond, I rushed forward. "It's partly the way politics is played, how the Shelby machine has everything tied up. I don't know where exactly Burns fits, but he's involved. It's not like it was in St. Luke. There, people spoke their minds. Sure, Mike Doyle wielded power, but he wasn't an absolute monarch, a dictator. Here, there's nothing but Shelby people. Is it any wonder that the Negroes have such a struggle? If it's not the factory bosses treading on their necks, it's the politicians."

Abby crossed the short distance between us and gestured for me to join her on the sofa. She put down the glass and took my hand.

"David, this is so typical of you. As soon as you have something good, you're looking to move on. You want whatever you think is around the next corner."

I tried to speak, but she silenced me with an upheld hand. I'd said what I needed to say, now it was her turn.

"Look what you sacrificed to come here. Are you really willing to give up your rights to own *The Monitor,* now that it's a success? And what next? Relocate the children again? Louis is a senior. We can't move him, not when his future depends on this year. We have to let him graduate without another upheaval."

I knew she was right, but knowing isn't the same as feeling. "It's only December," I said. "We could resettle Louis and Charlotte in Richmond and they can go back to their old school."

"But don't you see that is a stop-gap? And what about you? Are you going to settle in Richmond?"

There was an edge to her voice, reminding me that this was not going to be easy.

"I might," I said. "I could go back to *The Mirror.* I'm sure Nick would have me back. And you could teach at Richmond or Georgetown."

"David, I'm finding it good for me here, despite what happened with Louis. I'm productive and excited about my work. Unless you can give me a very convincing case, backed by more than your gut, we're staying. Think about what you could have here, owning the newspaper, having a real influence. You could pursue the fight for black civil rights from close to the center. Are you going to let one man cloud your judgment?"

I knew when I was beaten and stood up. "Let's forget this talk. You're right, it wouldn't be the time to move Louis." I smiled at my wife, hoping to soften the edge of our conversation. "Time for bed?"

"Do you mean sleep?" she said, smiling coyly.

"Eventually."

"Why, Mr. Driscoll, you are the very devil. And I thought you'd given that role to Jeremiah Burns!"

Chapter 21.

Suddenly it was Christmas. We left for our usual holiday in Miami Beach and the Flamingo Hotel. Abby's siblings and their families joined us and we stayed through the New Year. No matter how much I loved being with family and sharing the joy of the season, I just could not shake my concerns about, and dislike of, life in the Triangle with its prejudices, racism and the loss of the entire Butler family without comeback.

Shortly after we returned to Chapel Hill, Beau Burns' appeal against his prison sentence came before the North Carolina Supreme Court. The Burns clan occupied two rows in the well of the court; I sat to the side in the press box.

Before the hearing began, I felt sure that Burns would have everything locked up for Beau. The three judges listened with courtesy and patience as Bush Pollard made his case. I couldn't help wondering if it was all for show. When Pollard concluded his argument, Judge Montgomery spoke briefly to his fellow judges, leaned forward from the elevated bench and waived the prosecutor away. Had Burns bought the appellate court?

Montgomery addressed the state prosecution counsel. "There's no need for us to hear from you. The court is ready to deliver its unanimous ruling."

There was a murmur of surprise throughout the courtroom. I prepared myself for a "time served" verdict, which meant that Beau would walk away a free man. My thoughts of injustice were interrupted swiftly by Judge Montgomery's declaration.

"We are taking the unusual course of delivering our unanimous judgement from the bench. The defendant is a young man who has enjoyed every possible advantage life has to offer."

Montgomery continued. "But this defendant has wasted those advantages. His family has stood by him and he has let them down. Beau Burns involved himself in a get-rich-quick scheme, while ignoring advice from state law officers either to end the business dealings or face prosecution. I am aware Burns' uncle has settled the civil suits. However, this does not change one basic fact: the defendant broke the criminal law of this state and did so without a care for the people you hurt."

A low noise was beginning to move through the room. Was it possible that Beau would finally be held accountable? I had my doubts, but I made sure I was taking precise notes.

Montgomery sat straight in his chair, shoulders back as he delivered the court's decision. "This court sees no merit in the appeal. It is denied. It also sees no reason to reduce the custodial sentence given by the trial judge. Indeed, if this court had the power to increase the sentence, it would do so." He turned to his fellow judges, nodded and rose. The other judges followed him.

Emma-Jane, Burns' sister, was open mouthed. Bush Pollard turned to the family and shrugged, as if to say, "I told you he'd finally get his."

Emma-Jane yanked hard on the attorney's sleeve. "You can't leave it like this! You've got to appeal again. Get Beau out! He's not deserving of all this time inside."

Pollard removed her hand from his sleeve. "Mrs. Beaufort, there are no grounds for an appeal. Not to the Supreme Court of North Carolina nor to the Supreme Court in Washington. Even if there were, by the time an appeal was heard, Beau would have served his time. You have to accept that we have exhausted all legal grounds on his behalf."

Emma-Jane would have none of it. Her face was flushed red, sweat breaking out on her brow. I watched her closely and half-expected her to slap the attorney. She turned to the seat of power in her family.

"Jez, go to the Governor and get a pardon! Get Max Gardner to pressure the Governor. Do something!" Emma-Jane's voice was shrill, piercing. I almost felt sorry for her brother, but Burns ignored her. It was in the middle of her next diatribe that Burns lost his temper.

"Emma-Jane, you will never speak to me like that again. It's time to get it through your thick head that I can't tell the Governor or Max Gardner what to do." Before she could argue, he turned to leave. As if having an afterthought, he turned and spoke, his voice more in control. "We'll talk about this in the car." And then he looked around, his eyes stopping with me. "Too many prying eyes and ears," he added, walking quickly toward the exit.

Chapter 22.

Senator Andrews had taken over as chairman of the Senate War Investigations Committee and was quickly making his presence felt. He made good on his promise. I received a cable at the end of January:

> *Mr. Driscoll, as Chair of the War Munitions Oversight Committee, I'm informing you that I will conduct hearings into wrongdoings in North Carolina relating to military contracts. I have been advised of the activities of certain corporations whose names may be familiar to you and have subpoenaed a number of documents and witnesses. I'd be happy to provide a ringside seat for you. Time and place to follow.*

Committee Room D on the second floor of the Capitol Building is cavernous. At one end are three rows of elevated, well-appointed desks with substantial chairs, clad in deep green leather, for the legislators. On each desk is a microphone and nameplate. There is ample room at the rear of each row for aides to move about, carrying messages to and from their masters. The rows are positioned at a distance from the well of the room, where desks and chairs for witnesses and their advisers are placed in the first row. Each witness desk has its own microphone. Behind are rows of benches for the public and the press.

It was early. I took my seat on the press bench and watched as members of the public and fellow journalists drifted in.

I was amazed to find none of the other North Carolina newspapers were represented. Maybe it was New Year oblivion. Whatever, the Senator might have handed me a scoop.

At ten o'clock sharp, Senator Andrews and six other senators took their seats. Although the public benches were only one-third full, the tension was palpable.

Andrews banged his gavel and called the session to order. "Good morning to all," he began. "Although we are now a nation at peace, America has taken on the role of the world's policeman and we must face anything that threatens our existence, as well as the free world. Accordingly, we have rules and regulations to ensure that our armed forces are equipped properly with the arms and munitions they need." He looked around the room, reminding me of a teacher making certain all his pupils were paying attention. When he cleared his throat, I knew this was a sign that he was resuming what was promising to be quite an introduction.

Andrews leaned forward, his face solemn. "This Committee has the duty to investigate contractual relationships between private industry and our armed forces," he said. "In this manner, we can ensure that all contracts are proper, appropriate, within the rules and free from corruption. As ever with these inquiries, we are starting small and will seek evidence from the bigger players as the hearings continue."

I looked around and noted latecomers slipping into the last row of public seats. To my relief, I still saw no journalists I recognized from North Carolina. There were a few whispers in the room, cut short by the chairman's gavel.

"The first stage of this investigation is an inquiry into contracts for the supply of arms and equipment from North Carolina corporations," said Andrews.

"This state is an important link in the training of our armed forces, with bases such as Camp Lejeune. There are grave concerns that certain North Carolina corporations are flouting the rules. Today's investigations will center on the supply of equipment and munitions from these corporations."

There was now a buzz in the room, which caused Senator Andrews and his Democrat colleagues to look almost smug. The first witness entered and took his seat at the witness desk. He was a man in his late thirties, skinny, ill-shaven and looking like a rabbit caught in headlights. Everything about him reflected his state of nervous tension. He was accompanied by an attorney who spoke into the microphone. "Gerry Orback, Senator, counsel to Mr. Cletus Hooper."

"Thank you, Mr. Orback," said Andrews. "Mr. Hooper, you will be sworn in and then I will ask the first set of questions. Afterwards, I will invite my colleagues to ask their questions."

Orback nodded. Hooper, still looking terrified, was sworn in. I felt for the man. It was challenging enough to be questioned by the country's political leaders, but having this take place in the Capitol had to be especially daunting.

The Senator started with, "Mr. Hooper, where do you live?"

"Walnut Grove, sir. It's in North Piedmont, North Carolina."

"And what do you do there?"

"I have a grocery store."

"You sell groceries?"

"Yes, sir."

I could see Hooper relaxing, as if this might not be as threatening as he had imagined.

"Do you do anything else at your store?"

Hooper glanced at his attorney, who whispered in his ear. "I don't understand the question, sir."

"Well, for example, do you have a notice board where local people can place notices or advertisements?"

"Yes, sir, I do."

"Do you charge people for this service?"

"Sometimes...sir."

"Of course you do, you're a businessman."

Hooper smiled weakly at the Senator. For a small-town merchant, this was praise indeed.

"What other services do you offer?"

"Come again, Senator?"

"Is your store used as an accommodation address for North Carolina corporations?"

"I'm not sure what you mean by an accommodation address, Senator."

The Senator took a deep breath, exhaling loudly. "Do you allow other businesses to use your address as their place of business?"

"I did agree to this a while back."

"What corporations reside, if I may use that word, at your store?"

"There are four. Bee Balm Inc, Dotted Horsemint Inc, Indian Blanket Inc and Solomon's Seal Inc."

"Unusual names, don't you think?"

"Not for a country boy, Senator." There was laughter from the public seats. "They're named after flowers from our state."

"And your store is the registered address for these corporations?"

"I don't know about registered addresses. All I can tell you is that I have nameplates screwed to the inside wall of my store, with these names on them, if that's what you mean?"

The Senator made a note. "Now, Mr. Hooper, why did you do this business? It's far removed from selling groceries."

"One day, this feller comes to my store, buys a few things and starts talkin' to me. He asks if I'd like to make some easy money."

"Before you go on, Mr. Hooper, does this man have a name?"

"He said his name was David Smith."

"What did he look like?"

"He was short, maybe a little over five feet, kinda bald and tubby. I'm guessin' he was fifty or so. A nervy little guy, with a bit of a twitch and thick glass frames."

"Did you notice anything else?"

"He spoke like he was a teacher."

"After he asked you about money, what happened next?"

"He told me he needed an address for some businesses. All I had to do was screw on a few name plates to a wall and let him know if any mail came. For doing this, he'd pay me two hundred and fifty bucks for each business, plus a hundred every year my place was used after the first year. He said there'd be four nameplates."

"What did you say to him?"

"I told him no problem. Walnut Grove's not exactly flush with money these days, so when I found out there'd be a grand in it for me, I jumped at it. That's big money for a man like me."

"Did he make any other arrangements with you?"

"Well, he sure was prepared because he gave me the four plates there and then, and a thousand in cash. He also gave me a forwardin' address for any mail sent to the store."

"And what was that forwarding address?"

"Some mail box number at a post office in Durham."

"Did you think there was anything odd in these arrangements?"

Gerry Orback put a hand over the microphone and whispered to his client. Hooper replied, "Odd, sure, illegal, no. Listen, Senator, the war hit us hard where I live and times are still tough in North Piedmont. This money puts food on the table and clothes on my kids' backs. I wasn't doing anythin' against the law, so why not?"

Andrews asked his colleagues if they had any other questions. There were none. "Thank you, Mr. Hooper, you're excused." To the room, he added, "We'll take a ten-minute recess," and emphasized this with a rap of the gavel.

When the hearing resumed, Andrews announced that questioning would be passed to his colleague, Jason George, the honorable senior senator for Arkansas. Senator George was a diminutive fellow with a squeaky voice and beady eyes, but behind his spectacles those eyes burned with a fire of determination and purpose. He had a reputation as a fierce examiner.

The next witness was sworn in. "Please state your name?" asked Senator George.

"Harold Sanderson."

"What is your profession, Mr. Sanderson?"

"I am the senior clerk of the North Carolina Companies Registry."

"For the purposes of this hearing, were you asked to examine the records of Bee Balm Inc, Dotted Horsemint Inc, Indian Blanket Inc and Solomon's Seal Inc?"

"Yes, Senator."

"Do you have copies of those records with you?"

"I do," he said, holding up a folder. He opened it and removed several sheets of paper. The clerk was instructed to record the copies.

"Mr. Sanderson," continued the Senator, "what do these records disclose?"

"These four corporations were formed by the firm of Bush Pollard & Associates, Attorneys at Law, in July, 1947. All have their registered offices at Walnut Grove, North Piedmont. The forms required have been filed and fees paid, so the corporations are in good standing."

"Who are the directors of these corporations?"

"There is a sole director for all corporations, Professor Robert E. Lee Dixon."

"Do the records show a filing for shareholders?"

"Yes, and again each corporation has a sole shareholder, Firewall Inc, which is incorporated and registered in Delaware.

"And what can you conclude from the records?"

"That Professor Robert E. Lee Dixon is the sole director of record of these four corporations and Firewall Inc. is the holding company."

Have you looked into the records of Firewall Inc?"

"Yes."

"What did you find?"

"It is a corporation of good standing. Its sole director and shareholder is Robert E. Lee Dixon."

"Thank you, Mr. Sanderson. I'll yield the rest of my time for my colleagues."

Charles Young, senior senator for Pennsylvania and a Republican, indicated he had a question. "Mr. Sanderson, do you have any knowledge or information about Professor Dixon?"

"I believe he is a tenured professor at the University of North Carolina medical school."

The Senator nodded his thanks, as if having concluded his questioning. Before the witness could rise, he quickly added, "Is there any legal requirement for Professor Dixon to file documents with your registry or the Delaware registry to indicate he is acting as a nominee?"

"No, Senator, for the North Carolina corporations. I am not aware of any such requirement in Delaware but I am not an expert on Delaware corporation law."

"So, Dixon might be acting on behalf of someone else?"

"That's possible, yes."

"I have no more questions." Nor did any other Senators.

Andrews looked at his colleagues. "The next witness might take a while. Shall we recess for lunch?" When there was no objection, he announced the committee would reconvene in an hour.

As I rose, an aide tapped me on the shoulder and handed me a note from Senator Andrews: *I know this morning covered evidence, much of which you provided. Your report has been most helpful. I think this afternoon's witness will keep you interested.*

After lunch, the next witness was sworn in. He wore army uniform, the bars on his epaulettes indicating the rank of major. The examination was started by Senator Willy Lomax of Alabama, a man known as a powerful supporter of the military. One of his roles in Congress was to ensure lucrative military contracts were awarded to his state and he wasn't shy about voicing annoyance and jealousy when he took the view that other states were receiving too large a piece of the pie.

"Please state your name, rank and duties," Lomax requested.

"Bullard Quade, major. I'm attached to the Pentagon in charge of scrutinizing military contracts. My duties cover contracts awarded on the eastern seaboard of the United States, from Maine to Florida."

Senator Lomax nodded and asked, "Please explain why scrutiny of contracts is required."

"During the Second World War, there was central purchasing for the armed forces. However, this was found to be too bureaucratic, cumbersome and wasteful in many respects. Major weapons of war are still purchased centrally, subject to Congressional approval, but local bases now have the authority to buy goods, equipment, small arms and other weapons subject, of course, to budgets determined by Washington. If a base enters into a contract, that contract must be submitted for scrutiny to the state board. Without approval, funds are not released. Every state board has a scrutiny procedure because every state has at least one military base."

"Major Quade, please explain the criteria for contracts to be forwarded to your department."

The major shifted in his seat before responding. "One in five contracts must be sent to my department as a matter of course. Also, a contract is sent for scrutiny if the state board has any concerns."

"Do the names Bee Balm Inc, Dotted Horsemint Inc, Indian Blanket Inc and Solomon's Seal Inc mean anything to you?"

The major nodded and then held up a hand, remembering that a verbal response was needed. "Yes. The corporations you mention entered into contracts with bases in North Carolina to supply various items."

"Do you have copies of the contracts?"

"Yes, sir, I do."

"For the record, please tell the committee what was to be supplied."

"Bee Balm was to supply one hundred thousand pairs of boots; Dotted Horsemint was to supply fifty thousand gas masks; Indian Blanket was to supply one hundred thousand army fatigues and water bottles; and Solomon's Seal was contracted for fifty thousand howitzer shells."

The Senator paused, his eyes focused on the wall behind the witness, as if concentrating on something yet to be asked, or perhaps he was totaling the sum of these orders and weighing the implications. He turned to the witness. "Please tell this committee what prompted the investigation."

"Every military base in North Carolina supplied by these corporations lodged complaints about the quality of the goods. The soles of the boots were too thin and not fit for heavy use; more than half the gas masks leaked and the fatigues were far too flimsy; water bottles were not properly insulated and water turned brackish. Worst of all, the howitzer shells were sub-standard."

"Can you define 'sub-standard' Major?"

"On testing, more than twenty percent failed to explode."

A murmur ran through the room. I looked around to pinpoint the source and realized that there was general surprise and concern shared among the majority of attendees. It took no genius to understand that all these failures, especially the howitzer shells, would put soldiers at risk. Lives could be lost.

"What failure rate on howitzers is regarded as acceptable?"

"0.5% or one in two hundred."

The Senator edged closer in his seat towards Quade. "Major, how could all these failures have occurred?"

Quade leaned forward, as if about to impart vital testimony. "Before a corporation can supply anything to the military," he said, "that corporation must be approved by the state board, unless the Pentagon certifies otherwise. Likewise, if a corporation is proposing to use sub-contractors, those sub-contractors must also be approved in advance."

The Senator nodded. "And in the case of the four corporations?"

"Approval came from the Pentagon. However," he quickly added, his mouth pinched, "when investigations about supplies were carried out, two things became clear. First, sub-contractors were being used for every contract. Second, their identities were not disclosed to the state board. They were not approved. From this, one could only conclude the sub-contractors for these four corporations were not authorized to make the supplies."

"Were inquiries made of the four corporations?"

"Of course! And I regret to say Professor Robert E. Lee Dixon, who was on record as the sole director, refused to answer any of our questions until he was threatened with prosecution."

The Senator paused, as if for dramatic effect. "Professor Dixon has been subpoenaed to give evidence to this Committee, so I won't ask you to divulge what he told you, at least not at this stage. Please tell us the overall value of the contracts placed with these four corporations."

"It was in the region of eighty-seven million dollars."

There were no whispers in the room. Instead there was silence which I found meaningful. The public was stunned. The Senator proceeded as if nothing startling had been divulged.

"When the contracts came to you, what did you do?"

"I visited the registered offices of the corporations in Walnut Grove. A Mr. Hooper told me he knew nothing. It was clear to me that his premises were used merely as an accommodation address. After questioning, he gave me the name of David Smith and an address. I felt certain this was a false name, but I was able to uncover Professor Dixon's details from the corporation papers at the state Companies Registry. I arranged to meet Dixon."

"On what date?"

"Twenty-seven June, last year."

"What happened at that meeting?"

"I asked Dixon to identify the sub-contractors. He said he didn't know and referred to himself as 'just a nominee.' I took that to mean he was a stooge. When I asked him to identify the person or persons behind the corporations, he refused."

"And then what happened?"

"I reported my findings to my superior, General Nathan Forrest, who headed contract scrutiny at the Pentagon. His jurisdiction covered the whole country."

"What did he tell you?"

"He ordered me to stop my investigation, that he knew about the contracts in question and that there were good reasons not to take things further. Security issues meant he was unable to explain."

"How did you feel about this?"

"In a word, sick. I knew something was wrong and that my superior officer was blocking me."

"What led you to this conclusion, Major?"

"I could find no reason why...or what...security issues existed. I became suspicious of General Forrest, but there was no one I could go to for advice. In my line of work, whistle-blowing is frowned upon. In truth, it's a career breaker."

"So what did you do?"

"I went to see General Forrest again. I told him the details of my concerns and asked him to reconsider. He was pretty angry with me, said he had given me an order and was appalled that I had disobeyed. And if I continued to disobey, I would be stripped of my rank and posted to a remote location, where I would become a forgotten man."

I shook my head. What had been guarded respect for Major Quade was quickly shifting to compassion. I was already writing a story in my mind.

"How did you feel about that?" asked the Senator.

Quade took a deep breath and released it slowly, as if working to control his emotions. "Devastated," he said. "Either I had to turn a blind eye to protect my career or I could spill the beans and face a forcible exile. Caught between a rock and a hard place, as you might say."

"Major, what did you do?"

"I took some leave and visited my folks. My dad's as straight as they come. He gave me sound advice. 'Follow your gut and do what you think is right.' When I returned to base, I asked to see General Moody."

I was totally absorbed by Quade's evidence, but now I was on red alert. Kurt Moody was a three-star general and a war hero.

"Why did you choose General Moody?"

"He has a reputation as a man who would never get involved in anything corrupt."

"Did he meet with you?"

"Yes. He saw me in September. It was a very difficult meeting for me because I was disobeying a direct order from my superior officer.

"The general heard me out as I presented the evidence. I told him pretty well everything I've told you. I kept to the facts, except when I expressed my concern that my superior officer might be corrupt. Moody didn't like that. I remember telling him I was damned if I spoke up and damned if I didn't. At the end of the interview, the General told me to leave things with him and do nothing further to antagonize General Forrest."

"Thank you, Major Quade. I have no further questions at this stage. Anyway, my allotted time is over. Please wait. My colleagues may want to question you."

Quade continued to give evidence for the best part of another hour, most of it a repeat of information already divulged. Nothing significant was added, but it was clear to most of us that Quade was worried about his career and scared for his future in the Army. I made a mental note to follow up on his story. It would be grossly unfair if he were punished for doing the right thing.

When there were no more questions of Major Quade, Andrews gaveled the closure of the session for the day, announcing that the hearings would resume two days hence.

As I rose, Andrews' aide approached me again with another note. *Hope you enjoyed today. There will be fireworks on Wednesday, plenty to keep you amused. Strongly recommend you bring a photographer.*

Back at my hotel, I called Joshua Frost. "There's a story brewing here. I'll talk you through today's evidence later. On Wednesday, I've been told there will be a lot to write about. I think you should be here."

"How big is this story, David?"

I gave a precis of the day's evidence, much of which was new to Joshua. "Where do you think this leads?" he asked.

"If Dixon is a stooge, then I assume Burns is the puppet master. Whether there is any proof is another matter. However, the story is that the US taxpayers may have been cheated out of tens of millions of dollars by people from North Carolina." Before I hung up, I suggested he bring Molly Nolan, who would benefit from the experience. "And a photographer, too," I said.

My next move was to call home. I had a brief chat with the children and a much longer talk with Abby. Her advice was not to get carried away. "Make sure your people report the facts, not your prejudices," she said. Of course she was right.

On Wednesday, the Senate hearing resumed. I knew that word had reached Washington insiders because the public seats were filled. I also saw a reporter from another North Carolina newspaper. Andrews gaveled the session into order and called for the first witness.

A door on the side of the Committee Room opened and a soldier wearing the uniform of an army general walked in. He was flanked by two guards. General Nathan Forrest was handcuffed. I saw Joshua nudge the photographer, who took snaps as Forrest approached the witness desk where he was sworn in.

Andrews ordered the handcuffs to be removed and took up the questioning himself.

"Please state your name, address and rank."

"I am Nathan Forrest, two star General. I am currently detained at the Anacostia Naval Station Detention Facility here in D.C."

"What is the reason for your detention?"

Forrest hung his head. "I have been charged with a number of counts of corruption."

"I want to take you back a while, General Forrest. Do you recall an occasion last year when Major Quade brought a situation to you concerning four North Carolina corporations? I will name them if you like."

Forrest shook his head. Andrews continued. "He told you he had uncovered problems relating to sub-standard goods and equipment, as well as failed munitions, supplied to the military by these companies."

"I recall the occasion, yes."

"And what did you tell Major Quade?"

"I told him not to concern himself. The sums involved were small and the complaints were unproven. That is, from the evidence Quade produced to me."

"Did he tell you the corporations had used sub-contractors who were not approved?"

"He did, yes."

"And was this not a clear breach of the supply rules?"

Forrest shifted in his chair, as if the substance of these questions might prove threatening.

"General Forrest?"

"Yes," said Forrest, "he mentioned the sub-contract issue. But you need to understand these days, there are many sub-contracted suppliers who are accepted even though not approved. It's difficult to find manufacturers who make things on time, now that we're at peace. This rule is observed more in the breach, as they say."

"In other words, you saw nothing untoward about the complaint brought to you?"

"Not really, no."

"Major Quade persisted, did he not?"

"Yes."

"And how did you respond?"

Again, the witness shifted his position, his eyes focused toward the wall at the back of the room. "I ordered him to cease his investigation."

The Senator looked toward the seated visitors, his eyebrows raised as if to suggest they were finally getting to the heart of the case. "You ordered him to cease his investigation," he repeated, "but didn't you also threaten him with demotion and possibly a posting to some remote place?"

"I might have," said Forrest, "but that's just military bull, Senator. You know how it works."

That's when Joshua Frost leaned close to me and whispered, "Andrews isn't getting very far, is he?" I held up a hand, suggesting he wait for the axe to fall. I had confidence in the Senator's ability to go for the jugular.

The Senator poured himself a glass of water and, looking at the witness, gestured toward the pitcher. When the general shook his head, the Senator took a long drink, placed the glass on the table and faced his witness again. The crowd became suddenly still, anticipatory.

"General," said the Senator, his voice almost friendly, "do you have a safe deposit box at the First Bank of Durham?"

Forrest leant towards his lawyer and, head to head, they conferred for more than a minute, after which time the General resumed his erect posture. "I respectfully refuse to answer your question on grounds that it might incriminate me."

I almost laughed when Joshua jolted upright. The expression on the Senator's face barely changed. He was now in full control of this hearing and he knew it.

"General, you might consider conferring with your attorney, but surely he knows that army regulations require you to disclose the existence of personal bank accounts and safe deposit boxes.

"So I've no choice but to ask: Did you disclose your accounts at First Bank to army authorities?"

Forrest glanced at his attorney, who gave a barely perceptible shake of his head.

"I respectfully refuse to answer your question on grounds that it might incriminate me."

The Senator seemed unfazed. "What is your salary?"

"The Army currently pays me $12,250 a year."

"A good income, would you not agree? Bearing in mind, that is, you live rent-free in accommodation fit for one of your rank and have a car and driver at your disposal?"

Forrest's lawyer leaned into the microphone. "Senator, that's not a reasonable question."

Andrews waved his hand, as if brushing off the comment. "General, do you have other income apart from your pay? Do you have capital assets like shares and real estate?"

Forrest did not confer with his attorney this time. "I respectfully refuse to answer your question on grounds that it might incriminate me."

"So be it. Evidence will soon be given to this hearing about your personal banking arrangements. Is there nothing you want to say now in your defense?"

Forrest stayed silent for a long while and then returned to his mantra of hiding behind the Fifth Amendment.

Andrews yielded the rest of his time and nodded to Senator Lomax, who fixed Forrest with a steely look. Even from twenty feet away, I could see the muscles twitching in Lomax's jaw. "Lomax is furious," I whispered to Joshua. "I think a head might roll."

Lomax began his examination. "General, you have been given many advantages and benefits by the taxpayers of this country. Do you think it appropriate for a man of your rank and stature to hide behind the Fifth Amendment?"

Forrest had the grace to look embarrassed. "I respectfully refuse to answer your question on grounds that it might incriminate me."

"How can an answer to this question incriminate you? I asked for your thoughts about the Fifth Amendment!"

"Senator, my legal advisers have told me not to answer this type of question."

Lomax shook his head, as if repudiating both Forrest's rank and reputation. He announced, "General, you are a disgrace to your uniform. I have no more questions."

After further attempts to persuade Forrest to talk, he was excused, but ordered to remain in the building. The committee members took a short recess. Fifteen minutes later, the next witness was sworn in. Herman Wolz was in his fifties, well-dressed, his hair parted down the middle. He was nervous and had a habit of pressing his glasses higher onto the bridge of his nose. After the photographers did their work, it was Senator Young who questioned him.

"Mr. Wolz," said Young, "thank you for coming."

"This is the first time I've been asked to give evidence to Congress. It's overwhelming."

"All we want you to do is tell the truth." When Wolz nodded, the Senator continued. "Mr. Wolz, what is your profession?"

"I'm the assistant manager of the First Bank of Durham, in charge of customer relations."

"Do you know Nathan Forrest? If so, how?"

"Yes, I do. General Forrest is a customer of the bank."

"I'm going to ask you questions about General Forrest's banking matters. I realize that, under normal circumstances, you would be under an obligation not to divulge information. Have you resolved this issue?"

"Yes, the general manager of the Bank has taken legal advice. In proceedings of a criminal or quasi-criminal nature, disclosure is permitted."

A murmur ran through the room, as if to say, 'Now we're getting somewhere!'

"Very good. Now, please tell us, Mr. Wolz, what accounts does the General have at your bank?"

"He has a checking account and a savings account."

"Does he hold anything else at the bank?"

"Ten months ago, he rented a safe deposit box."

"With regard to the accounts the General holds, has there been any unusual activity in the past year or so?"

"What do you mean by unusual?"

"Have there been large deposits or withdrawals?"

Wolz removed folded papers from his inside pocket, unfolded them and gave a quick glance. "No, the deposits consist of his salary. If by large you mean anything over, say, two thousand dollars, the answer is no."

"Were you present when a subpoena was served on the bank to reveal the contents of the General's safe deposit box?"

"Yes. I was the one who opened the box in the presence of two officers from your committee."

"What did you find in the box?" asked Senator Young.

Again, he referred to the paper. "Private letters," he said. "Three stock certificates totaling 10,000 ordinary shares in B & M Tobacco, deeds to land in Virginia and cash."

"How much cash?"

"We counted two hundred and fifty-seven thousand dollars, all in hundred dollar bills." There was an audible gasp from the public seats. I noticed Andrews smile, knowing that this question had produced the desired effect.

"Two hundred and fifty-seven thousand dollars?" Senator Young spread out his arms, as if confused. "Where did this money come from?"

"I have no idea."

"Thank you. I have no further questions."

Senator Andrews yielded his time to other members of the committee, who indicated that they had a few questions. These were dealt with speedily.

"That will be all, Mr. Wolz," said Andrews. "The committee thanks you."

Fifteen minutes later after another short recess, Forrest returned to the committee room. Senator Andrews reminded him that he was still under oath. Senator Lomax forged ahead. A heightened tension filled the room. Some in the audience sat on the edges of their seats, as if fearful of missing the testimony.

"General," said Lomax, "we have just heard evidence from Herman Wolz. Is he known to you?" Forrest nodded.

"General, please give your answer for the record."

Forrest looked sick as he mumbled, "Yes."

"Mr. Wolz gave evidence of the contents of your safe deposit box at First Bank. Do you admit to having two hundred and fifty-seven thousand dollars in cash in that box?"

"I respectfully refuse to answer your question on grounds that it might incriminate me."

The Senator threw a scornful look toward the disgraced officer. "Come on, General, this is a question of fact. Is there or is there not two hundred and fifty-seven thousand dollars in cash in your safe deposit box?"

Forrest was rigid, his face pale. He conferred with his lawyer. After a long and deep breath, he said, "Yes."

"Please tell us where this money came from?"

Forrest growled, "I respectfully refuse to answer your question on grounds that it might incriminate me."

"General, was this cash a legacy, maybe a gift from a family member or friend, perhaps money you won at the track?"

"I respectfully refuse to answer your question on grounds that it might incriminate me."

"I see. Do you know Professor Robert E. Lee Dixon?"

"No."

"Do you know Jeremiah Burns?"

Forrest blanched again. "I respectfully refuse to answer your question on grounds that it might incriminate me."

"I don't understand. How can you be incriminated by telling this committee whether or not you know Mr. Burns? He's not a fugitive from justice, is he?"

Forrest, rattled, lowered his head, saying "Yes, I have met Mr. Burns."

"What connection is there between you and Mr. Burns relating to the money in your safe deposit box?"

Forrest glared at Lomax. "I respectfully refuse to answer your question on grounds that it might incriminate me."

"Did Mr. Burns bribe you to cast a blind eye to the irregularities in the military supply contracts that Major Quade brought to your attention?"

"I respectfully refuse to answer your question on grounds that it might incriminate me."

"On what occasions and in what circumstances have you met, spoken to, corresponded with or had contact or dealings with Mr. Burns?"

Forrest's attorney objected. "Without prior notice, Senator, how can you expect the General to be accurate in responding to this question?"

"Well, was it once, twice, several times?"

Forrest conferred with his attorney. "I respectfully refuse to answer your question on grounds that it might incriminate me."

In a theatrical manner, Lomax raised his arms, turned his back on Forrest and gestured to the other members of the committee. "I yield the rest of my time to the chairman. I am heartily sick of the sight of this witness."

Senator Andrews took over the questioning of Forrest, but made no headway as Forrest clung to his Fifth Amendment rights. Eventually, he was dismissed and the hearing broke for lunch.

I was halfway through a turkey sandwich when I asked Joshua if he was pleased he had come.

"Are you serious?" he said. "This is front page and three inside pages too, with pictures. I need to start writing!"

I put my hand on his arm, concerned that he might bolt from the cafeteria before finishing lunch. "Might I suggest you wait until this afternoon's session is done before you write?" I almost laughed when he grimaced. One of the many things I liked about Joshua was his eagerness to work. "I think there's a lot more to come out. You and Miss Nolan will be on for an all-nighter."

"If we can get it done in so short a time," said Joshua.

I assured him that I'd be there with them. "This is too big a story to miss the morning edition," I said. "Bring in anyone you need to make that deadline. I suggest you alert the guys at home and let the print room we will be publishing two, maybe three issues tomorrow." With that, I headed back to the committee room.

Senator Andrews called the committee to order and stated, "Next witness, please."

Robert E. Lee Dixon came to the witness desk, accompanied by Bush Pollard. He was sworn in, followed by the usual delay for pictures. Senator George commenced the questioning.

"What is your full name and profession?"

"Robert E. Lee Dixon, Professor of Health Medicine at the University of North Carolina."

"In addition to your college post, do you have any other appointments?"

"Yes, I am a health adviser to Burns & Murphy Tobacco."

"So you know Jeremiah Burns?"

"Yes."

"What exactly is your relationship with him?" asked the Senator.

"As an adviser to B & M, we have a professional relationship. In addition, I have known him for years and have been a guest in his home on many occasions. I hope he would regard me as a friend."

"A good friend?"

"Yes, I'd like to think so."

"A good enough friend where favors are exchanged?"

Bush Pollard placed his hand over the microphone, whispered to Dixon and removed his hand. "Please make your question more precise, Senator," said Pollard. "What favor or favors do you suggest have been exchanged?"

"I'll come back to this." Wind out of Senator George's sails. "Now, Professor Dixon, what can you tell us about four corporations where you have an interest? The corporations are Bee Balm Inc, Dotted Horsemint Inc, Indian Blanket Inc and Solomon's Seal Inc."

"Nothing much. I'm registered as their sole director. I have no financial interests."

"Did you not enter into four contracts with the military for the supply of goods, equipment and munitions?"

"If you mean did I sign the contracts for the corporations, the answer is yes, but did I negotiate those contracts? No."

"Who did?"

"I have no knowledge of that. As I said, I was a nominee."

"But surely you know who told you to sign the contracts?"

There was a delay as Dixon leaned toward Pollard for counsel, then he faced the Senator. "I respectfully refuse to answer your question on grounds that it might incriminate me."

There was a murmur moving across the room. Joshua leaned close to me and whispered, "Here we go again." The Senator shared Joshua's frustration.

"Professor, we understand that you acted as a nominee and now this committee wants to know the identity of your principal. How can you be incriminated?"

Dixon seemed about to answer and then his shoulders slumped. "I respectfully refuse to answer your question on grounds that it might incriminate me."

"Are you the sole director and shareholder of Firewall Inc, registered in Delaware?"

"Yes but I am a nominee."

"And does Firewall Inc own the shares of Bee Balm Inc, Dotted Horsemint Inc, Indian Blanket Inc and Solomon's Seal Inc."

"I respectfully refuse to answer your question on grounds that it might incriminate me."

"Good grief, Professor. How can you hide behind the Fifth Amendment on matters of record and fact? I ask you again, who is your principal in these matters?"

"I respectfully refuse to answer your question on grounds that it might incriminate me."

The Senator glared at the witness and looked at his colleagues. "Sir," he said, "if you persist in holding back information from this committee, much of which is already a matter of record, my colleagues and I may well hold you in contempt of Congress."

At this, Bush Pollard interceded. "Senator, with all due respect, it is beyond your powers to do this. A witness cannot be held in contempt if he is using his rights under the Fifth Amendment."

Senator George conferred with Seth Andrews, who took up the argument.

"Fine, Mr. Pollard," said Andrews. "You go find a judge who will help you. In the meantime, if your client maintains his refusal to disclose the name of his principal, he will be held in the cells in this building until he apologizes to the committee and tells us what we want to know."

Pollard conferred again with Dixon, who then leaned towards the microphone. "My principal in this business was not an individual. It was another corporation, which owns Firewall. I do not know who owns this corporation."

"Let me get this clear," said Senator Andrews. "You acted for people you don't know, on contracts with the military, from which you had nothing to gain. What were you paid for your modest services?"

"Twenty thousand dollars a year."

Andrews looked shocked. "That's a lot of money for a mere nominee. Did you declare this income to the Inland Revenue Service?"

After another conference with Pollard, Dixon replied, "I respectfully refuse to answer your question on grounds that it might incriminate me."

"How was your fee paid?"

"I respectfully refuse to answer your question on grounds that it might incriminate me."

"Was it paid in cash?"

"I respectfully refuse to answer your question on grounds that it might incriminate me."

"What did you do with the money?"

Dixon hesitated. "Senator, this is embarrassing, but if you have to know, I'm addicted to gambling. I needed to settle debts I owed to bookies."

"Professor Dixon, is it your evidence that you do not know who is behind Firewall Inc?"

Again, Dixon conferred with Pollard. "I understand that Firewall is owned by a corporation registered in the British Virgin Islands. I don't know the name of that corporation or who is behind it."

Senator Andrews grinned at Dixon. "Thank you. So we have a web of corporations inside and outside American jurisdiction, supplying shoddy armaments and goods to the US military and no one coming forward to accept responsibility and accountability. I want to know who owns these corporations, who is behind this business. You're hiding behind a veil, sir, a flimsy veil of incorporation. And this won't do. American taxpayers deserve to know the truth. So, here are straight questions. Who gave you instructions, who told you what to do, and who paid you?"

Dixon blanched, as if suddenly realizing that a pack of wolves were surrounding him and that nothing would save him from the onslaught. He looked downwards as he uttered, "I respectfully refuse to answer your question on grounds that it might incriminate me."

"I see." Senator Andrews paused for effect. "That is tantamount to your saying you do know, but you won't say. Subject to the views of my colleagues, I propose to hold you in contempt for failing to provide evidence to Congress. However, we will recess for thirty minutes in the hope that you will reconsider. I suggest you think this through very carefully. Take him down to the cells."

Bush Pollard leapt to his feet. "You, Senator, are abusing my client's due process rights and his constitutional protection. I appeal to you for justice for my client. I must protest in the strongest terms."

Andrews waived him off. "Your client is refusing to give information to Congress, information that it needs to deal properly with this Inquiry. Your client seeks to protect his own hide, but he also wants to protect others up the chain of command who are involved in this shoddy business. My committee will get to the bottom of what has happened and will have the identities of those using your client as a puppet. Your client has been warned of the consequences of his refusal to cooperate. It's up to him."

With that, the cadre of Senators rose and left the room, leaving behind a noisy buzz from the public seats.

*****

When the committee resumed the hearing, Andrews took control.

"Professor Dixon," he said, his jaws clenched, "my colleagues and I will give you one last chance to reveal the identity of the person or persons behind Firewall Inc and this whole disgraceful business. Again, I must warn you, if you choose to hide behind the Fifth Amendment, you will be held in contempt of Congress and returned to the cells in the basement of this building where you will remain until you purge your contempt."

Pollard jumped to his feet. "Mr. Chairman, I strongly protest!" he shouted. "This is unconscionable, a gross abuse of my client's rights."

"Your protest is noted," replied Andrews, his voice chillingly calm. "I might add that your client is grossly abusing the rights of a Congressional inquiry.

Dixon looked forlorn. I almost felt sorry for him. It reminded me of something Major Quade had said about being between a rock and a hard place. Dixon and Pollard spoke in whispers. Pollard's left hand covered the microphone. When Dixon finally spoke, he did so in hushed tones. "My instructions came from Senator Billy August, Junior."

There was pandemonium in the room. Members of the public were shouting. Andrews banged his gavel repeatedly "We will have order or I will have the room cleared." When the noise subsided, Andrews stared at Dixon, knowing exactly how to milk the moment. "I didn't hear that clearly, Professor Dixon. Please repeat your answer."

In a stronger voice, Dixon said, "Senator Billy August gave me my instructions and paid my fee."

I wondered if Andrews was as surprised as I was by Dixon's answer. Had Dixon lied? But why would he? Had Burns placed another layer of deniability between himself and this military business?

If so, how could I prove it? I was hoping that the committee would get Billy August to talk. Andrews declared the session ended and that the committee would resume hearings the following week.

I turned to Joshua and my team. "We're virtually the only North Carolina newspaper here, which means we have an exclusive. I want an edition published tonight and followed up tomorrow morning. I'll call Brutus. Let's give out tonight's paper free. Make sure it's shoved through every door possible. Call in the headline now: 'US Senator Billy August, Junior Implicated in Pentagon Corruption Scandal.' I want art, pictures of August, Dixon and Forrest. Josh, go with four or five pages. This could be our shining hour!"

The Durham Monitor – February 5, 1949
Senator Billy August Named in Pentagon
<u>Supply Corruption Scandal</u>

In an extraordinary turn of events, Billy August, Junior, one of our state's revered United States senators, was named by UNC Professor Robert E. Lee Dixon as the owner behind several corporations which allegedly supplied sub-standard equipment and weapons to the U.S. military. This was revealed today at the Congressional committee hearing in Washington DC.

Despite the end of World War II, the Senate War Investigations Committee (SWIC) retains considerable powers. One of its sub-committees, War Munitions Oversight (WMOC), has expressed concern that there may have been wholesale corruption between at least one senior officer in the armed forces and North Carolina industrial corporations supplying the military. The chairman of SWIC, Senator Seth Andrews, in a move to demonstrate the seriousness of the situation, is chairing the WMOC hearings and has engaged a heavyweight team of senators, including Willy Lomax of Alabama. "We want to get to the bottom of things," said another committee member, Senator George of Arkansas.

This week's hearings started with an investigation of the activities of North Carolina corporations. Evidence concerning the fitness of the supplies showed very poor quality standards foisted on the military. According to testimony, one in five howitzers failed to explode on impact. In breach of military supply rules, the corporations had engaged sub-contractors not approved by the Pentagon.

General Nathan Forrest is under arrest and faces a court martial for his part in this affair. He prevented an investigation into the sub-standard supplies from North Carolina corporations and threatened a junior officer with a reduction of rank and a remote posting if he persisted in his enquiries.

That officer courageously talked with Forrest's superior and is to be applauded for his part in exposing fraud.

WMOC unearthed evidence that the director of record of the four corporations was Professor Dixon. When Dixon was threatened with contempt of Congress for hiding behind the Fifth Amendment, he caved and, to everyone's amazement, named Senator Billy August, the junior US senator from this state, as his principal, the man who gave him instructions and paid him a large fee in cash for his services.

So far, Senator August has refused to comment on Dixon's assertion. His current whereabouts are not known. It seems he has gone into hiding. For every day that passes whilst August stays silent, the public will be concerned as to what he is concealing. This newspaper has asked Senator August to confirm or deny Dixon's allegation. To date, we have received no response.

Chapter 23.

In a private room at the Duke University Alumni Club, three men sat at a round table. The atmosphere was tense. Max Gardner spoke.

"Jez, Billy, you have really stirred up a hornets' nest." His face was blotchy with patches of red, his eyes narrowed. "You asked me here. What the hell do you expect me to do?"

Billy August, the junior senator for North Carolina, the coming man, the one with the film star looks who might have a run for president one day, was pale, sweat dotting his forehead. He was defeated, his career in tatters. He turned to face Jeremiah Burns.

"Jez, I did exactly what you told me to do. I pressed Forrest to keep those military contracts out of scrutiny. I gave him the cash. Now I'm in deep shit and it's your fault. Why in hell did you get into this business? Defrauding the military? Are you crazy? You're going to take the fall on this one. And I swear, if you don't own up, I'm going to the Justice Department and tell them everything."

Jez Burns studied Billy August's face for a moment, a taunting smile on his lips. "Everything, Billy, really, everything? Does that include what you've been paid by B & M and me personally? Or how Max and I broke the rules to get you into the Senate? And what about that girl you got into trouble a while back and how she disappeared? Mark my words, Billy," he said, waving a finger near the senator's face, "you start talking to Justice and everything will come out. You'll regret the day you were born."

August blanched. No one messed with Jeremiah Burns. As for regretting the day he was born, he already did. Burns turned to Max Gardner. "You can be as angry as you like, but you're involved. Instead of all this goddamned grandstanding, let's work out how to handle the situation."

Gardner stared deep into Burns' eyes. "Jez, what exactly do you expect me to do? My hands are tied, now that it's gone federal. I don't have the pull in D.C. for something like this and you know it. It's above anything I can handle."

Jez Burns was burning with rage. "You ungrateful bastard! I've bankrolled you and your machine for decades. I've paid time and again to keep you in power and I've made you a very rich man. Find a way to fix this...now."

Max Gardner rose. He was not a man to be spoken to as if he were a servant or some lackey.

"Gentlemen," he announced, "I'm leaving. This is your mess. It has nothing to do with me. I hope you find a way through the swamp, but don't call me again for help. You can threaten me, Jez, but do you really think the Shelby machine will leave me vulnerable? This shambles, this mishmash is entirely yours." He looked pointedly at Burns and August. "I wash my hands of it and both of you."

Jez stood, fists clenched, facing Gardner. "You complete, fucking shit, after everything I've done for you and this is what you do to me?"

"Jez, it's business. When you cool off, you'll accept." Gardner grinned as he said these words. It was as if he enjoyed the opportunity of twisting the knife. "And I'd recommend you don't pull any stunt against me. The machine won't like it."

Gardner left. Burns and August looked aghast at each other.

"So Billy," said Jez. "What are you going to do?"

Chapter 24.

The Monitor experienced its best circulation numbers since I'd taken it over. Two weeks after the Billy August story broke, we were selling 120,000 copies daily and it looked steady. The advertisers were happy; we were ecstatic.

I needed a breather, so Abby and I took a long weekend away with Louis and Charlotte. We headed for New York City to show the children the sights. On Saturday morning, I passed a car dealership on Third Avenue. A white Jaguar XK 120 with deep red leather interior and top to match was in the showroom. It was a beauty and, much to the amazement of my children and my wife's shock, I decided to reduce our bank balance by several thousand dollars. A test drive and an hour later, I was the XK's proud owner. My family thought I was mad. We returned to Chapel Hill in two cars.

Before I had time to unpack, I received a call from Emily Venn, my finance wizard. "Congratulations, Mr. Driscoll. You've done it again."

"Always happy to celebrate, Emily, but what exactly have I done this time?"

"The paper's so profitable, you can repay the bank loan and the working capital you borrowed."

I had the paper's head of finance cut a check for the amount owed. I signed it and sent it by courier to John Rayburn. I also wrote a letter to John, reminding him politely of the terms of our deal and asking him to transfer the shares of the paper to me. Despite my reservations about North Carolina, my future was now cast in this state.

*****

That weekend, Abby threw a party at our house for some of her UNC colleagues and acquaintances. I invited a few people from the paper. Altogether, we had nearly seventy guests. My only concern was the quantity of booze I ordered. Journalists drink an awful lot, but I have strong evidence that academics can match them glass for glass.

It was late into the evening. I was having an interesting discussion with a history professor, as we assessed the extent to which the South had recovered from the effects of the Civil War, when Abby grabbed my hand and apologetically pulled me away. The deep line across her brow told me that she was agitated. I was tempted to say something about my libido and needing time to prepare, but her expression stopped me cold. "What is it?" I asked.

"I have a very distraught Robert Dixon in the study," she said. "He's drunk, but he seems to be lucid. And he's got information you need to hear….now."

I followed Abby into the study. "Robert," I said, "I gather you want to speak to me."

Dixon reminded me of a caricature of a nervous wreck. His eyes were darting about and he was wringing his hands. He said, "I'm ruined, Mr. Newspaperman. After that hearing in Congress, UNC terminated me. I'm a tenured professor; I didn't think they could do this. I was wrong."

"I'm sorry to hear this."

"No," he said, "you're not. How could you be? Your newspaper has destroyed me and I've nothing left. And for the record, it's Abby I'm here to see, not you. But she won't talk to me unless you're in the room."

I looked at Abby and she nodded. "We're both here, so let's …."

He interrupted me with, "I want to confess everything. I have no job and my so-called friend Jeremiah Burns has cut me off. Do you have any idea what this means?" When I shook my head, he said, "It means my life is over!"

"Robert," said Abby, "there are avenues you can pursue."

"I can't do anything. I need to tell, to explain." He turned to me and added, "I don't like you and I don't trust you, but I know you'll print what I tell you."

I gestured for him to sit. Abby and I sat as well. We could hear our guests chatting on the other side of the door, going on with the party despite our absence.

"I've covered up for the high and mighty Jeremiah Burns for years," said Dixon. "I have incontrovertible proof that cigarettes are damaging people's health. They cause lung cancer and heart disease."

"What's your proof?" I asked.

"I got the evidence, but I suppressed it."

"What evidence?"

Dixon seemed suddenly sober, as if pulling himself together before delivering the goods. I wasn't far off in that supposition.

"I ordered extensive research be carried out at the medical school. When I realized what the results were proving, I stopped the research, removed all the paperwork and destroyed it."

"Surely, the tobacco industry would have found doctors to counter your evidence." When Dixon shrugged, I suggested that what he did was wrong, but not necessarily illegal.

"There's more," he said, "and it's much worse." Before I could respond, he looked at both of us and added, "I'm very sorry about what happened to Louis."

"What about Louis?" Abby asked. I motioned to her to keep silent and let Dixon talk.

"I didn't do anything to him, I swear. Jez Burns' man, Jackson Murphy, called me and said you and your paper had been making life difficult for the boss and you needed a warning delivered. That's when he told me that Louis would be visiting the campus and I was to make sure he was welcomed. That's all I knew. I should have told you. I'm sorry."

That was one mystery solved, but knowing how it unfolded did nothing to cool my anger. "Robert, of all the mean, underhanded and even dangerous things that my family and I have been subjected to since arriving here, this is the most despicable."

Dixon looked away and his hands began to shake "I know. I am really sorry. I have more."

Abby suddenly stood. "I hate to leave, but one of us needs to go back to our guests." Without awaiting a response, she left the room.

I turned back to Dixon, struggling to keep anger out of my voice. "If you want to tell me more, just say it. I doubt I can be shocked by anything now."

Dixon shifted in the chair, inching forward as if preparing to escape. "Do you remember the Butler family murders?"

I nodded, a numbness running through me. Surely Dixon wasn't mixed up in this. As if anticipating my thoughts, he quickly said. "I didn't kill Butler or his family, but I know who did. That evil man, Jackson Murphy, came to see me. He told me that Butler was getting into mischief at the plant, upsetting the colored workers and trying to find evidence to discredit the company. He said Butler needed to be brought down a peg or two and that he wanted me to use my Georgia connections to find people who could 'handle the problem' for him. He wanted people who would be hard to trace, people who would scare Butler and stop the investigations. I didn't ask questions. How could I? Murphy frightened me."

He edged back into the chair, as if relieved to be getting this off his chest. "My family's been in Georgia for decades, so I knew what to do. I had three wild Georgia boys, to whom I'm related, come to Durham and introduced them to Murphy. I don't know what happened after that, David, but I think it's safe to assume they killed the Butlers...and then Murphy killed them."

I needed time to process all of this information, to weigh my responsibilities as a newspaperman and a citizen. I'd be a fool not to run with the story, but the police needed to be brought in. "If you're right," I finally said, "then Murphy didn't just kill your relatives...he killed the waitress, too and the cook." And then I was struck by a terrible thought. "You've known about this for a long time, so why have you said nothing?"

Dixon closed his eyes. "I know, I know, but I was too scared to go to the police. And Murphy made sure that I knew what would happen to me if anything got out." Tears came to his eyes. "David, I can't see a way out. Everything is falling on my head. I've got no job, no money, no prospects and no friends and now I have to go to the police, who will put me in jail. Can't you see? My life is over."

I told him I knew everything seemed bleak, but I was sure he'd get through this. For starters, the paper would write the story and mention how frightened he was, but that he still came forward.

Dixon looked into my eyes. "I'm not like you; I don't have your inner strength."

In one sudden, swift movement, Professor Robert E. Lee Dixon opened his jacket, reached inside, produced a revolver, placed it to his right temple and fired. The shock of his actions and the report of the gunshot left me momentarily paralyzed.

I had never heard or seen a gun fired at close quarters before and everything I had eaten and drank that day came roaring up from my stomach.

I swallowed hard, but to no avail. I grabbed my waste paper basket and used it. Still bent over, I realized that I couldn't hear. I looked up. Blood, brain parts, gristle and skin were everywhere, splashed against the back of the chair and the walls.

I felt the vibration of running footsteps and I rushed to the study door to stop anyone from entering. Opening the door slightly, I blocked what view I could. It was one of Abby's colleagues. "Call an ambulance and the police," I told him. "And please find Brutus Elliott. He's here." The man turned and left. I positioned myself outside the door, now closed against all curious eyes.

Abby rushed up to my study. "David, what's happened?"

I whispered to her. "Robert's shot himself and I assume he's dead. The police and an ambulance are being called. Please take the kids next door. There's going to be a commotion here and I want them spared the trauma. Between the police and the press, it's going to be chaos, a zoo."

Abby's eyes started to well. "He took his life? Oh, his poor wife. Who's going to tell her?" Before I had a chance to answer, she pressed her hand to her mouth. "Oh, God, David, did he do it in front of you?"

My expression must have answered that question because she gave me a long hug. "We'll leave this to the police," I said and we held each other. I kept the door closed. I didn't want her looking at Dixon and his remains.

Brutus arrived and I disengaged from Abby. I preferred not to describe the suicide in front of Abby, but it needed to be reported. Briefly, I explained to Brutus what had occurred.

"I urgently need to speak with Chief LeGaillard," I said. "Call him and ask him to get here quickly. Before Robert shot himself, he revealed who killed the Butlers."

The rest of the night passed in a blur. Abby took the children to our neighbors. The guests had to remain until the police interviewed them. A police doctor confirmed Robert was dead and the police broke the news to Mary Beth, now Dixon's widow. Abby said she would visit her in the morning.

I divided my time between giving evidence to a detective and talking to my staff about the story they needed to get out. For the moment, I limited my account to Dixon's death, omitting what I knew about the Butler murders. I needed to talk things over first with LeGaillard. In a case like this, I was a citizen first, a newspaperman second.

The guests were finally permitted to leave and Dixon's body was removed. My study was off limits until the forensic team had finished. At around four in the morning, LeGaillard and I had time to talk and I told him exactly what Dixon had confessed to me.

"So, Chief," I asked, "now the Butler murder mystery is finally solved, when will you charge Burns and Murphy?"

"With *what* am I going to charge them? You say Dixon told you he got the three Georgia men for Murphy and assumed they would rough up Butler, scare him. That's all. Based on what you've told me, there is no evidence that would stand up in court against Burns. Where is there proof that Burns wanted Murphy to kill the Butler family? The link between Murphy and Butler is hearsay at best. As for Burns, there's no evidence of any link, at least not yet. Sorry, I just don't have a case."

"What about the business with my son? Doesn't this show a pattern of behavior?"

"There's no way to link what happened to Louis with the Butler murders. It won't wash."

"I need to tell you, Chief, I'm planning to run a story implicating Burns in the Butler murders."

"I can't stop you from doing that," he replied, "but are you sure you want to confront Burns on something where I can't touch him?"

I felt disgusted with a system that ignored the murders of all these people and how the law sat on its hands and did nothing. I told LeGaillard so, my voice shaking with emotion.

"Did I say we'd do nothing? Police work may seem slow and unsatisfactory, but it's methodical. Now we know where to look. The Butler case isn't over, Mr. Driscoll. Far from it."

I was too worn out to challenge him, so we left it at that. The next morning, I spoke with Nicholas Anslow. I told him everything I knew about Burns and the murders and asked him if he wanted to syndicate the story through *The Mirror*.

"Send me a draft of the story," he said. "I'll run it by our lawyers. If they're happy, so am I."

I drafted and polished the story and asked Joshua and Brutus to check it. After they gave the nod, I sent it to Nicholas, whose lawyers green-lighted the story. Jeremiah Burns' day of reckoning was approaching. I couldn't wait.

The Durham Monitor   March 7, 1949
Butler Murder Mystery May Be Solved
by David Driscoll

> In a tragic turn of events the night before last, Chapel Hill Professor, Robert E. Lee Dixon, took his own life. He died in my home, in my presence.

I had no idea he was armed. In a highly agitated state and declaring that he was a ruined man, Mr. Dixon pulled out a revolver without warning and shot himself. I was unable to stop him.

What would drive a man to commit suicide? He told me that he had lost his UNC job and his benefactor, Jeremiah Burns, had abandoned him. In the minutes before he died, he confessed to numerous wrongdoings, one of which was his complicity in the murders of Edgar Butler, his wife and young children, which took place at the Butler's Oak Grove home in October, 1947. Until now, the police have been unable to find the culprits.

Dixon told me moments before he died that he himself neither killed Butler nor Butler's family. He said that Jackson Murphy, the manager of the Burns' Silver Leaf Plantation, had come to see him, complaining that Butler was getting into mischief at the B & M plant, upsetting colored workers and trying to find evidence to discredit the company. Murphy said that Butler needed to be brought down a peg or two and forced Dixon to call on his Georgia mobster relatives to deal with the situation.

Dixon assumed that Murphy wanted to frighten Butler and stop his investigations. Assuming Dixon's confession is true, Murphy also killed the waitress and cook at the roadhouse where the murderers of the Butler family were shot to death. When all these killings took place, Dixon remained silent, fearing for his safety and that of his family.

Dixon's confession struck me as honest and heartfelt, coming from a shattered and remorseful man. I have no reason to believe he was lying. How tragic for him and his family that he felt he had no option other than suicide.

Yesterday, I telephoned the Silver Leaf Plantation to speak with Mr. Murphy and was told he was no longer employed there. My requests for details of his whereabouts were refused.

Murphy is the son of the late Leland Murphy and a contemporary of Jeremiah Burns. He has worked for Mr. Burns for decades and has earned a reputation as the enforcer for Mr. Burns.

Accordingly, it is reasonable to ask why Murphy himself considered Butler a threat, when Murphy had no obvious interest in B & M. This newspaper has put this question to Mr. Burns, but he has not responded.

I have reported all this information to the Durham Police Department. *The Durham Monitor* has every faith in Chief LeGaillard and his department and looks forward to reporting more on the investigations related to this ever-developing story.

It would have been one of biggest stories ever to break in North Carolina. What a pity no one ever read it.

Chapter 25.

There are things in life for which we cannot bargain or plan. From my first day at *The Monitor,* I suspected there was a mole, someone passing on information to Burns. I never discovered the identity of that mole, but he must have been the person who leaked the story about the Butler murders to Burns. Even if I am wrong, the end result was the same. The story didn't get published. This is what happened.

I knew the check I sent to John Rayburn had been cleared. I had a bank statement to prove it. However, I heard nothing from him, which surprised me. I had expected at least a thank you and a congratulatory message for bringing a moribund newspaper back to life and health, not to mention repaying the debt to the bank in full. There was also the issue of the *Monitor's* share certificates, which would establish my ownership of the newspaper. So I telephoned John Rayburn.

After usual pleasantries, I said, "John, I know you received my check because it has cleared, so I no longer have any obligations to the bank." When he agreed, I asked him about the share certificates. "I'm surprised you haven't acknowledged payment," I added. "Where are your famous Southern manners?"

There was a lengthy silence before he responded. "David, I have a problem," he told me. "This is very awkward."

This time, the silence came from me. I felt something crawl up my back. It was a shiver. "What are you talking about?"

"There's no easy way to tell you this," said Rayburn. "The bank received an offer for *The Monitor* from a third party and the board accepted it. I'm truly sorry."

There haven't been many times in my life when I experienced my blood running cold, but it did now. At the same time, I was seething. "Do I need to remind you that we have a legally binding agreement? The paper was not yours to sell."

"Actually," said Rayburn, "our lawyers advised us differently. In any case, it's sold and there's nothing I can do. The Board has asked me to speak with you regarding compensation. We accept that it was your expertise that added value to the paper, so it's only right that you should share in the profits."

I tried to process this. I had just been sucker-punched and was reeling from this news. I took a deep breath and reminded myself that level-headedness was required. "John," I said, "let me make this clear. I have no interest in money. What I want, and what I am legally entitled to, is ownership of the newspaper. If you will not agree to pass ownership to me now, I'll call in my lawyers and sue your bank. Trust me, the shares will only be the beginning."

"I'm sorry you feel that way," he said. "I understand you must do what is in your interest, but that doesn't change the fact that the newspaper has been sold. And we were within our legal rights to do so."

And that's when my head started to clear. "Who bought it?"

"I'm not at liberty to say, but I suspect you'll soon be told. Now, if we could just discuss..."

I slammed the phone back onto its cradle. That I didn't punch a hole in my office wall was surprising. So much for the myth of the Southern gentility. I opened my office door and, tempted as I was to yell, I politely asked my secretary to get Skyler Parker on the phone. I needed to speak to my attorney now, even though I was in the throes of righteous indignation.

"I'll call him," she said, "but Mr. Burns is here to see you."

You know that sinking feeling you get in your stomach when you anticipate you're about to hear really bad news. In this case, no one had to tell me. I just knew. Jeremiah Burns had bought back *The Monitor.* Why? That was easy. Someone had told him about the breaking story, accusing him of being behind the Butler murders. And this provoked him to buy back the newspaper. After all, if he owned it, he could control its content. Was he that scared? Then I remembered what Burns had done to the employees the last time he owned the paper. I feared for its people who were now my people and the teams I had built to rescue *The Monitor* and make it a success.

As I was telling my secretary to hold the call to Parker, Burns strode into my office as if he owned it, but then, I guess, the bastard did own it!

"Good morning, David," he announced, his voice booming through my office and into the newsroom. "But maybe it's not such a good morning for you, you might say? I'm here out of respect, to tell you in person that I have bought this newspaper back. This means that your presence is no longer required, so kindly clear out your desk." He glanced at his 18-carat gold watch. "You have fifteen minutes." Before I could respond, he walked around my desk and sat in my chair. With his elbows resting on the carved oak arms, he placed his fingers together, steeple-style, and smirked.

I wanted to shove him off that chair. Instead, I called in my secretary. She walked into my office, her eyes widening when she saw Burns in the seat of power. "Louise, I've just been fired by the newspaper's new owner, Mr. Burns here. Would you please pack up my belongings and send them to the house?"

I turned to Burns, who seemed to be enjoying himself. I admit it, I completely lost it.

"You are, without doubt, the most despicable man I've ever met and I have known a lot of despicable men. I know about you, Burns, and I'll make sure the public learns about your infamy and what a complete turd you are. You like to read about yourself in the paper? Then you'll love the articles about how you're killing millions of Americans with your cigarettes and how you use stooges in your plots to threaten people. Oh yes," I added, standing at my office door, "and wait until you read about how you have had people murdered just for investigating your business methods."

I got some satisfaction to see the smirk disappear. Not that Burns would cave in - I knew better than that - but I derived more than a little gratification planting doubt in his mind. "I'm going to speak to my team now," I told him. "You can try to stop me, but I have to warn you that it will require violence on your part."

I stormed out of my office and into Brutus Elliott's room. "Call everyone to a meeting in the yard right now," I said. "And I mean everyone: journalists, secretaries, print shop, everyone. Right this minute. Tell them to drop everything they're doing."

I saw his eyebrows shoot up and for a moment he struggled to speak. Then he jumped up from his desk and rushed out.

In less than five minutes, I was standing on a crate outside the print shop. "I have the worst news for you," I announced, looking into the faces of men and women I'd come to know and respect. I was happy to call some friend.

"The Bank has reneged on its deal and has sold *The Monitor* from under my feet. It grieves me to tell you that the new owner is Jeremiah Burns, the same man who almost destroyed this newspaper."

The faces before me expressed surprise, anger, indignation, sadness.

"This is the reward we get for our hard work and dedication. But don't despair. When I walk away today, my first step will be to see my attorneys. You have my word that I'll do everything in my power to stop this deal. If I fail, many of you might have to find work elsewhere. Count on me to give you stellar references. You've made me a part of your family, for which I'm deeply grateful."

Out of the corner of my eye, I saw four large men walking toward me. They were Burns' goons and they looked damned menacing. "If you look yonder," I said, pointing to the henchmen, "you'll see men determined to break up this meeting and perhaps a few heads, too." I stepped down from the crate. "I don't want them to have a beef with you, so I'll take my leave. I wish you all good luck and I thank you again for your dedication and loyalty."

I went straight to my car and drove to Parker's offices. As senior partner, Skyler Parker was one of the most experienced Triangle lawyers in business transactions and he would have no problem going toe to toe with the likes of John Rayburn, not to mention Jeremiah Burns. In his fifties, he stood six-five and towered over me. Fit and athletic, his grey hair, Roman nose and blue eyes made him Hollywood-star handsome.

After I related the morning's events, Skyler looked at my agreement with First Bank. He read it a second time and then pulled on his lower lip, as if considering the options.

"David," he finally said, "the first problem I have is that this contract is governed by Virginia law, not North Carolina law. I know a fair bit of Virginia civil law, but you'll need to engage the services of a Virginia lawyer if you litigate."

He paused, then continued.

"The second problem is the remedy you seek. In simple terms, you want a court to order the bank to hand back the shares of *The Monitor* to you. It follows that a court would have to order that the sale to Burns be ruled a nullity and set aside. I don't think this can be achieved under the Virginia civil code." Before I could protest, he held up a hand, "but there's someone local who will know how to proceed and that's Jimmy-Joe Burdett."

"Burdett," I repeated. "He's a viper. Worse, he's a Burns man. Why would I trust him?"

"I know of no reason that ties Jimmy-Joe to Burns in such a way that he has a conflict of interest. Also, he's one of the state's experts in this area of the law. I guarantee that he'll be straight with you. I'll call him now."

Two hours later, Skyler and I were seated in Jimmy-Joe Burdett's sumptuous office at UNC. I let Skyler run the show.

"Mr. Driscoll here has a corporation problem. Jeremiah Burns is involved," Skyler said. "Does this give you a conflict of interest?"

"Jez and I are friends and neighbors," said Burdett, "but I don't advise him on corporate matters, nor B & M for that matter. So no, there's no conflict."

I was a stranger here, a Northerner, asking one of the brotherhood to counsel against his own. Skyler trusted Burdett and I needed legal advice. I really didn't have much of a choice.

Skyler took Jimmy-Joe through the agreement with the bank, the time and resources spent ensuring the recovery of *The Monitor* and the bank's role selling the newspaper's shares to Burns. As the story unfolded, Jimmy-Joe leaned back in his chair, his hands clasped behind his head as he listened. When Skyler was done, he sat forward and looked at me. "Does that about cover it, Mr. Driscoll?"

I nodded, but I felt deep down that nothing good was going to come from the consultation. Burdett sighed and started to talk. "I wish I could help you. This is an appalling story," he added, drawing out his words like an old Southern gentleman. "And it is totally against the way Southerners should behave. However," he added, shaking his head in what seemed like resignation, "I fear Skyler has advised you right. The Virginia courts will not help you with the restitution you seek. You see, despite your agreement with First Bank, this remedy, namely having the share deal between the bank and Burns erased and those shares passed to you, is not available. Instead, the law of Virginia says your remedy lies in damages. In other words, money."

When I stared at him, saying nothing, he picked up a paper clip and began to unbend it. He added, "I believe you are entitled to a vast amount of dollars from The First Bank of Richmond, but nothing else."

"How should I proceed?" I asked.

"If I were handling this litigation," said Jimmy-Joe, "I would ask the Virginia court for an order requiring the bank to disclose what Burns paid for the shares. I would then ask the court to award damages in that sum, on the grounds that the bank should not benefit from its own wrongdoing. I would also seek additional, punitive damages for your loss of future profits."

I sat quietly, disappointed by his opinion. I didn't want money. What I wanted was *The Monitor*. As I pondered, Skyler and Burdett spoke quietly with each other. They were old friends. Skyler inquired about his friend's health and that's when the conversation shifted dramatically.

"Are we off the record?" Jimmy-Joe asked me.

I was taken aback, not sure where this was heading. "Of course," I said.

That's when Jimmy-Joe divulged that he had been diagnosed with leukemia and didn't have long to live.

"I've been feeling very tired, but I'm okay today."

I could see how hard this was for Skyler and how he fought to keep his composure.

"I'm real sorry, Jimmy-Joe," he said. "Is there anything I can do?"

"Pray for me. And if you have a prayer in you, Mr. Driscoll, I'd appreciate it too."

"You have it," I told him.

"The time I have to look after your interests is limited," he said. "With Skyler here, you're in good hands. I'm sorry I was unable to assist you in what you really wanted."

When we walked out of his office, I could only think about time wasted. I was sorry to hear about Burdett's illness, but the situation with the newspaper was urgent. I wanted to mention this to Skyler, but I knew how cold-hearted it would sound.

There were two conversations I needed to have immediately. The first was with Nicholas Anslow. Now that the Butler story would not be published in *The Monitor,* there was nothing to syndicate, unless Nicholas wanted to publish it in *The Mirror.* I didn't blame him when he had said that only a story printed in North Carolina would have value for his paper. Why would his readers be interested in a set of grubby murders in a Southern state? Had our roles been reversed, I would have taken the same position. I considered talking to other Durham editors, but I was certain that this story would be far too dangerous for them to touch. Jeremiah Burns had a long arm; the man could hurt anyone he chose...or worse.

The second conversation I needed to have was with Abby. I drove home and found her nested in the corner of the living room sofa, lost in the pages of a Victorian murder mystery. When I got her attention and explained what had transpired, tears came to her eyes.

"Oh, David," she said, taking my hand.

I felt sadness well up inside me. "You know the saying 'fool me once, shame on you, fool me twice, shame on me'? Well, this is the second time this has happened to me."

When she didn't speak, the silence became almost unbearable.

"Do you remember how Mike Doyle bought *The Bugle* to spike my story exposing his cheating of city taxpayers on a massive scale? Well, Jez Burns is the culprit this time. I feel like such a fool."

Abby leaned closer to me. "You're not a fool, David. You played straight and the bank played dirty. Remember how a while back we talked about leaving here? Let's do it. This is leaving a foul taste in my mouth and I can't see any reason to stay, once the school year is over."

I felt an enormous sense of relief and love for my wife. "Let's talk more about this, maybe tonight. I need to cool off and regain some perspective. But to be honest," I added, "I need to do something tomorrow morning and I don't want to be rational when I do it." Abby spluttered but didn't press me for details.

Early the next morning, I drove the Jaguar to Richmond. At nine o'clock, I stood on the steps of the First Bank of Richmond, ready to enter as soon as the doors opened. The guard arrived, unlocked the door and I strode through the foyer into the elevator and rode it to the third floor.

I followed the corridor to John Rayburn's outer office and would have entered his inner sanctum full speed, had his secretary not tried to stop me. I sidestepped her and shoved open Rayburn's door. He stood just as I reached him. I feigned a left hook, he moved to his left and I hit him with a right cross. Blood spurted from his broken nose as he fell.

"Get up, Rayburn," I demanded.

He rose slowly and I hit him with another right, this time in his ample stomach, causing him to groan loudly and crumple onto what was probably a very expensive Persian rug. His secretary came to the door and began shrieking, but I ignored her.

"Rayburn, I've hit you hard today, but trust me when I tell you this is nothing compared to the law suit I'm bringing against your bank and you personally."

Walking from the building, I could not suppress a grin, despite the severe pain in my right hand. I had dealt with the dispute, Southern style. Part of me wished I had used a whip. Now *that* would've been justice! My knuckles, now bloodied and bruised, were screaming at me. I found a diner, went into the men's room and soaked my hands in cold water. After a strong black coffee, I climbed back into the Jaguar. Despite the cold spring day, compounded by feelings of guilt for having begun to settle a score by using my fists, I drove back to Chapel Hill, the top down, and with a big grin on my face.

Chapter 26.

My family's reactions to my new-found pugilism proved interesting. Louis responded with, "Dad, how could you? You're the one who's always saying that violence is never the answer!" Lottie, on the other hand, was thrilled that her Dad had behaved like a Hollywood cowboy in a white Stetson.

"The jobs of everyone at the paper are in jeopardy," I told them. "I lost my temper, yes, but Rayburn's dishonesty and smugness...well, he needed to be taught a lesson."

Louis shook his head and I knew he was disappointed in me. But my daughter seemed downright excited. "Was there a lot of blood?" she asked. "Did any spill on you? Did you hear his nose break?" I was so tempted to share her enthusiasm, but I fended off her questions.

On the morning of my contretemps with Rayburn, Louis had received an acceptance letter from Stanford, welcoming him to his freshman year. As Abby tended to my bruised knuckles and wounds, I knew that her mind was spinning with questions about our future. She had already telephoned a friend on the English faculty at UC Berkeley and had received encouraging noises. She and I had talked briefly about our next move and pondered on the benefits of a move to the west coast. We could be near to Louis. She planned on flying to San Francisco the following week to meet with people at the college. It would also give her a chance to look at areas where we might live and check out high schools for Lottie.

I received a copy of *The Monitor* every day and looked for significant shifts in news reporting. To date, there were none.

The story about change of ownership did not mention Burns, listing instead a company name and nominees, which told me the new owners were more focused on increasing circulation and advertising revenue, with less emphasis on changing policy. That gave me hope that my people might keep their jobs. 'Long may it continue,' I said to myself and sent letters to the staff wishing them well. What more could I do?

*****

Skyler Parker liaised with Richmond attorneys to commence litigation against First Bank and, as he anticipated, the bank asked for a meeting. No surprise there since nothing good could come for the bank if their dirty secrets were aired in public. It was agreed that Parker would lead the talks. After my altercation with Rayburn, Skyler suggested that I remain in Chapel Hill. He would catch me up upon his return. Abby and I arrived at his office at the time he expected he would return and waited. I was twitching with curiosity, especially as he returned more than an hour later than expected.

"An interesting meeting," he said. "In fact, I'd say it was an astonishing turn of events." He went on to tell me what had happened. The bank was offered ten million dollars for *The Monitor* from a B & M subsidiary company, but only if the deal was done there and then. "The bank admits it didn't think clearly about what it was doing," Skyler said. "I think it got carried away by the numbers and profits. Anyway, the bank proposed the profits be shared equally with you."

"Five million dollars! What would I do with five million, compared to owning and running the paper?"

Skyler was very quiet for a moment and then he smiled. A big smile. A veritable Cheshire cat smile. And then he announced that there was more...much more.

"I asked the bank's lawyer to confirm my understanding of the law. A wrongdoer could not expect to benefit from his own wrongdoing when he broke a contract. He refused to answer. So then I suggested that, if positions were reversed, he'd be asking for, indeed demanding, the full ten million plus damages. The bank people were not happy. I'm not sure their attorney will remain long in his job."

I had to laugh at this. "Okay, Skyler, so what have they offered?" When that silly grin returned, I held my breath.

"Nine and a half million bucks and a large contribution towards my fees. Large enough that I won't ask you for a top up. In exchange, the bank wants confidentiality, a gag clause on you."

I ran that through my head. Over the days since the bombshell dropped, I had revised my thinking. Did I really want to own a newspaper in a town where its leading citizens behaved like bandits? Did I want to raise my children in a place where equality for Negroes would be a pipe dream for the foreseeable future? I now had an opportunity to bank nine and a half million bucks for the price of keeping my mouth shut and never revealing the terms of settlement. Hell, I could do that. Maybe I was not getting what I thought I wanted. But I could do a lot of good with nine million plus, even setting up a rival newspaper in Durham and taking all the *Monitor* people, leaving Burns with a potential ten million loss on the business he'd bought. I could also move to another city in America and start my own newspaper there.

"What do you think, Skyler?"

"I think we could go to trial for the full ten million plus punitive damages and make this all public."

"Really. How soon could you get a judgment?"

"That's another thing. You can bet the bank will drag out the litigation for years and appeal any adverse decision. If you take the settlement, all this business is behind you and Abby. And you get on with your lives."

"What would you do?"

"That's not really a question for me. What I would say is that with that much money, I could do whatever I liked."

I thanked him for doing such an excellent job. "Abby and I need to think things over," I added. "It's a lot of money. I was hoping to expose the bank for its underhanded tactics. Could we agree the deal without the gag?"

*****

A week later, Abby returned from San Francisco. She was energized. It had taken Berkeley no time at all to offer her a teaching post on her terms. They wanted her by early September, which would work fine, especially because Louis would be starting at Stanford later that month.

We talked again about the bank's offer. "Nine...what are we going to do with nine and a half million dollars, David? I can't even think of a million. What do you want to do?"

We looked at all sides of the deal. "The bottom line for me is I don't want this thing hanging over us for years. Abby, I think we should take the deal."

Abby nodded. When Abby's parents died, she and her siblings started a Foundation for sick children in her parents' names, so I suggested we make a hefty donation there. Abby's face lit up and she hugged me.

Then we discussed a donation to Howard University. It was the only all-Negro college in the States that had a School of Journalism. "We can create a trust fund," I said. "The interest generated will provide scholarships. And I'd like to consider what we can do for staff at *The Monitor*. There's still a risk some of them will be left high and dry."

"We both need time to think about all of this," said Abby.

"Sure," I said, "but the bank wants my answer pretty soon." I laughed. "Stuff them! We'll respond when we're ready. And by the way," I added, "my altruistic days are over. I worked hard to bring *The Monitor* back to life and I earned my reward, so I'm going to keep quite a bit for us and the children. We deserve some treats."

The next day, Abby agreed I should settle with the bank. I instructed Skyler to do the necessary. I had to accept the gag. You can't have everything.

"There's one other thing." I described to Abby what I had in mind. She approved and wanted to listen in when I made the phone call. I telephoned Emily Venn. We exchanged the usual greetings and then I got to the point.

"Emily," I said. "I no longer want to be paid by installments for *The Bugle* shares." I anticipated this would catch her off-guard.

"Oh dear," she responded. "I'm not sure we'd manage to pay a lump sum right now. I'll have to look into our taking a loan."

I was enjoying this and Abby's expression told me that she was, too. After all, she knew what was coming.

"Emily, I'm afraid I wasn't clear. I don't want any more payments. I want to give the shares to you, Henrietta and Peter immediately. No more installment payments. You'll own the paper outright."

Emily went quiet and I wondered if she understood what I was saying. "We owe you nine hundred and fifty thousand dollars," she said.

"Not any longer, you don't. The truth is, I'm suddenly worth a lot of money. The three of you, especially you, helped me make my first fortune. This is something that Abby and I want to do. In fact, we're thrilled to do it. Please ask that husband of yours to draw up the legal papers and send them to me."

For a moment, I thought I heard Emily crying. However, when she spoke her voice was strong. "Thank you so much, Mr. Driscoll, you and Abby. Your generosity will make a huge difference to our lives."

"It's our pleasure but it comes with one condition. You have to stop calling me Mr. Driscoll. It's David."

"Okay, David." I heard a giggle.

After I hung up, I turned to Abby and grinned. "Now, that was fun."

*****

I was now at loose ends. With school schedules, we couldn't leave Chapel Hill for a few weeks. I was out of work and needed to keep busy. I wrote the occasional article for *The Washington Mirror*, keeping my hand in the business I knew and loved. There was life in the old boy yet.

Chapter 27.

Jimmy-Joe Burdett telephoned me out of the blue. "Mr. Driscoll, you know I'm unwell and the doctors are telling me I don't have much time left. I need to leave this life with a better conscience and someone knowing what I have done."

"How can I help?" I asked.

"I'm in Chapel Hill General, room 416. I don't want a priest to take my confession. I'm not a religious man, never was. Please come and hear me out."

The man was struggling to speak, his voice weak, gasping. How could I refuse him? I promised to come later that day.

Jimmy-Joe's room was the epitome of modern medicine: linoleum floors, white walls and a hospital bed that could be adjusted up and down at both ends. There were tubes attached to bottles. The disinfectant smell that always made me want to rush outside for fresh air was strong. There were prints of the North Carolina coast and mountains, which added a little color and life to this play of dying. And Jimmy-Joe had a radio sitting on a table between two overstuffed leather armchairs. One was empty; Jimmy-Joe sat in the other. Around him were assorted pillows and a blanket draped over his legs. His feet in slippers rested on a footstool. I was shocked by how he had changed in just a few weeks. He was jaundiced and looked a good twenty pounds lighter. His eyes were now deep in their sockets, red, unfocused. This vital man had been reduced to a shell.

He gestured and I sat down. There was no reason for me to speak: we both understood the gravity of this meeting.

"Thank you for coming," he rasped, pointing to a pen and sheets of paper resting on the table. "May I call you David?" I nodded. "I want you to take down what I say and have me sign."

"Why me?" I said. "You have friends, attorneys..."

"I trust you," he said. "You're...honorable." He took a moment to catch his breath before continuing. "Under our rules of evidence in this state, a dying man's declaration is admissible in court," he said, struggling to complete the sentence. After a long moment, he added, "That is, if offered in a criminal prosecution ...or even a civil action...provided it's made when death is imminent."

It took Jimmy-Joe five minutes to get through his preamble, stopping every few words to gasp for breath. At one point, he asked me to call for a nurse to come in and administer oxygen. He started to talk more freely. I wrote down his testimony, every word.

He warned me that what he had to say might appall and disgust me. He also expressed his concern that his revelations would be a burden for me, especially because they related to Jeremiah Burns.

The story was fascinating, a kind of saga of disreputable and dishonorable actions. Jimmy-Joe Burdett and Jez Burns grew up as friends. Jimmy-Joe was two years older. He knew Jez's father and all his family. Both boys were dirt poor and their lives weren't easy. He revealed how the story told by Jez that his step-mother had bankrolled him as he turned B & M into a major force was a lie. When Jez was nineteen, he married an older woman, a wealthy woman and she gave Jez the funds he needed to get the business moving. The problem was, she was as ugly as sin, and, to use the words Jez said to me, 'she was a bitch, evil from head to toe.' Jez couldn't stand her. He married her for her money, nothing else.

I found the story interesting, but it sounded like nothing more than gossip. And then Jimmy-Joe's face changed. Color came into his cheeks and he looked so hard at me that I wanted to avert my gaze. He grabbed my free hand.

"One night," he said, "Jez went out drinking and carousing. He caused such a disturbance, he spent the night in jail."

I listened closely. Jimmy-Joe told me how, that same night, while Jez was behind bars, an intruder broke into the Burns house, stole some things and murdered his wife.

"Being in jail is a solid alibi," I said.

Jimmy-Joe gestured toward the sheets of paper. "Keep writing. The intruder was me. I killed Jez's wife."

He explained how a plot had been hatched to get Jez both the money he needed for his company and freedom from the woman he hated. In exchange, Jimmy-Joe received a block of shares in B & M. By then, Jimmy-Joe was a young lawyer specializing in corporate law. He knew how to create shares in a corporation which entitled him to huge dividends and special voting rights, as well as the ability to block the votes of all other shareholders.

He shuffled his papers and produced an envelope which he handed to me. Inside were his B & M share certificates and a short document. It was a form for transfer of the shares.

"Sign this," he told me. "And give me a dollar bill."

"I don't understand," I said. "You've just confessed to murder and now you want to do a share deal?"

"Not just murder, David, a conspiracy. Jez and I planned the killing together."

Jimmy-Joe stressed how the sale of his B & M shares to me for one dollar would give me enormous power in B & M, as well as control over Jez Burns.

"Jez will be really scared of you," said Jimmy-Joe. "If you want, you can wreck the company and ruin him into the bargain. Even better, he'll know he's been out-smarted."

Jimmy-Joe told me that Jez would never dream of touching me or my family because my holding the shares could create havoc and disaster at B & M, if I were so minded. He knew that Jez would quickly understand how he was in jeopardy. Still, I wasn't sure I wanted any part of it.

Using immense effort, Jimmy-Joe sat up in his chair. "Listen to me. You need to look at these shares as protection for you and your family. They are also pay-back for what Jez did to you at *The Monitor.* You're only doing to him what he did to you. He'll respect that."

"How so?"

"He thinks these shares are going to him when I die."

Quickly, I decided to act first and think later. Nothing would be lost from doing as Burdett asked. I asked the nurse to return. In her presence, I gave Jimmy-Joe a dollar bill and we both signed the share transfer documents. The nurse acted as witness. I slipped the documents back into the envelope. I thought our conversation was over, but he gestured for me to stay.

"What I have to tell you now is embarrassing and I am truly sorry. I'm the one behind what happened to your son last year."

I felt heat rise to my face. "You were the one who hurt Louis?"

"I'm sorry, David. Jackson Murphy is just the enforcer, a thug with shit for brains. Over the years, I've often helped Jez plan his dirty tricks."

Spasmodic coughing took over and I had no choice but to wait for this dying man to catch his breath. It didn't take a genius to predict what else he wanted to reveal. When Jez Burns wanted something nefarious done, Jimmy-Joe was the man he turned to.

"He wanted you scared, terrified," said Jimmy-Joe, "you and all your family."

"So I'd back off?" I asked.

"It was my idea to make Louis sick. I'm so ashamed. Maybe those B & M shares will go a little way to apologize for what I did. I'm relieved that your boy suffered no long-term damage."

I was angry, livid. I wanted to rip up the share documents and leave the hospital there and then, but the journalist in me made me stay. I felt there was more to come, so I said nothing and waited.

"That business with the Butler family was partly my doing too. Jez wanted Butler stopped. I told Jackson Murphy to have him roughed up, but I never told Murphy to murder anyone. I was shocked when it went so wrong."

"Why do these things?" I asked. "You're a respected law professor. You had plenty of dirt on Burns. And the laws that were broken could be traced back to him. What does he have on you?"

Jimmy-Joe started to shake. Suddenly, tears rolled down his cheeks. I waited.

"I don't know if I can bear to tell you the rest," he finally said.

"I've heard some terrible things in my time. You called me here to share your awful secrets; this may be your last chance to unburden."

Jimmy-Joe took a deep breath. "I never married. I never seemed able to make a connection with someone of the opposite sex but I am not a homosexual." Jimmy-Joe stopped to catch a breath. "From my early twenties I developed a liking for young people."

"By young people, do you mean children?" I knew new depths to the sinking feeling in my stomach. Jimmy-Joe lowered his head as he nodded. He stayed a while with his head in that position, wheezing.

"One drunken night, I told Jez of my predilection. He procured a twelve-year old colored boy for me. I abused this boy sexually for weeks. I got bored with him so he was removed."

"What exactly do you mean, 'removed'?" I didn't really want to hear the answer.

Jimmy-Joe sobbed as he spoke. "I killed him, the boy and buried him on my plantation. When Jez and Lou opened the orphanage at Silver Leaf, Jez hinted there was a ready supply of children for me in exchange for my continued abilities as his brains trust." His breathing got more difficult. "Over the years, I must have buried more than twenty young people from the orphanage, mostly colored kids no-one would ever miss."

"Apart from Jez, who else knew what was happening?"

"I suspect Lou knew," he gasped. "I never talked about it with her."

I wrote everything down but had to excuse myself, pleading a need for the men's room. I found one and was violently sick. This man, this idol of the North Carolina legal establishment, was a mass child murderer. I had been given the orphanage story but ignored it. Was I equally responsible for the deaths of some children because I had failed to do a proper job and act quickly? How would I tell Abby?

The journalist in me took over. I returned to Jimmy-Joe's room. I asked him for names of the children he killed. Jimmy-Joe waived me away. "I can't talk no more."

"You have to. Where are they, Jimmy-Joe? Where did you bury them?"

He tried to pull himself up. Using staccato-style speech, he mumbled, "A field to the south-east of my plantation, half a mile from its farthest corner. By the Spanish oaks."

Jimmy-Joe crumpled in his chair. I called for the nurse. She and an orderly put him into bed. He gestured to me. "Write the statement now. I need to sign it. And you and the nurse need to witness."

I just did as he asked. I forced myself to complete the statement, omitting nothing. The murder of Burns' first wife, the Butler murders, the Louis incident, the orphans and everything else he'd told me, it all went in. I called the nurse into the room. Jimmy-Joe managed to sign and we witnessed his signature. He laid back and shut his eyes, as his breathing became shallow. I found a rest room. I spent the next ten minutes throwing up again until my stomach was empty. The heaves still continued.

Eventually, I left the hospital and went straight to the Durham Police Station. I didn't know it, but Jimmy-Joe had already passed away. He would face nothing further on this earth.

LeGaillard wasn't there. I asked to be connected to him, saying it was most urgent. We spoke on the phone. He was not best pleased being summoned during his dinner and he made sure I knew it. The language he used is often referred to as 'rich.' I assured the Chief that what I had to tell him could not keep. Fifteen minutes later, LeGaillard sat with me in his office.

"This better be good, Mr. Driscoll."

"Read this, Chief." I handed LeGaillard the statement Jimmy-Joe had signed. I watched as he read, seeing his eyes widening. He finished reading and put the statement down on his desk.

"Do you think all of this is genuine?" he asked me.

"Yes, I do. He knows he's dying. He wanted to clear his conscience although I don't know how he could manage this. The statement implicates Jez Burns in the Butler murders.

"I'm no criminal lawyer, but it looks to me there are crimes everywhere around here that lead right back to Jeremiah Burns. I know now what Burns had on Jimmy-Joe. Sorry, Chief, but what I have seen in these parts while I've been here tells me nothing, no matter how foul and disgusting, is beyond your good ol' boys."

LeGaillard didn't contradict me. He read the statement again, stroking his chin. Eventually he spoke. "One step at a time, Mr. Driscoll. One step at a time. This is not one to rush. Can't make mistakes. But you can rest assured I'll be havin' my people out at Burdett's place at dawn."

Chapter 28.

I spoke with Skyler about the transfer of Burdett's B & M shares. He advised that they lawfully belonged to me and that I should register ownership with B & M's company secretary, which I did in person. I had no intention of letting the documents out of my possession. After I handled this, I sat back and waited, knowing that Burns would not be able to control himself. He would want the shares back and would feel compelled to contact me.

I was right. I had a call from Burns' secretary, asking me to meet with him. I refused to go to him at either Silver Leaf or the B & M plant. Neither venue suited me. I wanted to be in a public place. I informed her that I would see him at noon at the Grand Avenue Restaurant in Chapel Hill. When I arrived, Burns was waiting for me at a corner table. "Shall we eat first and talk later?" he asked.

I sat and moved my head towards him. "I have no intention of breaking bread or drinking with you. You called this meeting, so tell me what you want?"

"I know we've had our disagreements, but it was all business. David, can we behave like civilized gentlemen and talk things through?"

I suppressed the urge to reach across the table and grab the bastard by the throat. "Just business! Drugging my son was just business? Murdering the Butler family was just business? You're delusional! And what about your fraud in supplying the military?"

"That was Billy August!"

"Like hell it was," I said, disgusted with this man's pretense at innocence. "My sources tell me August has been singing to the Justice Department choir."

Burns stared at me without emotion. "Do you really think he won't give you up?" I asked. "From what I'm hearing, he's done so already. Which means you're about to have the Feds on your back. Why on earth did you cheat the military?"

Jez smiled at me, a sardonic and taunting expression. "Why are you bothered?"

"I'll tell you why. If I was an infantryman fighting in swamps or deserts, I'd want boots that didn't leak or disintegrate. I'd want water in my water bottle that hadn't turned stagnant. And those howitzers? You think I'd want to jeopardize my life knowing they were defective? Why are other people's lives so meaningless to you? You have so much money, why did you need to make more by cheating taxpayers and putting soldiers' lives at risk?"

"There's no evidence that I did any of this," he said. "That's not why we're here. Let's talk about those shares Burdett purportedly transferred to you?"

"What about them?"

"I had an agreement with Jimmy-Joe. If he died before me, the shares would be mine. It's in writing."

I laughed in his face. "And because of this agreement, you think you have the right to those shares? So, sue me! Might I remind you that I had a written agreement with First Bank giving me ownership of *The Monitor*? You weren't bothered by that deal when you stole the newspaper out from under my feet. Seems to me there's a double standard here as wide as the Missouri river!"

Burns held up both hands, as if in surrender. "Fair point. So here's a proposal. I'll give *The Monitor* to you, lock, stock and barrel, in exchange for those shares. And you can keep the settlement funds you got from the bank. Great deal, yes, a win, win for you." His smile was more of a leer. What confounded cheek!

I leaned back and smiled broadly. "The thing is, Burns, I no longer want *The Monitor*. My time in North Carolina has taught me that there are some wonderful people here and that it's a beautiful part of the world, but there's too much evil for me to stomach. My family no longer wants to live here. We're leaving."

Burns looked as if couldn't believe my response. He had been so certain that I would leap to accept his offer. "Think this through," he urged. Then he tried to threaten me. "If you know what's good for you, you'll take the deal."

"Another threat?" I fired back, knowing this time he was running scared.

"You'll have all the money in the world," he pleaded. "Plus ownership of a thriving and reputable newspaper. What more could you possibly want?"

"Peace of mind," I said. "And peace of mind is something I'll never get if I stay here. How could I be certain that you wouldn't try to harm my children again? You have a track record. Or you might have me murdered. By the way, I know what happened with your first wife."

Burns' face paled to grey-white.

"Burdett told me everything," I continued. "Forget about doing any deals with me. I don't know what I will do with the shares, but one thing is for sure. You won't get your hands on them. You can stew in cow's blood, for all I care."

Burns abruptly stood. "Think real hard about my offer. You don't actually want them and I'm prepared to give you whatever you ask."

"Anything? Really?"

"Within reason, yes."

"Okay. I want my son never to know he was drugged and poisoned just to get at me. I want my wife and daughter not to remember that they were used as pawns and terrorized as part of the same game. I want to remove from my mind the sight of Robert Dixon taking his life and spraying his blood and bones all over me.

"I want the Butler family to have their lives back. I want all the workers at your factories to be paid properly, not forced to live on the bread line. I want all those innocent orphans murdered by Jimmy-Joe to have their lives back. How could you and your wife have let this happen? I want all the people you've hurt, damaged, destroyed and killed to have their lives restored. Give me all these things and you can have the shares back for nothing. But you can't do any of it, can you?"

"No." Burns suddenly looked crestfallen, crushed, a broken old man.

"In that case, Burns, I'll keep your shares. I know how your mind works, so I've delivered the original certificates to my lawyers, together with a notarized statement which documents everything I know about your activities; all of them including Burdett and Murphy. If you ever try to damage me or one hair of the head of anyone I love, that statement will be released to the nation's press and I will use those shares to wreck B & M. Make sure you understand and believe what I'm telling you."

With that, I walked out of the restaurant, not giving Jeremiah Burns another look. I felt a little satisfaction, knowing that unless I gave evidence at a trial, I would never have to set eyes on him again. I also felt deep sadness for all those people who had not survived as a result of his awfulness.

Chapter 29.

I needed to go somewhere I found relaxing, somewhere that would remove the taste of Burns, Burdett and this accursed town from my mouth. I also needed to think through the next steps of my life. It dawned on me that, unlike when I lived in St. Luke, New York or DC, I had nowhere special to go and no close friend to talk to, except Abby. I found a pay phone, rang Abby at her office and asked if we could meet. I heard my voice. It was weak and almost pitiful.

"I can get away in about half an hour. Go home, David, put some coffee on and I'll be with you as soon as I can."

The coffee was ready when Abby got home. I was not. As I reviewed my life, I felt tears welling. Then I started to sob. I cannot remember crying when my parents died or when my children were born. The last time I cried was when Abby and I got married. But this time was different. I now lived in a place where I had no close friends, where I had come face to face with excessive greed and cruelty, as Burns and his friends enriched themselves at the expense of workers who could barely exist on their wages and where people's lives were expendable; not just the Butlers and the poor orphans murdered by Burdett but so many workers at B & M lived a life far shorter than it should have been. The countryside of North Carolina might be beautiful but its way of life was not, unless you were white and wealthy.

Did Abby see me as a broken reed? Not at all. I told her of Burdett and his outrageous conduct, of Burns and his craven offer for the B & M shares, of all the things that had made me feel sick.

"You warned me, Abby. You told me at the outset I didn't know the South, that I should not come. You were so right. I'm sorry I brought us here."

"Yes I did warn you but I was complicit. I wanted the position at Chapel Hill. Let's think this through. The authorities may want you here as inquiries take place and people are prosecuted. Maybe your journalist instincts will come to the surface. There is a lot here to write about, stories that will pique the interest of people you know in New York and DC. You can go freelance. And you can donate any fees you earn to charity. No need to take blood money."

"Do you think so? Will people want to hear of scandals in this backwater?"

"Yes, of course. Call Nicholas Anslow or Lucas Vine if you don't believe me. Speak to Brutus or Cass. *The Monitor* won't publish your work but they have good instincts."

Nicholas edited a DC newspaper but I didn't think he was the best fit. I had worked for Lucas years at *The New York Standard*. He was a great editor and proprietor. He might make an excellent choice.

"I want to sleep on this. If I call Brutus or Cass, they might be compromised. They might feel they have a duty to tell the bosses and it would get back to Burns. But Lucas is a really interesting possibility. Thank you. I've not blabbed like this since we got married. It's a relief to get it out of my system."

Abby cuddled me and we kissed. Further developments had to wait because Lottie came home but that night, I did my best to show Abby how grateful I was.

*****

The next morning, I called Lucas Vine. "Hi Lucas, it's the prodigal journalist here."

"Mr. Driscoll, the latter-day crusader, as I live and breathe. How the hell are you? I read about your victories at *The Monitor*. Congratulations. But the word is you are no longer the editor-in-chief. I'd like to know more."

"What you heard is right but it's quite a tale, not fit for a phone call. I am indeed freelance now and I have some stories that might interest you. I'd rather not talk over the phone. How is your availability?"

"For you, Mr. Driscoll, I have no availability during the day. It's so busy right now. But I'll ask Mrs. Vine to spare me on Thursday night. Come to New York and spend some time with me. I'll book you in at The Plaza. In the evening, take a walk to 44th and 5th. I'll book for 7:30. I am sure you know the place. I hope Abby will be with you."

"Abby will want to stay here. We had an incident a while back and she likes to be around for the children when they're home from school. Do you know, I've never stayed at The Plaza? Now just a room, not a suite. I'm not a Rockefeller"

"If the stories are good, I might be persuaded to have *The Standard* cover the cost. Business has been good. Dinner is on me."

"44th and 5th? Let's see how good my memory is. Delmonico's?"

"Yup."

"Just so you know, while you may have misplaced expectations about my stories, one includes a US senator who's in big trouble and is likely to resign."

"Thursday, my friend. I'll bring my notebook. That's what journalists do, isn't it?"

*****

On Thursday morning, I took the train from Raleigh's Union Station, arriving at Penn Station in New York around three o'clock. I took a cab to the Plaza.

I have been to impressive places over the years but this hotel was an institution. I resisted a stop and a scotch at the famous Oak Room and after a quick break to unpack my luggage, I decided to take a walk in Central Park. I might spend time tomorrow at FAO Schwarz, the famous toy store on 5th Avenue by Central Park. Were the children too old now for toys? Probably but I could look.

It was a chilly but fresh early May day. After half an hour, I decided that exercise was overrated. Time for a shower, change and a cab to Delmonico's. I was hungry and yearned for a New York strip steak.

Lucas was at the table when I arrived. We shook hands. He had been my boss in New York years before when we became friends. He had accepted my move back to St. Luke to run my own show. He gave me encouragement of sorts when I took over *The Monitor.*

"As I recall, when I bought *The Bugle,* you told me I was completely mad and would come crawling back within weeks."

"I gave you weeks? Generous of me!"

We chatted about life, newspaper stuff and families as we ate clam chowder, followed by Delmonico's finest steaks.

"Want a dessert," Lucas asked.

"I'll pass, thank you but you go ahead."

Lucas patted his stomach. "I like to stand up and see my feet. I'll just have a coffee."

"Good idea but let's do this at The Plaza. We can talk business there."

Lucas settled the bill. We both had overcoats and decided to walk the eleven blocks to the hotel.

We found a corner spot in a quiet lounge. A coffee pot and a bottle of cognac materialized. "This part of the evening is on me," I told Lucas. "Shall I start?" Lucas nodded.

"If you know your Aesop's Fables, there is a story but I can't remember which one that talks about a nest of vipers. That's what I walked into in North Carolina. There is an inequality in Raleigh/Durham the like of which I have never seen. The bosses, usually in the tobacco industry, make large fortunes at the expense of workers, most of whom live at or below subsistence levels. The strike at B & M was about life and death, yet management, who knew exactly what was at stake, kept the workers a bay for weeks.

"One of the bosses was involved in a scam, supplying substandard equipment and munitions to the army for profit. This man is a multi-millionaire. The state's Junior US Senator was heavily involved and I expect him to be forced to resign his position and be charged with fraud. In addition, I uncovered murders of several orphans, not to mention the killing of a tobacco union man and his family who got close to another B & M scam.

"I was fired from *The Monitor* to prevent the newspaper publishing what had been uncovered. Jeremiah Burns bought the newspaper from under me and spiked the stories I would have published. You should know that as a result, he managed to make me a very rich man, hence if you engage me to write these stories, I will want no fee. Instead, I'll want donations to Children's charities that you and I agree on."

"Let's start with the rich man thing. How rich?"

"Not your business but in the millions."

Lucas blew air through his teeth. "Maybe you should buy *The Standard* and I can put my feet up."

"Not a chance. Louis is probably going to Stanford, his mother has been offered gainful employment at UC Berkeley and I am heading for a west coast life of ease and pleasure, some of which will include an investigation of California beaches."

"But you have time to write these stories now? Will you want to do this here in New York?"

"No. I'll stay in Chapel Hill for the time being. Events are likely to move fast. I need to be on the spot. My guess is that before the end of August, we'll head for the west coast but things will almost certainly be done and dusted by then."

I freshened Lucas's coffee cup and snifter. He gave me that look which was so familiar. "Okay, I'm interested. Where do we start?"

I outlined my plans. Three articles, to be published over a week or two.

"Not that it matters much but do I run any risk of being sued? I prefer not to defame the living."

"I don't see a problem but run them past your lawyers. The first story concerns two people who are admitting to a crime. The second story is mainly about murders by a dead man. If memory serves, under the law, you cannot defame the dead. As for the others mentioned, I will be quoting from the dead man's last statement given in contemplation of death. The last story about the Butler murders will implicate a man who will not want to take me on. I have something that he desperately wants and he won't risk his company's future by taking me on in a law suit. Lucas, I am totally confident that there is no risk but, like I said, talk with your legal team. I'll be happy to attend."

Lucas checked his wristwatch. "Past my bedtime, Mr. Driscoll. I'd rather not get into more hot water with my beloved. She was expecting me an hour ago. I'd better call her."

"Be my guest."

Within a few minutes, Lucas's domestic affairs were in good order. We said our goodbyes. "Is there anything else?"

"Yes, one thing. Would you speak to Nick Anslow at *The Washington Standard* and include him in any syndication deal, free of charge? Like you, he was very good to me and was responsible for my getting the army supplies scandal. It would be nice to give back a little."

"Okay. When can I expect the first article?"

"Next week. I just have to check some facts with a friendly Senator."

"My, you Southern boys mix in exalted circles.

*****

The next morning after breakfast, I strolled over to FAO Schwarz on 5th and Memory Lane. When Abby and I lived in the city in the 30s, I would take Louis there to see all the toys and maybe buy him one. As I toured the floors, looking at all the goods for sale, I realized there was nothing at all that would do for either of my children. They were now young adults. Not for the first time, I kicked myself that I had missed big chunks of their childhood.

I walked down 5th to Tiffany's. I bought Abby a relief brooch and wristwatches for the kids. Tiffany's is so over-priced but they make up for it in customer relations and gift packaging. Holding the Tiffany bag, I returned to the Plaza, settled my bill and checked out. At Penn Station, I had to wait thirty minutes before the train left. I'd be back in Chapel Hill in time for tea.

Chapter 30.

That night at home, I gave the children their gifts. Lottie loved hers. Louis was circumspect. "It's really nice, Dad, but I have a watch. The new one is far too good."

"Lottie, you're welcome. Louis, Mom and I are very proud of your approach to your studies and this is a present you deserve."

After the children went to bed, I gave Abby her brooch. She went all Southern.

"Why, Mr. Driscoll, a pearl necklace for our anniversary and now this beautiful Tiffany brooch, ah do believe you are spoilin' me. Or just maybe, ya'll are feelin' a little guilty about somethin'. You go out lots at night. Is there somethin' you want to get of that manly chest of yours?"

"Well, Mrs. Driscoll, I do indeed want to confess all to you. I did spend a night in New York City, that's the place where the city never sleeps. And I had a very late night."

Abby giggled. She knew that any suggestion that I would 'stray' was preposterous. She gave me a hug.

"So, how was Lucas?"

I took a while to tell Abby my plans. She thought my ideas were solid, only pausing to express concern that I would be crossing swords yet again with Jeremiah Burns.

"I have those B & M shares. If I want, I could cause serious damage to the company, even wreck it. Burns won't dare do anything to us because he knows that one false step and B & M might go bankrupt.

"I trust you but does this mean we stay here for a while?"

"I have to. I may be needed to give evidence and I don't want to keep criss-crossing the country. But if you want to take the kids to California now, I don't object."

"We are a team. We work much better when we are together. Best to stay here." As always, Abby was right.

*****

Next morning, I placed a call to Senator Seth Andrews. He came on the phone with little delay.

"Why, it's my favorite North Carolina journalist. Good morning, David. To what do I owe the pleasure?"

"I am writing an article on the denouement of the North Carolina arms scandal. I am aware that there has been a settlement. Would you have time now to run through the terms of the deal the defendants made?

"Sure and I'll make it on the record. My Committee owes you big for what you did. The court hearing is on Thursday next week to announce the sentences. I'd have no objection to your publishing the day before. But where will you publish? My spies tell me you are no longer at *The Monitor.*"

"Long story, Senator. Next time I'm in DC, I'll be happy to share a mint julep or two with you and explain. The article will be published in *The New York Standard* and I expect it will be syndicated to many newspapers."

The Senator told me the terms which Burns and August had agreed. "Please suggest to your friends at that fine New York newspaper that good stories about South Carolina and its political leadership are always welcome."

I had to laugh at the man's brass neck.

*****

The New York Standard   June 12, 1949
US General Forrest Jailed.
Ringleaders of War Munitions
Scandal to be sentenced.
By David Driscoll

Several months ago, Seth Adams, senior Senator from South Carolina, presided over hearings of the War Munitions Oversight Committee. The first case heard by the committee related to the supply of sub-standard military equipment and munitions to North Carolina bases. During the hearing, evidence was introduced of the duplicity, fraud and criminal conduct of General Nathan Forrest. At his court martial last week, Forrest was found guilty on all charges and sentenced to a dishonorable discharge from the army and three years' imprisonment. He was also fined $300,000, half the penalty for accepting a bribe and half for his improper conduct.

At the Congressional hearing, the junior US Senator from North Carolina, Billy August Junior, was named as the ring-master of the plot to defraud the military. Faced with ruin, he approached the senior US Senator for North Carolina for help but was given short shrift.

August, defeated, had little choice other than to deliver a letter of resignation to the North Carolina governor, Michael Richards. It is understood that Governor Richards will appoint a replacement shortly, rather than hold a special election. No doubt, the Shelby machine, which has enormous influence over North Carolina politics, will play a major role in the appointment.

August became a state's witness and in a court hearing two weeks ago, he implicated B & M tobacco baron, Jeremiah Burns, as the one who conceived, instigated and financed the illegal actions. Initially, Burns pleaded not guilty to the charges but sources close to the court have told this reporter that tomorrow, both Burns and August will enter guilty pleas. Both have accepted the court's sentences.

Each man has accepted the court's requirement to sign a statement unequivocally acknowledging his guilt and apologizing to the state of North Carolina, the US Congress and the American people for wrongdoing.

Mr. August will be given a four year prison sentence, suspended for two years.

He will also acknowledge that the slightest infraction of federal or state criminal law, excluding minor traffic violations, during the two year period will find him before the court when he will serve the full sentence, as well as any additional punishment. Finally, Mr. August will be fined $500,000. Half of this sum equates to the gains made by August for his part in the fraud and half as a penalty for wrongdoing.

Mr. Burns will be given an eight year prison sentence, suspended for four years. He will acknowledge that the slightest infraction of federal or state criminal law, excluding minor traffic violations, during the four year period will find him before the court when he will serve the full sentence, as well as any additional punishment.

Also, Mr. Burns will be fined twenty million dollars. Half of this sum equates to the gains made by Burns for his part in the fraud and the remainder as a penalty for wrongdoing.

Finally, Mr. Burns will be banned for life, whether as shareholder, executive or employee of any firm, partnership or corporation, from supplying any department of the US government with goods and products, in particular tobacco products.

> In future, if anyone in the military wants to buy a carton or pack of New Holborns or Gordons cigarettes, they will have to pay full price, like any other US citizen. No longer will PX stores stock B & M products.
>
> The Adams Committee must be congratulated for bringing the North Carolina affair to light. Hopefully, what will happen tomorrow in court will discourage any potential fraudsters, be they ever so high and elite, from following the path of Burns, August and Forrest.

The reaction to the article was immediate and explosive. At first, the North Carolina establishment dismissed the article as misleading and plain wrong. Later in the day, the state newspapers printed a retraction and went quiet. *The Standard* received bags of letters, mostly from veterans, who criticized the perpetrators harshly. Lucas published a selection of the letters over the next few days.

Television and radio decamped outside Seth Adams' office waiting for Seth to give an interview. Eventually, he offered his congratulations to the prosecutors and the courts. By then, President Truman offered his congratulations too. In doing so, he gave praise to "the journalist who broke the story." He also reminded people that he had played a leading role in the War Investigations Committee from its inception and that he was proud to say he had saved millions of dollars for the taxpayers.

Four days later, Lucas published the orphan story.

The New York Standard   June 15, 1949
Grizzly Murders of Orphans
Uncovered in Durham, North Carolina.
By David Driscoll

On the surface, Raleigh/Durham in North Carolina is a model community. Within a radius of seven miles, it houses two of America's highly rated universities. It is the centre of the tobacco industry, employing many thousands of men and women. But the community has a dark side.

James (Jimmy-Joe) Burdett was a law professor at the University of North Carolina. He was one of the state's foremost experts on corporate law. He lived quietly on a plantation adjoining Jeremiah Burns' Silver Leaf plantation. They were neighbors, and although the two homes were miles apart, they were good friends.

But the relationship went much further than just neighbors. Burdett gave a 'statement in expectation of death' to this reporter when he confessed that he was the brains behind many of Jez Burns' dirty tricks.

> It started with the murder of Burns' first wife decades ago. Burns contrived to get himself jailed for drunken behavior, thus gaining the best of alibis while Burdett did the deadly deed.

Later, when the Silver Leaf plantation expanded and included an orphanage, Burdett told this reporter that he confided to Burns about his 'fondness' for young people. Burdett created the Raleigh Orphans Foundation, a charity that supposedly placed orphans with families in the West. The regulations for the orphans' transfer were weak and few records were kept.

Over the years, the Burns orphanage provided many children to Burdett, supposedly for adoption. There are no records to prove what became of these children. When Burdett gave his dying statement, he confessed to the murder of at least twenty children and told this reporter where to find the graves on his plantation.

The exhumations started the day after Burdett's death and they still continue some three months later. It is slow, painstaking and emotional work. So far the bodies of thirty two children have been discovered.

According to Burdett, Jeremiah Burns knew the likely fate of the orphan children sent to his care. Burdett's statement included an assumption that Louise-Beth Burns also knew of the children's fate but this is something for prosecutors to decide. This newspaper makes no such assertion.

Durham Chief of Police, Buck LeGaillard, is unwilling to comment on future prosecutions. "All I can say is that federal prosecutors are discussing jurisdiction and other issues with the North Carolina attorney. I would not want to speculate on the outcome."

This reporter is disturbed that a criminal investigation seems to be hampered by turf wars. If Burdett's evidence is to be believed, Burns' role in the matter needs close examination as an accessory both before and after the fact.

This newspaper is calling on both the US attorney and the North Carolina attorney to decide the extraneous issues and either move a prosecution forward or say there is no case for Burns to answer. If the latter, they need to state how such conclusion has been reached.

Lucas Vine, the editor of *The Standard*, has been so moved by the plight of the late orphans and any orphans who have not been adopted that he will match, dollar for dollar, all contributions from this newspaper's readership in aid of The New York Society for the Prevention of Cruelty to Children.

Mr. Vine will cap his contribution at a massive $250,000. He is to be thanked and praised for such a generous gesture.

By the time this article was published, syndication had reached more than 400 outlets. The reaction was astounding. All kinds of organizations, charities and political groups clamored for action and a review of the law relating to orphans 'so this can never happen again.' The charity appeal hit $500,000 in two days. I was so energized by what had happened. My final article dripped off my pen, so to speak. A week later I sent Lucas my final article.

The New York Standard   June 22, 1949
Is the Murder of Edgar Butler and His
Family Solved?
<u>By David Driscoll.</u>

Over a year ago, tobacco union official, Edgar Butler, was murdered in his home in an attack by three men dressed in Ku Klux Klan robes. The killers also ended the lives of Butler's wife and two young children.

After the murders, the three killers went to a roadhouse in the adjoining county where they were to be paid. Whoever the paymaster was, he took the lives of the Butler killers, as well as a waitress and cook working that night at the roadhouse.

It took several months for the Raleigh/Durham police to get anywhere with their investigations. As there were no witnesses and no clues, the trail was cold. The logjam was broken a few months ago in this reporter's Chapel Hill home, where a party was being held for colleagues of myself and my wife, a literature professor at UNC. Among our guests was Robert E. Lee Dixon, a Professor of Medicine at UNC.

I spoke with Dixon privately at his request in my study. He told me that Jackson Murphy, the plantation manager at Silver Leaf who was also Jez Burns' enforcer, ordered Dixon to bring members of his family who lived in Georgia, for a job Jackson wanted done. Dixon's Georgia relations were criminals with reputations for delivering beatings.

Dixon realized that his family members had carried out the Butler murders and that, almost certainly, Murphy had murdered them but was too frightened to go to the authorities.

I asked Dixon if he knew why it had happened. He told me that Jackson acted because Butler was getting too big for his boots and causing unrest at the B & M factory. Murphy would have taken orders direct from either UNC Law Professor Jimmy-Joe Burdett, of whom I wrote last week, or Jeremiah Burns himself.

Tragically, Dixon, who was also involved in the army munitions and equipment scandal, took his life in front of me. I made a detailed statement to the Raleigh police of what Dixon had told me but no prosecution followed.

As Burdett is dead, he can no longer be charged with incitement to murder. Murphy has gone to ground and cannot be found. The North Carolina attorney has refused to charge Murphy in absentia and says there is insufficient evidence to charge Burns, although no reasons have been given for such a decision.

America is a nation of laws. There is a case to be answered here. Eight people died that night and it can neither be right nor in the interests of justice that nobody has been charged with the murders. This reporter challenges Jeremiah Burns to answer questions in relation to the Butler deaths and the killings of those who perpetrated the murders.

1. Did you tell Jackson Murphy to rough up or kill Butler and his family?
2. If not, why would Murphy have this done of his own volition? He has no stake in B & M Tobacco.
3. If you say that Burdett gave the orders, why would he do so? Burdett played no part in the management of B & M Tobacco so why would he know about Edgar Butler?
4. What was Butler doing that got you so riled up? Was it the disclosure of a medical insurance scam at B & M where you benefited hugely at the expense of your poorly paid workers?

North Carolina is a beautiful state and in the course of eighteen months, I met some very fine people but I am not sorry to be leaving. I have too many bad memories to make staying worthwhile.

As expected, the Shelby machine came to the aid of Burns in political statements and newspaper articles but the federal government has shown interest. I doubt the FBI will get anywhere. The North Carolina mafia will block them.

Epilogue.

So far, no prosecution has been mounted against Jeremiah Burns for incitement to murder the Butler family. This comes as no surprise to me. No doubt the Shelby machine intervened. They would have told the states attorney this was not a federal matter and that a state prosecution would never have succeeded. What benefit would come from washing Burns' dirty linen in public?

No anti-trust suit was commenced against B & M, but the Truman administration intervened. A reorganization of B & M took place late in 1950, splitting the marketing and sales side of the business away from production. The reorganization was just window dressing. The shareholding remained as it had been. I receive dividends from B & M for my shares. I donate every cent either to charity or Local 31 of the tobacco union.

Burns seemed to have faded away from Durham. He no longer attended his place of business and Silver Leaf was shut. It was rumored that Lou-Beth went abroad, probably the South of France, and that the marriage was over. Burns was no loss to the taxpayers of North Carolina, who continue to be ruled by the Shelby machine.

I am writing this account in the late fall of 1950. Jackson Murphy disappeared and has not been found. He is on the FBI's wanted list. Some believe that he went to the Smoky Mountains where he has family and that he has become part of its rural life. My own guess is that he is in Chicago or some other big city.

The Driscoll family saga is writing its next chapter. Abby will thrive at Berkeley, Louis is at Stanford and he will succeed in his studies through intellect, determination and grit. Lottie is heading toward an unknown future that promises adventure and creativity. She loves the relaxed life that California offers. Like her father, she is a survivor and always open to new adventures.

One thing that did not go to California with us was my XK150 Jaguar sports car. Louis made a telling argument: "Dad, imagine you are on a Texas road where nothing exists for miles except critters. It is a British car, so oil leaks are a racing certainty. If you have to stop where there is no human existence within a fifty mile radius, what will you do?" I accepted the point, sold the car for a $250 loss but I made a mental note to buy another one when I got to San Francisco.

It is about a 3,500 mile drive from Chapel Hill to San Francisco. We left in early August and made some detours. We stayed a few days in Richmond so Abby could see family and then at St. Luke to re-acquaint ourselves with old friends. We finally reached our destination on 9th September, giving us time to get Louis settled in Stanford and Lottie enrolled in her high school.

The drive gave me time to reflect. First and foremost, I knew I was a very lucky man. Despite the horrors of Raleigh/Durham, I had re-built my relationship with Louis and Lottie. There was now mutual respect as well as love. My marriage was stronger, either despite or because of the events of the past eighteen months.

After years of pressure as an editor and owner of a newspaper, I had no job and no career to worry about. I had done it all. I had nothing left to prove.

I felt confident that something would turn up but when it did, it would be on my terms. Of course, none of our futures are assured, but I'm looking forward with great anticipation to whatever awaits us down the road.

THE END

TRADE-OFF

Prologue

December, 1950

The Man sat at a huge oak desk, reviewing costs and incomes for the past month. The Man's office was designed to be welcoming to some and feared by others. His office was air-conditioned on low. In one corner, there was a well-stocked bar. There was a sofa and matching armchairs in another corner. The room was designed for comfort.

As general manager of The Beachcomber Hotel and Casino, the largest complex on the Vegas Strip, The Man was not just the boss. He was a Vegas personality alongside made men who had made Vegas their home. Pictures of well-known personalities were displayed on bookshelves. However, if a gambler owed the casino and was invited to the Man's office, the debtor knew trouble and pain would follow.

More than three hundred and fifty people worked at The Beachcomber, including cleaners, janitors, cooks, waiters and entertainers, as well as the dealers and casino staff. The Man was a tough manager. He ran a tight ship. If staff erred, they knew there were no second chances.

The Man was dressed Las Vegas style. Light blue cotton shirt, matching pants and two-tone navy blue and white loafers. A navy blue blazer hung over his office chair. There was a gold chain around his neck, a Jaeger LeCoultre watch on one wrist and a gold identity bracelet on the other.

The Man was hefty, mostly muscle. At six feet two inches and 192 pounds, he was an imposing figure. He checked his watch. 11.20 pm, time to walk the casino floor and make sure all was as it should be before the midnight show.

Suddenly, the office door swung open. There was no knock. A slim, tall, grey-haired man walked in unannounced. The Man stood and hailed his visitor. "Max, what a pleasant surprise. Come on in."

"Two Fingers, what's up?"

Only the most senior people in the Organization addressed The Man as 'Two Fingers.' This name resulted from a shooting incident twelve years earlier when The Man's Mauser misfired.

"I didn't know you were in town, Max. You should have told me. I'd have taken care of you."

Max Torino, smiled to himself. He had been in Vegas for two days, doing business under the wire. If Two Fingers was unaware, it followed that pretty well all the other Organization guys would not have known of his presence.

In the twenties, Torino had been Al Capone's right hand man in the Mid-west. When Capone went to Sing-Sing, Torino had risen in importance in Our Thing, becoming second only to Frank Costello and Charles 'Lucky' Luciano, the Capi di Capi. In 1946, the Feds caught up with 'Lucky', offering him exile or state-side jail time, long jail time. Quietly, Lucky left America for Sicily, leaving Torino in charge of Chicago and the Midwest and West Organizations. Frank Costello remained as Number One in the East. Lucky knew divide and rule was in his interests.

Max Torino had a scary presence. He liked to give the impression that he was a highly qualified accountant, the senior partner. He dressed conservatively, straight out of Brook Brothers. It was his uniform. Navy blue, dark grey and black, three-piece pin-striped suits, wing tip shoes and crisp white shirts with button-down collars, and conservative ties. He spoke in a quiet, deep voice. He treated all around him with apparent respect but there was always underlying menace. Now in his early fifties, he was slightly balding. He had a fading scar on the side of his left eye, a relic of the Capone days.

In Max's youth, he had not been averse to using guns, knives, iron bars and all manner of weaponry to enforce his wishes. His reputation as one of the most vicious and violent of the inter-war years Chicago gangsters rested lightly on his shoulders but resonated with his associates and those lower in the Organization. Nowadays, others did the dirty work but nobody crossed Max Torino unless they had a death wish.

While Two Fingers seemed relaxed on the outside, his internal organs shrieked. Max Torino turning up like this was not good.

"You and I are going for a ride," Torino ordered Two Fingers. "You drive. Let's go."

"It's Saturday night, it's busy here. Couldn't you just tell me what's bothering you? Whatever it is, Max, I'll fix it?"

"You want to know? Two Fingers, you already know. You've been skimming and I have the evidence. A few thousand bucks here and there is one thing but you've taken a million plus from us. We want it all back. Tonight! So get your car keys. We're going to the Safety Deposit."

"Not so fast. Who says I've been skimming? Where's this evidence?" The Man looked Torino in the eye. "I tell you straight, I've not taken one red cent that's not rightfully mine. Who's telling you this bull-shine? Let's get him in here. I'll see him with you and get the truth. Max, this isn't right."

Torino was impassive. "Last chance, Two Fingers. Get your car keys. Now!"

"Look at the time, the Safety Deposit place is closed," The Man pleaded.

"This is Vegas. Make a call."

The Man shrugged, checked his rolodex and made the call. Protest was hopeless. Fifteen minutes later, the two men were escorted into the Abercrombie Guarantee Safety Deposit Bureau. The Man and a Bureau employee unlocked a large safety box. The employee left and The Man opened the lid of the box. There were some papers but mainly, the box was stuffed with one hundred dollar bills in $10,000 bundles.

Torino removed one hundred bundles of dollar bills and put them in a pilot bag. He looked at The Man and raised his eyebrows. "You don't think you'll be let off with only paying back what you owe, do you? I want the vig."

"How much?" The Man was resigned.

"The rest of the box."

"But that's more than the same again. It's my money. I earned it!"

"Stop wasting my time. Put the cash in the bag."

The Man shrugged his shoulders. He knew complaint and argument would fall on deaf ears. Best do as he was told. Five minutes later, the safety box was locked and stored. The two men left the Bureau.

The Man drove Torino back to the Beachcomber. In the hotel lobby, Torino made a show of greeting staff before saying goodbye to The Man in a very public and friendly fashion as he whispered, "you're fired. Clear out your office tonight."

Torino's car was driven to the front entrance by a valet and within twenty minutes Torino arrived at McCarran Airport. He returned the hire car and spent a few minutes chatting with airport staff in the VIP lounge before boarding the United Airlines red eye to Chicago.

It was after three in the morning when The Man left the Beachcomber for his home. His personal stuff was in boxes on the back seat of his Cadillac. He relaxed a little as he thought of the contents of two other safety deposit boxes he rented. He knew he was finished in Vegas but he could lie low for a few months. Maybe go to Lake Tahoe or Sun Valley. Myra liked Idaho and it would be okay for the kids. There would be other openings for him, maybe California. He had heard about a new casino ship operation in 'international waters' where the ship moored three miles off-shore from the Los Angeles coast. Maybe his skills could be useful to the owners.

He parked at his ranch-style home on the edge of the desert and started to walk to the house. He didn't make it to the front door. An AK-47 emptied its magazine of 30 rounds. The Man was cut to pieces. He died instantly. By then, Torino's plane was over Nebraska.

Acknowledgment

This is a work of fiction and any resemblance to any person living or dead is entirely coincidental. However, I have borrowed elements from real historical incidents, for example the tobacco workers strike happened.

When I considered writing a second book about David Driscoll, one of the questions I asked myself was where should it be set? I like going to America on research trips and I chose North Carolina. It is a lovely part of the world, with the added interest of staying in a Southern state. On my first visit, I spent a month at the University of North Carolina, better known as Chapel Hill. I also explored the beautiful coastline and the Inner and Outer Banks. I have returned since and would love to make another trip but not at a time of year when the Mosquito Coast earns its name.

At Chapel Hill, I met several librarians who were eager to advise and direct me. I virtually took up residence at the Wilson Library where I read local newspapers from the late 1940s. I would like to thank the people there for their many kindnesses.

I met many academics who introduced me to Southern customs, including the preparation and sipping of mint juleps. I made my trips in 2013 and 2014. Sadly, records of the people I met have been destroyed in error. I am very sorry not to be able to name the individuals, especially as they were so helpful. However, I remain in touch with Dr Jon Oberlander, who teaches at UNC, who has become a friend. I treasure his political and medical knowledge.

I am indebted to my editors, Victoria Zackhein and Mary Woods, both of whom spent many hours correcting my drafts. Victoria taught me a great deal about writing an American "thriller" and Mary was invaluable in many ways, including helping me remove the 'Englishisms' from the manuscript.

Thanks, too, to my dear cousin, Ann McCaughan, and sister, Janet Solomon, for proof reading the final version.

The history of the tobacco industry is both fascinating and fearful. The factories in Raleigh/Durham are no more but the buildings stand. Perhaps this is an appropriate epitaph.